Comes the End

Comes the End

A Christian Futuristic Thriller

William S. Creed

House of Stuart Publishing
PUBLISHING THE BEST OF NEW FICTION

This book is a work of fiction. Names, characters, places and events are products of the author's imagination or are used fictitiously. Any resemblance to actual events, locations or persons, living or deceased, is purely coincidental. We assume no responsibility for errors, inaccuracies, omissions, or any inconsistency herein.

First printing 2003
Second printing 2004

ISBN 0-9722891-3-5
LCCN 2002110152

ATTENTION CORPORATIONS, UNIVERSITIES, COLLEGES, AND PROFESSIONAL ORGANIZATIONS: Quantity discounts are available on bulk purchases of this book for educational, gift purposes, or as premiums for increasing magazine subscriptions or renewals. Special books or book excerpts can also be created to fit specific needs. For information, please contact House of Stuart Publishing, editors@houseofstuart.net; ph. 586-752-0137.

— TABLE OF CONTENT—

CHAPTER 1

They're Coming

THE HUMID FLORIDA night draped itself over the small squat white building. Inside, however, the station was comfortable thanks to the valiant air-conditioning, which, even during these early morning hours, struggled.

These dark, early hours were Ron Borders' favorite time to work: No calls, no distractions, and best of all, no officers—unless one considered the OD boss, but Ron didn't since the officer of the day was in another building, almost a mile away. Here, despite his boyish face and sun bleached hair, he was the boss. He had attempted to conquer his youthful seventeen-year-old appearance by growing a beard on his twenty-two-year-old face. It was only partially successful: It was neither growing fast nor evenly, giving him a haggard unshaven look.

He shuffled through his CDs, looking for the appropriate one. Although playing the radio and occasionally a CD helped pass the hours, Ron was always careful not to let the music distract him from the monitors. The thought passed through his mind that a crossword puzzle could help, but he dismissed the notion before it could become a temptation. It was a rule that full attention should be paid to the data. He knew others on the day and afternoon shifts read books or played games to pass the time, but he didn't allow himself those luxuries.

One of the monitors beeped. With a groan, Ron put his feet on the floor, enabling him to reach the control panel. Several times each shift, these beeps would sound. Any stray signal necessitated the inconvenience of small adjustments. He slowly adjusted the dial as usual, but the signal was strong. Ron watched carefully, feeling his heart beginning to pound.

"Oh no," he muttered, fiddling with the dial again. "No, no, no!"

He grabbed the alert phone. He didn't have to dial; it automatically rang at headquarters. It was answered immediately. "Give me the OD!" he shouted.

Another voice came on quickly. "This is the OD. What's up?"

"Sir, this is Airman Ron Borders at STAT OPS A. I need you here immediately, sir, immediately!"

"What's up, airman?"

"Sir, you know that thing we joked about? It's happening. They're coming!"

THE CONFERENCE ROOM at the Hyatt was crowded—fifty yapping reporters stuffed in a room meant for half that. Andy Moore paused a moment before entering the room. Slowly he looked around at the group of reporters while listening to the increasing din of their voices. He clasped his notebook between his arms and folded them across his tall body. He was a distinguished-looking man; the years had been kind to his forty-year-old face. His chiseled features were showing signs of deepening lines, but otherwise he looked thirty. Finally he made his way into the room, feeling instantly clammy, his forehead quickly glistening under the overhead fluorescents while his nostrils told him more than he wanted to know about the bathing habits of others.

"This shindig better be worth it," he grumbled to himself. A laughing man backed into him. Each apologized, both thinking the other was an idiot. Maneuvering his six-foot-two frame between bodies, Andy headed for the only space in the room that was sparsely populated—the very back, near an open window. He suddenly wished he weren't there, but then he considered the rare paycheck. Where he should be was covering the war. He should be on some barren ridge in

Israel or Iraq writing a column by shaded flashlight with the sounds of gunfire in the distance. But here he was covering something he had no expertise about. He'd like to blame Edward Poll, his editor at the paper. But it wasn't Ed who drank all that booze, wouldn't get outta bed, spent mornings over the toilet. No it wasn't—but who cared? He'd blame him anyway. It made him feel better.

So a new comet had been discovered, sure it was important, but big deal. He shouldn't complain and he knew it. He was lucky to get the story, and with some clever writing, he might be able to stretch it into a couple of columns, two paychecks: one grocery and the other rent.

Nodding at others, he squeezed through the crowd, managing half smiles for familiar faces as well as strangers.

"Andy...hey, Andy Moore!"

Andy caught a glimpse of Tommy Jenkins slowly making his way toward him, though not having much luck at the moment. This was the first time he'd seen TJ, as he was known, in almost a year and he didn't want to now. He hadn't changed much. Still had the good looks Andy wished he enjoyed himself. At least he was taller than TJ's five-foot-nine—that was something. Tommy's short brown hair always bounced as he walked, whereas Andy had to plaster his own down, another reason not to talk to him. And there were other things that made Andy jealous of TJ—his square face, and Greek nose, and eyes that sparkled when he laughed then narrowed to slits when thinking.

Quickly Andy turned away, feigning deafness, while pushing a little faster through the crowd, bowing his head to make his silver streaked hair less noticeable. It wasn't that he disliked TJ—he was a nice guy, really. It wasn't TJ at all. In fact, he'd known the man for years, and found him to be honest, churchgoing (maybe too much of that), and always of good cheer. The problem, Andy knew, was with himself. Having TJ see him now was like an old schoolmate seeing him as a bum. Gone were the days of headline stories, insightful analysis, and insider contacts. Now he picked up stories here and there as a stringer. He couldn't bear the humiliation. TJ was everything he used to be and now wasn't.

Catching a glimpse of John Trombley, he made a path in his direction. Trombley wasn't a friend, simply a body he could hide behind. Short, pudgy, in his late forties, and as usual standing alone, rocking back and forth while embracing a briefcase beneath his nearly bald head. His appearance was that of a mad-scientist, which was close to true. Though Andy considered him wacky, he also knew Trombley was brilliant. If anybody was aware of the news in space, it was this weirdo. Hanging from Trombley's vest pocket was his press pass; received by publishing a not-always-monthly newsletter, which other wacky people read.

"John," smiled Andy. "What's going on here?" He stood behind Trombley, hunching over a bit and looking beyond to see if TJ was still coming. He wasn't.

Trombley grunted, as usual. "A show—just a show," he snapped with his squeaky voice. "If you want the truth, you won't find it here. I just showed up to see how they're gonna handle it."

"The comet?"

Trombley snorted. "Comet. Yeah, that's what they're calling it, all right."

"What do you mean?"

Trombley's eyes focused on Andy. "Never mind. Find out for yourself."

Andy's antenna began to twitch, but before he could answer, a crackle came from the overhead speakers.

"Ladies and gentlemen." The voice was young—maybe late twenties—a typical political groupie, hanging around Washington scooping up unimportant appointee jobs for the resume. "We're passing around some releases for you. Please read them over. Richard Kirkland of NASA will be out shortly to answer a few brief questions. Thank you."

Out of nowhere, someone handed Andy a stack of stapled papers. Taking the top package, he passed the remaining to his left into nowhere. Semi-silence crept over the room as reporters began reading.

Trombley leaned toward Andy. Andy could smell his foul breath when he spoke. "Told ya."

"Told me? Told me what?"

"This is a bunch of crap!" snorted the little man.

"You think it's not true?"

"Think? I know it's not!"

Again Andy felt his antenna twitch, this time stronger. "Really? Now John, you don't really know it's not true. I remember three years ago when you said you knew NASA was building the Tri-Max engine…"

"And they were!" snapped Trombley. "They just got it under wraps. Besides, I know what's true here. I got the proof."

"I'd have to see it to believe it," mumbled Andy, appearing barely interested.

"I got it all right here," retorted Trombley patting his clasped briefcase.

Andy's eyebrows crawled together.

"You don't believe me?" snapped Trombley. Without waiting, he reached into the tightly held case, withdrawing an inch of fan-folded computer paper. Only half the pages came out, the rest unfolding like an accordion "Take a look at this!"

Trombley rapidly flipped through the pages, stopping here and there to point out supposed proof to Andy, but the expression on Andy's face showed his confusion.

"I don't get it," he confessed.

Trombley let a breath of exasperation escape. "Why do you even cover space news? You're an idiot," he gasped. "This is a spectrographic wave analysis of the so-called comet's path." Quickly he retraced the pages he'd just shown to Andy. "These paths are not natural."

"Not natural?"

"Are you gonna listen to me or not? Not natural! This is not a comet. No comet moves like this one does."

Andy was silent; stunned by the implication Trombley was making. It would be the story of the century, if true. "Maybe it's natural and the paths you see are just some kinda gravitational pull from somewhere?" Andy ventured.

Trombley shook his head slowly while imitating Andy's voice, "Some kinda gravity from somewhere doing something to something.… There isn't any such 'something' out there—and even if there was, it wouldn't make angular movements."

"So you're saying it's something else? Something not natural?" Andy lowered his voice. "Like a spacecraft?"

"I didn't say that!" exploded Trombley. His sudden outburst turned a few heads.

Trombley waited a few moments, then resumed almost in a whisper: "I didn't say that. I suppose it could be, at least it's something that's not natural. Maybe a probe—you know, like the ones we send, but this one is huge."

"Big, huh?"

Trombley nodded.

Andy grabbed Trombley's elbow, which the scientist instinctively tried to jerk away while stuffing printouts back into the briefcase, but Andy held fast, his big hand easily surrounding Trombley's arm. He found himself half pulling, half leading Trombley toward the back wall.

"Hey, wha—"

"Come here. I want to tell you something."

Finally Trombley shook his elbow loose but continued to follow Andy. Reaching the rear of the room, Andy hesitated, then motioned Trombley to follow him into the corridor.

Once in the corridor, Andy waited for the door to close.

"So what's with you?" demanded Trombley.

Andy cast a glance first one way, then the other, assuring himself they were alone. "This information you got, you know, that graph? Where'd you get it?"

"None of your business. I'm gonna blow this trumped-up news conference apart with it. About time this Nazi government started giving out the truth!" Trombley made a motion to leave, but Andy put his hand on the little man's arm.

"Wait. I agree, John, I agree," ventured Andy, exercising his best attempt at bridge building. "But this is not the place, it won't work. I'll tell you why: They simply are not going to believe you."

"Yes they will," retorted Trombley, holding up his briefcase. "I got the proof!"

"John, listen to me. Most of the jerks in there think you're nuts. They don't know you like I do."

"Last year you called me 'wacky' in your column."

"I was joking, John—I know how smart you are. Listen to me. I think I have a plan that would work."

Trombley lowered his head, tucking the briefcase closer to his chest, while giving Andy a hard look.

"First, if you lay all this out on the imbeciles inside, they'll just think its some sorta goofy stunt. Those guys will have you looking like a weird scientist on the loose." Andy paused, but Trombley kept silent. "Now, on the other hand, if I report it as a hard news story, people will pay attention. The Washington *Dispatch* has real clout."

The thought of such a story, under his byline and copyright, flashed through Andy's mind. All the syndicates would pick it up, for sure. In fact, if he were fast, he might maybe even get some articles in *Life, Time*—but he would need pictures. "Pictures. You got pictures?"

"Pictures? You nuts? By the time they are able to take pictures, it'll be all over. If this thing hits us, it'll be like every nuclear warhead ever made going off at once. There won't be anything left on Earth." Trombley wheezed, "Pictures. Where'd you learn about space—comic books?"

"Hit the Earth? It's gonna hit the Earth?" Andy was stunned. It hadn't occurred to him that such a thing was possible. Till now it was just a story—possibly the greatest story of his life, but now he felt a pang of fear.

"Well, not right now, it'll just pass close, real close. But if it changes course a little bit more, bull's-eye."

Andy rubbed his cheek, considering. "But if it isn't natural, like you said, if it's alien, wouldn't it avoid us?"

Trombley shrugged his shoulders. "Maybe, if it can. But suppose it's just some sorta probe? It wouldn't know we were here until it was too late."

"Is it possible there might be aliens inside?"

Trombley shrugged his shoulders again. "Could be, I suppose—but I'm not saying there is, and don't go saying I said there are aliens!"

From inside the room, Andy heard someone start speaking through the loudspeaker. Moving Trombley further from the door, Andy gave him his best pitch. "Now, John, don't say anything at all here. Believe me, these guys will blow you out of the water. Best thing to do is for us to team up and put this story out ourselves. I'll write it up just the way you want. The wire services will gobble it up, especially when I use the word 'alien.'"

"I told you, I didn't say there were aliens!"

"I know, I know. I'm not gonna say you used the word, I'll just sort of hint at it, like a speculation. It will give the story longer legs. I guarantee you, a lot more people—people from all over the world will hear it. And…they will know it was you who found it out, John! Think of it—'John Trombley, space scientist!'"

Trombley was silent for a moment. "You'll use my name? Give me credit?"

"Oh course."

"What's in it for you?" challenged Trombley.

"I won't lie to you, this is the biggest story I or anybody else ever had, and I want it. But I also want to get out the truth, same as you."

Trombley considered for a moment, then slowly nodded.

"Great! Now, here's the plan. We wait until those NASA people get their stories reported. Let their stories run, see. That'll get the public's attention. Then we'll zap them with ours. It's gonna be beautiful, John, just beautiful. You're gonna love it." He paused for a moment. "Now, John, this is for real, right? I mean, you do have the facts right? You aren't a nutcase like they say?"

"Who says I'm a nutcase! I'm no nutcase—and I got the proof right here! Just read it yourself—oh, forgot, you got no brains. So you don't believe me?"

"No, no, just checking." Then, reassuring Trombley he would have the story ready to release after the morning edition and would give him all the credit, Andy took two of the chart pages, the accompanying explanations, and bid Trombley goodbye. Quickly, he headed for the Washington Suites Hotel where he was staying while in town.

Outside, the evening's heat enveloped, then clung to him, but Andy was oblivious to the assault as he hailed a cab; already he was putting together the lead sentence of the story. It was a thirty-minute ride to his hotel, but Andy didn't notice, nor was he aware that he had arrived until the cabby tapped on the glass and asked for the money. Quickly thrusting his next-to-last twenty into the driver's hand, he rushed into the lobby's cool air.

"Mr. Moore? Oh, Mr. Moore!" His name came floating across the lobby. Andy stopped and waited for a dapper man hurrying toward him. His gait gave him an awkward appearance as he tried to maintain some sophistication. Approaching Andy, the clerk leaned close.

"Mr. Moore, I'm the day manager here and I have some awkward news. As you instructed, we put through your credit card for an extension covering the next two nights. Unfortunately, it seems you've exceeded your credit limit."

"I have?"

"Yes, sir. If you have another card I could use, I would be happy to put it through."

"I don't have another card." In fact, he was lucky he had that one.

"Oh, I see." His tone dropped a bit. "Well, I'm afraid we'll have to ask you to vacate the room. You're only paid up through last night."

"Vacate? Now?"

The manager nodded sympathetically.

"I can't. I got a story to write. How about if you put it through for one more night and I throw in some money too?" he asked, fishing in his pocket and withdrawing his last twenty.

For a second, it appeared the manager was going to object, but instead he sighed, "Very well, Mr. Moore, if I have any problem I'll call your room; otherwise, checkout time tomorrow is eleven A.M."

Andy nodded and hurried to the elevators. He was tired of people always hounding him about money. He'd show them—it wouldn't be long until he could carry hundreds just for tips. This story was going to make him some real money. The thought brought a rare smile.

Reaching his room, he attacked the laptop computer, framing ideas decided upon during the ride over. He paused for a moment as the thought flashed through his mind that he might be writing a story that a crazy man told him. Retrieving his old address book, he fished for a phone number. Grabbing the phone, he dialed. She didn't answer until the third ring.

"Hello?" Her voice hadn't changed.

"Carla?"

There was a brief pause before she answered. "Andy? Is that you?"

"The one and the same. So how are you?"

"Well, I'm fine. Why are you calling? Have you been drinking?"

"No, Carla, girl, I haven't. I'm still as dry as a bone. I called to ask a favor."

He heard her exhale into the receiver. "A favor. I might have known. Not a word from you in four years, but now you need a favor."

"Yeah, ain't it the pits?"

"So what's the favor?"

"Well, you're still the admin for the science department, aren't you?"

"So?"

"Isn't that astronomer Gregory Tole part of that department?"

"Yes."

"I thought so, and doesn't he sorta know something about radio telescopes?"

"Well, I guess so. He's one of the leading authorities. A lot of places call him as an advisor, but you know that."

"Yes. Here's the favor, a question really: Are you aware of any special goings on with him and the radio telescopes?"

There was a brief silence. "What do you mean?"

Andy detected a subtle change in her tone: A bit more professional, a little more distant.

"Well, like maybe there is something coming at us from out in space." There, he said it. Now she was probably going to call him an idiot.

"I can't talk about those things."

Andy's spirits jumped. "You can't talk about those things—you mean something is out there and you can't talk about it."

"Goodbye, Andy."

"No, Carla, wait. Give me a break here, this is big!"

Carla did not respond, but Andy could hear her breathing for a moment, as she hesitated, then hung up.

Slowly Andy replaced the receiver, and smiled. Carla had told him all he needed to know—that weirdo had really found something!

He attacked his laptop again with the story writing itself. How couldn't it? It was the biggest piece of news since Jesus Christ. In fact, bigger. Back then they didn't have the wire services, TV, or best of all, residuals.

He wrote until almost midnight. When finished, he actually had three stories: The first, a news release; second, a piece for the magazines; and last, his in-depth story. This one he liked the most. It talked about himself, how he had tracked the story, squeezing it out of a reluctant source, and so forth.

Finally, Andy leaned back in his chair, stretching protesting muscles as he reached for the ceiling. It felt great. He was going to make it big again, at last. Maybe he'd look up TJ and invite him to dinner. He was really a delightful guy and Andy felt bad about ducking him. Rising from the chair, Andy stretched once more then flopped down on the bed. He felt great. He felt exhausted. Sleep pounced on him without warning.

Sunlight jolted him awake, though not until it was well into the sky. He'd assumed this day, this very special day, he'd be awake before the sun rose. Jumping out of bed he showered and dressed. Checking his watch, Andy saw there was still time to make the deadline at the Washington *Dispatch*.

The phone rang.

"So where's my story!" Trombley's squeaky voice demanded.

"It's on its way, John, just keep cool. I'm releasing it to the *Dispatch* this morning—check the evening edition, you'll see."

A click was Trombley's response.

Andy dropped the phone on the hook. Who cared? The guy was probably nuts anyway. Life was good. His story would blow the media apart. He could already feel his hands around the steering wheel of his new Corvette—and he wouldn't have to watch the games on an old 21-inch TV either. One of those big screen jobs with a zillion channels. Finally his ship was coming in, but would it be full of aliens? Who cared?

Making a quick call to the lobby, he arranged to extend his checkout time until three P.M. Good, that's when the evening editions would be available. In the lobby, Andy checked the newsstand for the morning papers. Sure enough, they were reporting the story given of the newly discovered comet. It wasn't the main story—the war still was that. Today the headlines were of Iraq's talk using the word nuclear. Yet, it did make the front page. What a setup. He was going to buy a paper, then remembered giving all his money to the greedy hotel guy. He was reminded again when he instinctively started to hail a cab. No matter. He set off walking to the newspaper office, six blocks away.

Slightly flushed, Andy pushed through the front double doors into the air-conditioned lobby in time to see the editor, Jim Morgan, about to leave.

"Hey, Jim. Hold on!"

The editor paused and looked. Seeing it was Andy, he resumed his exit, but too late. Andy was on him.

"I've got the greatest story of my life—and yours too!"

Morgan's brow furrowed. "Again?" he replied flatly as he continued walking.

"I'm serious, it's all right here—read it!" His voice rose as he shoved the papers in the editor's face.

Perhaps it was the intensity of Andy's voice, or the fact that Morgan secretly liked—or felt sorry for—Andy that he took the papers. He scanned through the story quickly, then reread. This time slowly.

"Not for me," was his announced judgment.

"Not for you? What do you mean, 'not for you'?"

"Did you think I'd scoop it up?"

"Did I think? I knew you would. It's the biggest thing since 'and then there was light!'"

"Yeah right. I'm tired of your blockbuster promises and do-nothing results. Aliens? Are you nuts, and you use that goofy so-called scientist for a source and authority? Goodbye," he said, taking a couple of steps, but Andy positioned himself in front, blocking Morgan.

"Listen a minute. I got it confirmed."

"Confirmed? A second source? Not a flying saucer freak?"

"Hell no, absolutely not."

Morgan looked at Andy then took a deep breath. "Okay, who?" he asked.

Andy hesitated; he couldn't say it was a feeling he got talking to his wife. "I can't reveal the identity."

Morgan turned away. "Goodbye."

"Wait, I'll get that second confirmation. Listen a minute. I've been in this business over twenty years. Okay, so lately I've been slipping, but I tell you this is the real thing. The *Times* wants it," he lied, and it worked.

"The *Times?* That rag?" Morgan said with disgust. But Andy knew he'd struck a soft spot. Though Morgan didn't like the *Times,* if they were going to print, that added pressure. The editor paused. "You gotta get me another source to confirm it—and I don't mean some goofy fruitcake. Get someone from the university to even admit it might be possible and I'll go with it."

"Done. How long I got until deadline?"

Morgan checked his watch. "Five hours."

"That's time enough. Uh, I'll need to get over to the university and I just lost my wallet, could you let me have twenty or so, until I can get to the bank? Promise, I'll have that second source wrapped up by deadline."

Morgan sighed. "Lost your wallet, again? You should tie a string on that thing." He fished in his pocket, pulling out a twenty-dollar bill, and was about to hand it over, when he grabbed another, shoving both into Andy's hand.

Morgan was a good guy. Andy smiled his appreciation.

"If you don't have that second source on my desk within five hours—don't show your face around here again!"

Andy nodded. Well, maybe he wasn't such a good guy after all.

Andy's first instinct was to go to the university and interview one of the professors, then he remembered someone he'd known a long time ago. Having been in the reporter game for twenty years gave him a mental Rolodex. Hailing a cab, he went back to the hotel, and rushing to his room, pulled the old address book from his briefcase. It'd been a long time since he'd needed it, and it was good to use it again. The black fake-leather was so thin in places the color had worn off, exposing the white paper beneath. The pages were bent and dirty from years of pawing. They felt good to the touch, though the years of human oil and dirt had turned them almost gray in places. He located the name he was searching for, Ron Borders. Quickly he placed the call. It had been more than ten years since he'd spoken to the man, but surely he would remember him. For crying out loud, the man and his wife had stayed at his place when they visited Washington.

A male voice answered on the third ring. "Tracking," was the short greeting.

"Ron? Is this Ron Borders?"

"Yeah. Who's this?"

"Andy. Andy Moore. Remember me? We watched the *Challenger* blow up when it launched."

There were a few moments of silence. "No, I don't remember. I think you have the wrong number—"

"Wait! Sure you remember, you and your wife Karen stayed at my place when you visited Washington."

The response was a single click.

For a moment Andy stood still, staring at the phone in his hand. What was that all about? Surely, Borders remembered. No one could forget staying at someone's house on a trip. Moreover, they had gone to bars together, seen the *Challenger* blow up, were almost thrown in jail one time. No, something was not right. Borders did remember, Andy was sure of it. Replacing the receiver on the telephone set, he knew whatever the reason for the man's behavior, would have to wait. There were more important things he needed to do right now. He grabbed the envelope containing the information he would need to show to a professor. He was his last hope. Quickly he made for the front door. The telephone ring stopped him. Turning back, he picked up the receiver.

"Yes?"

"Andy? Good, you're still there, good."

"Borders? How did you find me here?"

"All telephone calls are traced now."

"Since when? Where are you calling me from?"

"My cell phone. Security is real tight since they found that thing. That's why you called, right?"

"Yeah, if you mean that comet—whatever it is."

"I thought so. Look, Andy, we go back a ways, so let me tell you to be careful. Something is really going down, and you might get hurt if you aren't careful."

"So tell me what *is* going on?"

"Not sure, but it looks like that comet isn't a comet."

"Aliens?" ventured Andy, unable to hold back.

"Aliens? I never said that. Aliens? You never heard that from me! We tracked it for about a week now, and it sure doesn't behave like any comet I ever saw or heard of." Borders was silent for a moment. "Yeah, okay, some of the scuttle mentions aliens—it's why everything is getting so crazy—and they don't want anyone to know."

Andy let out a low whistle. "I'm about to write a story blowing the lid off this thing. Will you help me?" Andy asked.

"You crazy? I'm not gonna stick my neck out and get canned."

"I won't use your name—an unidentified source is what I'll say. Only myself and my editor will know."

"Look, Andy, I would like to help you, but I can't. It would mean my job, for sure."

"So? After these boys land, who's gonna worry about a job—I think chaos will break loose."

Borders was silent for a second, and Andy did not prod him, he had to do this on his own. Finally Borders inhaled, "Yeah, you're right. everything will go down the tubes when they land. Okay, look, here's what I can do. I have some graphs on this thing: its course both projected, and actual. They show that this thing is not natural, it's something that was made, and is directed."

"Great, Ron, I appreciate it."

"Wanna know why I'm doing it?"

"'Cause we're buds?"

"No. I think the world deserves to know. This is big, Andy, and a lot of people could get hurt if they aren't told in time. I don't think any government has the right to withhold something like this. Now, you won't use my name?"

"No, I won't. The only person I'll tell, if I have to, is my editor, and only if I have to, Ron. Believe me, neither he nor I will ever release it."

Borders was silent for a moment. "Okay. Now it'll take me a little while to get this together. Then I have to fax it, and that could be a problem too. I'll have to find a place where I can do it, and not be traced—I'll figure that out. When you get the fax, cut off any identifying info, okay?"

"You got it." Andy gave him the fax number and hung up. He was excited, more than he'd been in years. This was it. This was the story of a lifetime, and it was his. Quickly he gathered his belongings; it was time to check out of the hotel and then go get the fax. Fortunately, he hadn't packed heavy and the two small suitcases weren't burdensome. He made his way to the lobby and then to the hotel's familiar bar where the longtime bartender, Robert, with his white gloves, was wiping down the bar. Andy suspected the gloves were Robert's idea, and not the hotel's. Perhaps they were his way of standing out as a professional.

"Hey there, Andy. How long you been in town?" greeted Robert.

"Got in night before last. I was trying to cover the NASA news conference."

"Umm," muttered Robert. It was his standard reply to all news, good, bad, funny, or sad. "What's up? How come no-see until now? What's with NASA—they launching a new shuttle or something?"

"Actually, Robert, what I found out at the conference is gonna blow this town apart."

"Terrorism?" asked Robert, a trace of alarm in his voice.

"No, no, not terrorism—something even bigger than that. I just can't tell you right this second. You'll find out about it tomorrow."

Robert held up his hand. "No problem. I'll probably hear all about it across the bar tonight," he said, smiling.

Andy smiled and nodded. "Say, Robert, your fax in the back is still working, isn't it—the one customers use to send in their lunch orders?"

"Andy, you using my fax again? When you gonna get one of your own? I swear, I never heard of a newsman using a restaurant fax for his business. I should charge you, big-time. And you, not even gonna tell me what it's all about." Robert smiled broadly.

"Yeah, I owe you, Robert."

"When is that fax comin'?"

"May be here now, you wanna check?"

"Sure, you want something to drink while you wait? Coke, milk? You stayin' off the sauce still?"

"You know I am."

Robert grinned, setting down a coke before disappearing through two double doors behind the bar. Returning a minute later shaking his head, "Nothing yet."

Andy nodded. He and Robert exchanged small talk for an hour before Robert checked again. This time he returned with a sheaf of five pages.

"These what you're looking for?"

Andy thumbed through them. A couple of the pages showed graphs similar to the ones he'd taken from Trombley.

Andy jumped up and grabbed Robert's black face, pulling it across the bar where he gave him a big kiss on the cheek. "Thank you, darlin'!"

"Hey, you fool!" protested Robert, jerking back and looking around the empty room. "You lost your mind?" he snapped as he wiped his cheek vigorously.

"No, found it. Hey, I'm gonna throw these bags behind here for a couple of hours, okay?"

"No it ain't okay, what do you think this is? You waltz in here after a year, turning this place into your private office, sexually assault me, now you want to make it your closet too." Robert shook his head. "Put them behind the door there. If you aren't back by tonight, I'll sell them."

"Why don't you put them in your room? You still have a room here?"

"Sure. Can't give up my lucky number one-two-two-five. I used to play my room number in the lottery every week. Too bad they stopped that."

"Hey, Robert, my man, thanks a lot—I really appreciate it."

"Okay, fine, but don't kiss me again, fool! You're losing your marbles!"

Andy laughed, waving as he left.

Arriving at the Washington *Dispatch,* he took a vacant desk and telephoned the astronomy instructor at the university. It took a little while, but he finally reached him and briefly brought him up to date.

If he sent him some graphs and accompanying text could he interpret them for him? He then faxed the documents over and waited. It took less than thirty minutes until he got a fax that confirmed everything he'd promised. The misspellings on the fax betrayed the author's excitement. An hour later, it was done. In another three, Andy held a copy of the newspaper in his hands. He got front-page headline! The story even pushed the Middle East War down the page. It'd been ten years since he'd had a front-page story. His name should have been bigger, perhaps. On the other hand, he had a two-thousand-dollar bonus in his pocket and didn't even have to pay back the forty he'd been given by Morgan. And he'd gotten his old job back, plus a raise. Life was good.

Over the next few days, Andy was in a daze and loving it. There were interviews with UPI, CBS, NBC, and the Sunday news programs. And then there was the money; it started coming fast, with promises of more to follow. Each day he wrote, and each day his ideas flowed, as they had years ago. But he could only take the maddening crush for so long, then slipped back to his apartment outside Washington. He had to escape, to think, to recharge his aging batteries with sleep, and then sleep some more.

Finally rested, he found himself on his patio reading the paper. The space news and the war news seesawed with the headline news. Today the war was back on top. It seemed the entire Muslim world was at war with the West. The headlines repeated the word "nuclear" more often now. It was getting scary. The talking heads on the tube had bantered it about here and there. Folding the paper Andy forced the war out of his mind—his concern now was his story. He sat staring at the old oak tree whose roots were raising the sidewalk. The story was getting old, at least for him. Now he was just one among many trying to find new ways to say "boo!" He needed a new angle, something really good. In this business, you need a new story every day, or comes the slippery slope. But where else could he go with this story? If he had his choice, the new story would be that his first story was a mistake. It was as though he wished the story had been discredited, and everyone could resume his or her normal lives without it being his fault and, of course, not having to refund any money.

On the other hand, having the UN debate his story and then verify it was a real rush. But it also made his skin crawl. It was real, and the world was about to undergo a trauma, the likes of which it had never collectively known in all of human experience.

He was startled by his phone's goofy ring filtering through the doorway. He disliked the new electronic phone rings. Why didn't they keep the old ones that shouted, "Answer me, stupid!" The new rings seemed too politically correct, as if they were saying, "I hate to intrude upon your space, but there's someone who wishes to speak with you." Ugh.

Andy grabbed the receiver. "Hello!"

His editor's voice surprised him; he couldn't recall ever receiving a call from him at home before.

"Andy. Get the first train in here; I need you in here now! Something is breaking and I know you'll want to be a part of it. Bring an overnight case with you."

"Sure, I'll—" but Morgan hung up before Andy could finish.

Andy replaced the receiver. There had been a sense of urgency in the voice. He didn't like that. The thought of calling back and declining flashed through his mind but faded before he could seriously consider it. Taking a deep breath, he hurried to leave. Something big was ahead. Although he rushed, he feared he would be too late for the train. Fortunately, the five o'clock commuter was late too.

The departing side of the station for passengers headed to D.C., was empty. It was time for the rush of people out of the city to arrive at the opposite side of the tracks. Only he and a sad-looking fellow occupied the departure side. Andy doubted the other man was a passenger. From his clothes and demeanor, he was most likely a vagrant.

Suddenly the man looked at Andy and spoke. "Hey, mister." It was low and not unpleasant.

Ignoring the call, Andy turned his back toward the stranger. He would go away. From the corner of his eye he saw the man rise. He was tall and appeared surprisingly well muscled. Slowly he made his way toward Andy.

"Mister?"

Andy couldn't ignore him any longer, but without looking toward him replied, "Yeah?" He hoped his voice sounded surly enough.

"You got some money I could have for a dinner?"

Andy began to turn and move away, then stopped. Suddenly, he felt sorry for the man. Perhaps it was something in his voice. He reached into his pocket, grabbed a few bills, and thrust them toward the stranger. He got his first real look at the man. He did not look like a typical station rat. He wore a dirty suit, at least a size too small, with two missing buttons; however, his open-collared white shirt appeared spotless as was his face, which had almost-beautiful blue intelligent eyes. He took the bills then looked at Andy. Andy could feel his gaze reach inside of him.

"Thank you," the man said softly. "And one good turn deserves another, friend."

Slowly he put the bills into his pocket, without breaking his penetrating, disconcerting gaze, "God loves you. You are going on an adventure, and God is with you, Andy." The man smiled then turned and walked slowly toward the exit and around the corner.

Andy was stunned. How did he know his name? He watched him silently and was so engrossed in his thoughts, he didn't hear the approaching train until startled by the breaking wheels on the tracks. Who was that bum? What story was behind him? His reporter antenna jerked; but he realized he'd never know.

TOMMY JENKINS WAS mad, and his walk showed it. Passing through the *Times* newsroom, he ignored the "Hi, TJs," even brushing past a few people without realizing it. Reaching the editor's door, he strode through without knocking. "Just what do you think you're doing?" he demanded of Drexton as he entered.

His editor looked up, startled by the sudden entry. "Wha—"

"You know I'm the one that should be going—that story should be mine."

Drexton's eyes closed for a second as he caught up with the question. "Close the door, TJ, and sit down."

For a brief moment TJ did not move, then he slowly shut the door.

"That's better, now sit." There was no anger in Drexton's voice, but TJ could hear a tone of sternness creep into Drexton's normally soft-spoken voice. The editor got up slowly from the chair, his seventy years requiring help from his hands, and shuffled to the window.

"You're right," he said finally. "This should be your story, son. But I don't want you to take it." He turned, looking at TJ while leaning against the windowsill. "If this were a story about a bombing, a murder, kidnapping—you name it, you'd be gone. I'd send you. If this were a war, you'd be gone. But this is different." He sighed, putting his hands in his pockets, then stood silent for a few seconds. "Yes, this is very different. Things are going to change around here. I don't mean just a little, they're gonna change big-time. The whole fabric of society is gonna get torn."

Turning back toward the window, he looked down on the busy street. "Look here," he said motioning TJ over. "See those people down there? They walk when the light says they should, they pass by each other without a thought. They all feel safe and secure inside a whole matrix of society's checks and balances that say they can go their way safely, can sleep tonight in peace, wake tomorrow and have food—all without fear." Drexton turned and reached out, tapping his knuckles on the desk. "That's all gonna change."

"What are you talking about?" asked TJ, his voice subdued. Drexton had always been strong-willed, tough talking, and brusquely kind—now, his tone was of a sad old man sharing a secret.

Drexton returned to his chair, sitting heavily in it. "Look, I got word two hours ago we could send a reporter out with the ships. Some say they're going to land, some say not. No one knows for sure—don't know what's inside of those things, if anything. Either way, life around the planet is going to change."

"So it's true…the ships are going out to where those space things are suppose to hit," TJ interjected.

Drexton nodded. "I guess the *Dispatch* is sending Andy Moore and we're allowed to send one man also. That should be you, I know. But TJ, I think your place is here with your wife. I don't know if any of those ships are coming back—nobody knows. The way I see it, one of two things is going to happen. First, those things headed toward us are pieces of rock, big enough to split this planet in two. If that happens, you should be with your wife. Second, I guess it could be some sorta alien ship. Now, if it is, if there are aliens out there about to pay us a visit, pandemonium is gonna strike. Every screwball, malcontent, half-baked philosopher, anti-social loser, and criminal is going to simply opt out."

"Of what?"

"Society! The rules are off! There's a new game plan. It might start slow, but it won't take long before the streets are gonna be empty, stores empty, factories empty. Two kinds of people will emerge: Those that prey upon the weak, and the weak." He stopped for a second, reading TJ's face. "Don't agree? Look, m'boy, I've spent more years than you've been alive watching people and then writing about them. I may not know about a lot of things, but I'm in the people game. I know people. Your wife is going to need you near."

TJ silently sat back down in his chair. Drexton had done more than he realized. He confirmed what Sarah had already told him. And the risks—Sarah knew all about the risks. Should he tell Drexton Sarah already knew about the coming aliens long before the news broke? TJ rose from the chair slowly. He knew he couldn't tell anyone, no one would understand. This was something he had to do, and Sarah knew it. Looking his old friend in the eye, TJ reached out and touched his arm. "I know what you're trying to do here, but I don't need protect-ing, nor does my wife. This is a story I can't let pass, and you can't let it pass me by. I want to go." TJ held up his hands as though trying to frame his sentence. "When the war started I wanted to go, but you talked me out of that. I understood why, and I appreciated your con-cern. This is different. This is bigger. My Lord, this is a visitation from outer space! I've got to go. You know that!"

Drexton looked down at the desk a few seconds, then nodded. "Okay...I hope for your sake it's the right decision."

In thanking his editor, TJ found Drexton's handshake firmer than normal and reluctant to let go. Then TJ was off, hurrying to pack and say goodbye to Sarah.

Opening the backdoor to their house, he found her waiting in the kitchen. Her hair was done up in the usual bun and she was dressed in blue jeans and the white blouse with roses, her favorite flower. Silently she watched him come into the kitchen. TJ wasn't surprised to see her waiting. Sarah always seemed to know.

"Well, honey," he began, "I leave immediately."

Sarah nodded, then looked down.

"We knew this is the way it had to be," TJ said.

Sarah looked quietly into his eyes for a moment. "No, this is not the way it has to be. This is the way you think it should be."

TJ walked over, placed his arms around his wife, and held her close. "We need proof, honey. We need to know for sure. I'm convinced we need to say we know for sure."

Sarah stepped back. "No, we don't. You just won't trust me, and what I already know." She took a deep breath, looking up at the ceiling. "But if you've made up your mind, there is nothing I can do."

TJ embraced her again. "I think I need to do this. Who's gonna believe you? I believe you, 'cause I love you. But others, I think they are gonna need proof before they make a commitment."

Sarah nodded. "I know you think you should, but I don't feel good about this. I just don't feel good."

TJ smiled. "Don't worry, I'll be careful. My guess is we will be gone no more than a month. When I get back, we'll do things your way, promise."

Sarah smiled small. "You promise to make me breakfast for a week?"

TJ smiled. "Promise."

LEANING BACK ON the Lazy Boy, Bernie felt the leather responding graciously to his round body. He ran his fingers through his mostly white and uneven beard, then removed his rimless glasses from beneath his balding head, before closing his eyes and breathing deeply. Bernie loved Sundays. On Sundays he felt safe. No telephone ringing. No knocking at the door. No station manager complaining. Today he was absolutely safe from the outside world. The only thing he might complain about was so much religious crap and war news. Every re-tired general since Grant was telling him what was happening, why it was, what would be next, ad infinitum. What he needed was a good baseball game. Or maybe what they needed was a pre-pre-pre-game show. They were the best napping shows.

Clicking the TV, he scanned a few channels. Though he couldn't see the pictures clearly, he could tell what programs were on—war crap, religious crap, war crap, religious crap, cartoons, chic flick, ah—here's one: soccer game. He didn't like soccer, but the noise was right as was the drone of the play-by-play. Bernie lay the channel selector down and closed his eyes, taking a deep peaceful breath. Life was good.

Suddenly a loud knock at his apartment door startled him. Not only was it unexpected, but the strength of the knock was alarming. To Bernie there were different categories of knocks: Some were Police knocks, made with fists, shaking the door and surrounding wall; others were Grandma knocks—a little tapping at the door, and one just knew it was a kindly person, smiling in anticipation. And there were others: Schoolboy knocks, Relative knocks, and the old Morse Code—knockity-knock-knock…knock, knock. There seemed even to be a number associated with the type of call about to be made. Two knocks: "I know you know it's me"; three knocks: "I'm friendly and you'll like me"; four knocks: "I'm coming with authority, you'd better answer me."

This was a firm four-knocker.

Bernie snapped his chair shut, maneuvered out, and approached the door suspiciously. Grabbing the doorknob, he paused, then put his eye to the peephole. It revealed two men in suits with ties, dressed almost like twins, and looking somewhat that way, too. Both were very tall, even taller-looking through the peephole, which also made both men look fatter than Bernie. Bernie liked that. Putting the chain in place, he opened the door an inch or two.

"Are you Bernard Krantz?" The voice came deep and flat.

Bernie nodded. The speaker reached into his suit coat's inner pocket, retrieving a plastic case the size of a business card, which unfolded easily, revealing an ID card on the lower half and a badge on the upper half. His partner duplicated the action.

"I'm Special Agent Grogan and this is Agent Hennings. We are with the U.S. State Department. May we come in?"

As the two stood with their ID cases extended, Bernie felt his chest tighten and his intestines turning liquid. Was this about his income tax? His bedroom was his office. He tried to look at the badges, but what should he be looking for? They looked official, but so did all that stuff today, including letters selling magazines that looked like they were from God himself, but rarely were. He took a chance.

Unlatching the chain, he opened the door without speaking. The two agents walked in, giving quick, professional scans of the apartment. In person, they were even more impressive in appearance than through the peephole. Both were well over 6 feet tall, with bodies that appeared to be in excellent shape, topped with faces chiseled straight from a Louis L'Amour western. They looked like recruiting posters for Greek gods.

"Mr. Krantz, we've got a letter for you from the secretary of state. I'd appreciate your reading it now."

"Secretary of what state?"

"The United States, sir. Will you please read it?" He extended a new manila envelope with a seal over its flap and return address of Washington, D.C.

Bernie slowly unsealed the envelope, careful not to rip the flap, and withdrew a single, neatly typed sheet of paper from inside. Carefully he read the short letter, then looked up.

"This letter is from the secretary of the United States," he announced as though they didn't know, "he wants me to come to Washington." Bernie stared at the letter for a moment then looked up at the agents. "Why?"

"I'm afraid I can't go into the details; however, I am authorized to contact the White House for you to confirm this invitation."

"Our White House?" Bernie stared at first one, then the other agent.

Finally, agent Grogan stepped forward, putting his hand on Bernie's shoulder. "Mr. Krantz, believe me, what's about to happen will thrill you beyond your dreams. There are many people being contacted, not only here in the States but around the world. I assure you, they are every bit as puzzled as you are. This is your lucky day."

"It is?"

"Yes. I can say this: Are you aware of the objects in space that are headed this way?"

Bernie nodded. "Who isn't? That's all they been talking about—can't get a decent game on TV, nothing but specials."

"I can't tell you everything, but they have intelligence."

"Intelligence. You mean people?"

"Well, I can't go into that.

"Aliens?"

The agents exchanged glances.

"What's all this got to do with me? You sure you got the right guy?"

"We—that is the United Nations—received communication from them. They invited certain people to come and meet them, one hundred forty-four thousand, to be exact."

"Me? I'm one?"

Grogan nodded. "Have you ever seen aliens before?"

Bernie shook his head, then put his hand to his forehead as if the effort was too much. "Seen aliens? No, never. What a screwy question."

The agents remained silent, allowing Bernie time to think.

"I can't understand what I have to do with aliens. The closest I ever got to the government was an audit about twelve years ago. How do I know they don't want me 'cause I got the kind of blood they drink, or they want my liver or something?"

"Do you attend a church? Do you consider yourself a religious person?"

"No, not really."

The agent nodded silently, looking over to his partner who smiled small. He turned back to Bernie, "Well, you won't be alone in that, I assure you. The others invited feel the same way. They are all agnostic or atheist."

"Well, God knows I am."

CHAPTER 2

Plans

RELUCTANTLY TJ OPENED his eyes as he felt the bus come to a slow squealing stop. Looking out the window he saw they'd reached Tyndall Air Force Base, and the bus was now parked in front of some long, plain-looking barracks. The bus doors opened and an Air Force sergeant with an "MP" armband boarded, taking an envelope offered by the driver. Without looking inside, he put his hands on his hips, surveying the three passengers as though the bus were full of new recruits.

TJ yawned. He was dead tired. Although the flights and the bus trip together only took three hours, the experience seemed to drain him. A glance at his watch revealed it was just past midnight.

The MP approached the first man, a reporter from the *Dallas News*. Glancing first at the photo he'd withdrawn from the envelope and then at the passenger, he grunted, apparently satisfied. Moving to the UPI reporter occasioned another grunt, and finally to TJ, who felt uneasy under the stare. Apparently he passed inspection because the MP gave another grunt before moving forward in the bus.

"Follow me!" he commanded in a well-practiced military voice. He made his way off the bus without looking back, and headed for the barracks door to their right. TJ waited until the other two passengers made their way forward before following. The night was darker than usual because of the new moon. Except for an entryway light at the door of each barracks, there were no other visible lights. The barracks, a line of one-story wood, oblong buildings, obviously put there to perform the single function of housing bodies, did not have a permanent look about them. It appeared as though, at a moment's notice, they could be torn down and dispensed with, and no one would consider it a loss. The number painted on the front of their barracks was 262B. Following the others up three cement steps, then through the door, he saw the unsmiling MP waiting for them in the dimly lit entry hall.

"Okay. Inside are your bunks for the night. At oh-eight-hundred in the morning another bus will pick you up, you'll be given breakfast and then driven out to the airfield where you'll board transportation. Inside you'll find plenty of bunks, pick whatever one you want. Goodnight, ladies." With that he disappeared out the door and the sound of the bus departing followed moments later.

Carefully, the three made their way through double swinging doors into the darkened room where only a few snores disturbed the night. TJ couldn't wait to join them and a half hour later, almost did. But then he heard another bus pull up. He heard the outside door open and shut, voices, and finally one of the double doors creaked open. A big man shuffled down the dark aisle between the cots, obviously searching for an empty one. His silver streaked hair was TJ's first clue. It was Andy Moore.

"Hey there, stranger," TJ whispered, fighting his way back from near-sleep.

Andy stopped, and leaned forward, attempting to identify the voice. "Hey, yourself," he responded finally, with a smile. "Guess we're barracks mates, huh?"

"Guess," replied TJ. "I heard you were coming. Hope you can fill me in on some details, I don't know much. Just grabbed my bag, and here I am."

Quietly Andy approached, dumping his small suitcase on the bunk next to TJ. He tested the mattress with his hand and found it too hard and too thin. Cautiously he sat down, uttering a low satisfied groan before answering TJ. "Don't know much myself. Heard we catch a flight out in the morning. Understand we're gonna stop in Japan and then be flown out to a ship." said Andy, patting the mattress again and shaking his head. "It's been twenty years since I slept on one of these, they haven't improved," he grumbled.

"It must be coming down in the ocean," whispered TJ.

"That's the word—in fact, my sources tell me it's in the Antarctic Ocean" replied Andy, as he sank into the metal springs on the bunk.

"Really. The Antarctic—I don't know if I like that. I was hoping for something warmer like maybe the Caribbean"

Andy smiled as he rubbed the top of his head. "Yeah, it's gonna be cold. What I learned actually were the coordinates. Six degrees east and sixty-six degrees south. And that puts us in exactly the middle of nowhere—except iceberg land."

"Sounds like you looked it up."

"Yeah. We aren't far from the Antarctic Circle, just off Queen Maud Land—whatever that is. Hope you brought your longjohns, TJ, my boy."

TJ sat up in his bunk, swinging his legs over the side. "Andy, what do you think—are we gonna see some true-blue aliens? Sarah doesn't think so."

Andy didn't reply immediately. TJ referencing his wife always bothered him. Who'd he think Sarah was? Andy knew her as a nice girl, pretty girl, gracious, smart—but so what? Why did TJ treat her like she was some kinda mystic all the time? "Sarah says, Sarah feels, I think Sarah knows." A man shouldn't be under a woman's thumb like that. Not right. But he was too tired to make an issue of it. He replied simply, "Who knows?"

TJ nodded slowly.

Andy stretched. It felt good after the trip. "From what I hear, Washington thinks we might. I talked to a guy I know at NASA, down at the Cape. He says these things—these spaceships—aren't solid. Maybe they're a mirage."

"Not solid?" TJ's voice began to rise.

Andy held up his hand to quiet TJ. Looking around, he lowered his voice. "That's what he says. Seems they can't get any radar readings on them, only light readings. I'm wondering if maybe they are some sort of projection, you know, like an image we're supposed to think is real." It was comfortable talking to TJ now, now that Andy felt successful again. In fact, listening to the young man talk, Andy wondered why he ever avoided TJ. He was a delightful man, with enthusiasm Andy enjoyed.

"Hmm. A projection?" mused TJ.

"Just a thought. Goofy. At any rate, in the next few days we're going to hear a lot of speculation from everyone here," he said, gesturing to the sleeping bodies around them. "My guess is, the facts aren't going to reveal themselves until the last moment," said Andy.

TJ nodded. "Look, what say we team up on this thing? There's too much going down, and in such a short time span, I don't think either of us can be everywhere to get the whole story. Maybe if we team up we can both get a better story." TJ felt a second of regret knowing he wouldn't be able to share everything he knew—that Sarah knew.

Andy thought for a moment as he pulled off his shirt. "I think you might have something there—a shared byline?"

TJ smiled, he didn't care about bylines this time. Offering his hand, he said, "Done."

Andy shook his hand, then lay back on his bunk. It was obvious TJ wanted to talk more, but he was dead tired. There was nothing that couldn't wait until the morning. Morning would come soon enough, probably too soon.

It did, rudely.

"Up and at 'em, ladies!" The loud voice cut through the dark, followed instantly by bright lights and a chorus of groans and expletives.

"Now, now ladies—I know you love me," was his practiced reply.

TJ stretched, massaging his face. Finally he looked toward Andy, who was sitting silently on the edge of his bed, looking into middle space. "Andy," said TJ as he leaned over. "There was something else I wanted to ask you last night."

Andy grunted.

"Remember the NASA guy you talked to?"

"NASA? Oh, yeah."

"What was it he said about there being more than one spaceship?"

Instantly, Andy was no longer sleepy. "I didn't say he said anything about that." That little piece of information was classified and he'd been sworn to secrecy. "Are you sure I said that?"

TJ knew he'd made a blunder. No, it wasn't Andy who'd told him; it was Sarah.

Andy considered a moment, then shook his head. "I must be getting senile, but you gotta promise me this goes no further."

TJ nodded.

"I suppose I should tell you anyway since we are gonna be partners. Yes, he told me there are seven of them. They aren't sure, but it looks like six are grouped together and one—a huge one—is still behind them."

"A huge one, huh?" Sarah hadn't said anything about a big one. TJ thought for a moment as Andy resumed dressing.

Andy, glancing around to see if others were paying any attention to them, motioned for TJ to come nearer. "There's something else I just remembered," he said, "There's this guy in Washington, says some mighty strange things going on there."

"Like?"

"They got the FBI, CIA, and Justice Department running around the country interviewing a whole bunch of people for clearances—nobody seems to know why."

"And you make something of it, like…"

Andy shrugged. "Don't know. But I do know that's not natural—since when do those three agencies do anything together? They've got thousands of agents from all sorts of departments flying all over interviewing these people. Why? The only thing going on, is this. I mean, they aren't concerned about filling job vacancies in Washington, or polling people—it has to be this. This is the number one thing right now with this government, or any government on the face of the planet."

"Yeah…so?"

"Maybe Washington knows more about this than we thought."

TJ nodded thoughtfully. "Maybe they know this is no meteor or unguided spaceship."

Andy stopped and nodded. "Yes. I think this just reinforces the old position of, "don't believe what Uncle Sam says until you get a second source."

"Or third," smiled TJ.

Andy nodded. "And did you see those barracks down the road from us we passed last night? They didn't open those for us. Last night coming in, I noticed soldiers working late fixing those places up—for who?"

TJ zipped up his bag, then threw it over his shoulder. "Something's going on that we aren't supposed to know about."

The two men made their way outside, and found themselves in back of a line that was filing, slowly, into three waiting buses. Andy and TJ began the slow shuffle forward.

TJ punched Andy in the side, and pointed to their left. Buses were arriving, stopping a hundred yards short of them. As they watched, the buses began to empty.

"Who are they?" muttered TJ.

Andy watched as these new arrivals stepped down from the buses. All were dressed as civilians except for three Air Force escorts, who were directing them toward the barracks to their left.

Andy shook his head. "Dunno. Maybe more reporters, but like I said, I don't think so."

TJ grunted. "You're right, we're the only group of reporters. This must be the mystery group all those barracks are being fixed up for."

Andy nodded. As they watched, two figures exited one of the buses and stopped, returning their gaze.

"They look as confused as we do," smiled Andy.

The line in front of Andy began moving again, and both men followed it aboard the blue school bus. Immediately, the doors closed and the uniformed driver began grinding through the gears as the bus bumped and swayed toward the mess hall and a breakfast both men needed. Following others inside, they found two long serving lines running down each side of a large hall filled with eight-foot tables and their attending chairs. Andy estimated a couple hundred people could easily sit at the tables. Now, only one line was open and the reporters, who were alone in the large mess hall, began filing down it. Andy watched as his plastic tray received scrambled eggs, sausage, bacon, some gravy on biscuits, and finally an empty bowl.

"What's this for?" he asked of the enlisted server.

"Milk," came the short reply with a finger pointing to the beverage islands in the center of the room. "They give us bowls so we don't break glasses," he said with a shrug of his shoulders.

Andy accepted the bowl and leaned toward TJ. "You think they could afford glasses with all the taxes we pay."

TJ smiled as he followed Andy to one of the tables. For a few minutes both men were silent, concentrating on downing their breakfast, which was surprisingly good. Even the milk from his bowl was good—nice and cold.

"Andy, " said TJ finally, "I got something really weird to tell you."

"Like?"

"Well, you know when we were getting on the bus? Remember those MPs, directing those people off the buses?"

Andy nodded, then downed the last of his milk. It felt foolish drinking out of a bowl, but everyone was doing it.

"I think I recognized one of those MPs, the tall one—or at least he was a dead ringer for somebody."

"Really?"

"I think I might have seen him somewhere before. Back at the paper, he was a new reporter. Came from the *Panagraphic News* in Bloomington, Illinois, someone said."

"We were a little ways from them, how could you tell he was familiar or not?"

TJ nodded. "Yeah, you're right. Yet, I'm just sure it was the same guy. Don't know why, just sure."

"Make anything of it? Is that your point, you make something of it—like he shouldn't be here or something?"

TJ shook his head softly. "No, can't say I make anything of it, but, well, it seems weird—rather it makes me feel weird for some reason."

"You are weird. Didn't anyone ever tell you that?" Andy smiled.

Suddenly the voice of their sergeant echoed through the building. "Okay, ladies, time to go!"

With that there was a sudden increase in noise as everyone rose at once and followed the sergeant out the door and back on the buses for the ride to the runway and waiting planes.

Reaching the tarmac, there were no flight preliminaries. The buses drove directly up to two gigantic 747s that sat brooding in the early morning sun. As each person in the group got off the bus, their ID was checked. Then they were directed to one of the two waiting aircraft. It took a little less than an hour to board the plane and take off. Despite the fast beginning, the following flight was long, boring, cramped, and seemingly endless. Within the windowless cavern of the plane there was much speculation among the reporters. It struck Andy more as a verbal sparring match as each reporter tried to glean what others knew without revealing his own information. But in time, even this conversation died and each retreated into private thoughts or sleep for the duration of the trip.

Once they landed, all were transported to waiting navy ships for the voyage to Ground Zero. Andy and TJ found themselves aboard a destroyer, sharing a small cabin with two other reporters necessitating every inch of the cabin be accounted for in use.

Securing their bunks, and the few items they brought, both reporters made their way on deck in time to see the mooring lines snaking from the wharf to within the ship, followed by a long, deafening ship's whistle. TJ pointed out the other ships leaving their moorings. It was clear the task force would consist of many ships. Within the hour a second deafening blast of ship's horns was given and the rumble of the ship's engines reverberated through the ship.

Once offshore, two other, even larger groups joined them, each group with an aircraft carrier. It was difficult to estimate how many ships were involved, but over a hundred would not be far off. As far as they could see, there were navy ships. Had they pulled every ship outta mothballs and the war zone? Whatever waited beyond the watery horizon, it was going to see them coming.

Andy inhaled the sea air and it tasted good. He turned to TJ. "Tell me, friend, are you ready to see aliens?"

TJ's face grew serious. "No."

THE UNEVEN ROAD made the bus lurch left, then sharply to the right as it entered the Tyndall Air Force Base. Bernie nearly slipped from his seat before catching himself. It had been a long ride and he was hungry, tired, sore, and sleepy—and most of all, fed up with not knowing what was happening. He closed his eyes in an effort to re-group. Keeping calm was important, though he could feel his excitement, with a splash of fear, growing as they entered their destina-tion.

Looking forward, up the aisle of the bus and through the wind-shield, he could see the road ahead and that they had turned down a row of squat, one-story buildings, obviously used to house soldiers. Behind them were other buses, he hadn't counted them, but knew there were more than fifty. At last, their bus turned down a lane and began to slow. The brakes protested shrilly as the bus driver slowed their bus to a halt. Immediately, a soldier in fatigues rapped on the bus' doors, and the driver opened them. He was tall—very tall—and muscular. By his armband, Bernie saw he was an MP. He was the perfect picture of a soldier: His brown uniform was tailored with crisp, starched lines. Slowly, his gaze scanned the bus as he walked down the aisle. Bernie watched him approach and for a spilt second, when the MP's eyes rested on him, the light made one eye appear to have a reddish glint to it.

"Good afternoon, ladies and gentlemen," he said finally. His tone was flat—not unfriendly, but practiced. "This will be your home for the next few days while you are processed and await transportation. We don't have more comfortable quarters, but on such short notice, this is the best we can do. We'll try to meet all of your needs." His voice was droning, sounding more like a bad impression of a worn speech. "If you will step off, we will assign you individual sleeping quarters. Once off, form a line and on my command follow me. Any questions!"

The bus was silent.

"Okay then. Follow me."

Silently they started filing out. Though on their bus there were only men, once he stepped out, Bernie could see some women among the faces on other buses. He paused a moment as he noticed ahead of them were several other buses, but they were loading people.

"Bet I know who they are," said a voice.

Bernie turned. "Who?"

"Press. Most of them are carrying shoulder bags. I recognize the bags as designed for serious camera people."

"Press? I thought this was hush-hush. How come they found out?"

"They always do," he smiled.

Bernie smiled, extending his hand. "I'm Bernie Krantz."

"Hi, Bernie. Yeah, I know who you are. You're a DJ on radio, right? I'm Durk." He smiled back.

"How do you know me?" asked Bernie, astonished.

"Oh, I happen to see a roster of the folks on the bus—I got sorta a photo memory. Once I see something, I don't forget."

"I missed you getting on the bus, did you board in Washington?"

Durk smiled, "Yeah, and believe me, I can feel it!" He stretched his large frame. He was tall, maybe six-foot-five and well built, with long-ish, rich, dark black hair. "What do you think of all this?"

Bernie was prevented from answering by the sergeant's call of "Okay, follow me!" With that, the line began to move toward the barracks directly in front of them. Other busloads of people were already making their way to the buildings on either side.

"I don't know," said Bernie, finally. "It sure as hell is the most exciting thing that has ever happened to me."

Durk nodded. "Yes, it's that." He laughed out loud suddenly, tossing his head back. The sun catching his eyes gave their deep brown a glint of red. "It sure is that. I haven't had so much fun in a long, long time."

"Aren't you scared, just a little?"

Durk shook his head, and laughed. "No, not a bit. This is wonderful. I've been looking forward to this for a long time."

"You have? For a long time?"

"Yep, I just knew there was something like this coming."

"Aliens?"

"Uh, aliens? Yes, aliens—or something. I'm just very excited. And look, you get to be part of some elect group—now tell me, isn't that exciting?"

Bernie smiled again. "Yes, yes it's certainly that. I've thought about it and wondered, why me? Have you figured it out? Why you?"

"Don't care. Don't worry about it, we'll all find that out soon enough. Enjoy the moment. I certainly am."

Bernie chuckled, "I guess you're right. Let's enjoy it."

"Exactly."

The line entered the barracks but the sergeant cut off Durk after Bernie had passed. Bernie looked back and saw the sergeant holding Durk and directing them toward the next barracks.

Bernie was disappointed Durk wouldn't be in the same barracks; he would like to have a friend in this. Through the double front doors of the barracks was an entry hall fifteen-foot square. Off to the left an open door led to the latrine area and to the right, showers. Those in front went through a second set of swinging doors to the sleeping quarters. Here a number of double bunks lined either side of a long room. Perhaps enough for fifty people.

"Okay folks!" Barked a waiting soldier. "These are your bunks. Behind each bunk are lockers you will use in stowing your personal items. In half an hour, you will be taken to the mess hall and fed, following that you'll be taken to the orientation briefing. Any questions?"

"Yeah," someone said. "Why not eat now? I'm starved!"

A ripple of laughter followed.

The sergeant's demeanor was unmoved, but glancing at his watch he answered in a monotone voice; "The mess call will begin at oh-nine-hundred. That gives you half an hour to get your gear in order." He didn't wait for more questions but left them to find their own bunks and lockers.

True to his word, he arrived exactly thirty minutes later to lead them outside. Bernie's stomach was ready for some eggs and bacon, or cereal, or toast, or anything he could get. Outside, the line met up with the other lines, all walking slowly toward some food. As they passed one barracks, Bernie spotted Durk on one of the barracks's small porches. He waved at him.

"Hey, come on! Let's get some chow!"

Durk smiled. "No thanks, I'm not hungry. Don't like breakfast."

"Well, come on and have a cup of coffee with me then."

Durk shrugged. "Why not," he said, coming over to join Bernie.

"How do you like your digs?" Durk asked

"All right, I guess."

Durk nodded slowly. "Can I give you some advice?" he asked. Bernie saw he was in a much more serious mood than earlier.

"Sure."

"Pay attention to everything. Don't allow yourself to put aside anything told to you, accept it, become part of it."

Bernie was silent for a moment. "Why so serious all of a sudden? Do you know something I don't?"

"Perhaps, perhaps not. But I know this. Your life will never be the same, and the more you absorb, the more you can turn this to your benefit."

The rest of the walk to the mess hall was taken up with small talk, very small talk, as Durk became less communicative. Bernie got eggs, bacon, toast, and milk, which he had to drink from a bowl; however, Durk got only coffee, and let that sit until cold. Their conversation revolved around Tyndall Air Force Base with which Durk was familiar from some previous experience. Bernie was not clear what it was except that he was assigned there in the past. Durk seemed like a good guy to know. He had a logical mind, a pleasant personality, could obviously handle himself if bad came to worse, and all that was coupled with a sense of humor. Finally, they drifted into a silence, which ended with Durk rising from the table.

"Well, gotta go."

Bernie nodded, extending his hand. Durk's hand seemed as cold as yesterday, a sure sign of poor circulation, which Bernie was tempted to talk to him about, but didn't.

"I might not see you for a while Bernie," continued Durk, "but I'm sure you are going to enjoy what's ahead."

Bernie smiled. "Yes, I'm sure I will. You know, at first, I was a little apprehensive, but lately, I'm feeling good about it. Actually, I'm really excited."

"You should be, a lot of people wish they were in the position you are in now. And in a little while, millions of people will envy you, I promise. Goodbye, friend."

Bernie said goodbye. Somehow he knew he wouldn't be talking to Durk again. Shortly after, at some unheard signal, people began rising from their tables, taking their trays to a long window on the left of the serving area. Here there were several barrels. One for paper waste, one for food waste, a large tub for silverware, and the rest was placed on an aluminum counter where waiting hands scooped them up to be washed.

Bernie made his way back to his barracks only to be turned out with the rest and marched, if it could be called that, to the large cinder block auditorium behind the barracks. The outside of the building led Bernie to suspect it was a gymnasium, a guess that was confirmed when entering he saw basketball backboards raised up and out of the way. The sides of the gym had bleachers into which his group was led. On the gym floor, folding chairs occupied the entire area. It was hard to estimate how many were in the gym, but several thousand would not be far off.

The loudspeakers came to life with an anonymous voice, the speaker hidden somewhere among the bodies ahead of him. Finally Bernie saw a soldier to the side holding a microphone. Briefly, he explained they would be processed for the next three days, then transported to ships at sea and finally flown to their final destination. He was careful not to be specific on that point, and ignored several shouts asking him what and where that final destination would be. Rumors had been flying among the guests. Some said they were going to be taken into space, some said they were going to be ambassadors for the aliens, or workers. There was no end of speculation, and some ideas were not encouraging; one in particular claimed use of body parts for alien study, but none took it seriously. All waited patiently until group by group they were led away for processing.

At last, his section of the bleachers was led outside and to the infirmary where they all were given thorough physicals. On his way, he caught a glimpse of Durk some distance off, and though he tried to yell at him, Durk did not notice. He seemed to be engaged in conversation with another man who could have been his brother. He was too far away to see their faces clearly, but they certainly looked similar including their athletic builds. Perhaps they were brothers, after all.

There were physical exams, which no one seemed to fail; although obviously there were people unable pass any kind of physical examination. Photos were taken and ID cards issued. They were cautioned never to let the ID card out of their sight. The ID card was a plastic affair with computer read code on the bottom. In the left-hand corner of the credit-sized card was his picture. Not a very good one, but identifiable. His name was in large, boldfaced letters and beneath the name and above the UPC code was a number. His number was 5102. On one edge of the card a hole had been punched and a loop with a fastener had been inserted. This card was to be fastened to overalls, which he was issued. The overalls became the uniforms of the "guests," which was short for their official title, Elected Guests. He'd been given several pairs of these dark blue, loose-fitting overalls, which had black piping down the legs and around the wrists; a lighter blue jacket, actually more than a smock; and shoes—resembling tennis shoes.

In addition to the ID card, their identification number was also written on their forearms in indelible black ink—a fact Bernie discovered later, to his dismay, when he took a shower. Later, each was helped in writing their will. This was something that unnerved a few, including Bernie, yet even this worry faded, as he grew more excited. Finally after the third day, they were given twenty-four hours off and told they would be leaving the following day.

Bernie lay in his bunk flicking channels of the TV at the foot of his bed. All the shows were the same, the coming spacecraft. Every talk show had weirdos giving views and predictions. Bernie smiled quietly. If they only knew what was about to happen to the men around him. Surprisingly, the thought of meeting these space guys no longer brought any fear or even apprehension. He was excited, to be sure, but he felt confident, curious, and well, special.

Cutting the TV off, he wished he were back in his Lazy Boy. There would never be a better place to take a nap. He mused whether aliens knew the benefits of a Lazy Boy.

CHAPTER 3

The Arrival

DESPITE THE HEAVY following sea, she had an easy motion to her, swaying her stern gently in a slow midnight dance with the black waters. Occasional whitecaps peeked out from the dark, and were instantly bathed in the growing light of the approaching spacecraft. The brisk Southern Ocean wind gave a nip to the air. Even though it was summer in the Southern latitudes, this far south it was still cold at night.

The objects above appeared as one brilliant orb, though all knew now there were actually seven. On deck, a constant, though changing, group of sailors came to watch silently, intently. There was nothing left to say. Only the engine's low hum, deep in the ship's bowels, disturbed the silent night. Whatever it might be, all aboard knew their fate was sealed.

"Lousy blips!" Slogan's voice came from behind. The ship's radar man stood holding a life vest in his hand, automatically swaying with the destroyer's motion as the ship rolled slowly to the port, hesitated, recovered, then rolled to starboard. "Here, you forgot to put this on— it's orders, you know."

Andy took the offered preserver, slipping it on reluctantly over his sea coat. He hadn't forgotten; it just seemed a waste of time. If these things were to hit, no preserver would do any good.

Slogan looked up. "I've been at sea for almost ten years, Andy, and I gotta tell ya, I ain't never seen nothin' like this."

Andy shrugged. "That's an understatement, if I ever heard one. Besides that little gem, is there any other news?" Slogan was usually good for some gossip, a lot of it turning out to be true. Andy looked out as far as the night would allow, interested in seeing that the sea, which had been choppy, was calming. The whitecaps were slowly disappearing, replaced by a smooth, ever present swell, as if the sea was preparing to receive the oncoming craft, and taking a deep breath in her anticipation.

"Not really, 'cept there was some talk going around about how these things were strange."

"Yeah, I guess they are—you are just full of info tonight."

"I don't mean goofy strange, they say the size of these things should be having some effect on us, but ain't."

"Like what?"

"Tides, high pressure, something."

Andy thought for a moment and decided what Slogan was saying was probably true. The combined size of these things should be affecting the Earth in a lot of ways, not only tides, but weather and who knows what else. "Yeah, so why aren't they?"

"Dunno, no one can figure it out."

"Listen, has anyone suggested that maybe they are just mirages? You know, maybe not real at all?" asked Andy, recalling his short conversation with Ron Borders at the Cape.

"What are you talking about? Mirages? I don't think so—maybe you better start drinking again, coffee is turning your brain to mush."

Andy shrugged, then telling the radioman he'd see him later, began to wander the ship, unable to remain in one place too long. Finally, he made his way through narrow companionways to the enlisted mess hall, where he knew hot coffee was always on hand.

The mess hall was a small space in the ship, capable of seating only a fraction of the crew at any one time. To his left, as he entered, was an even smaller space reserved for the NCOs of the ship. It impressed him that such a space was almost humorous. No more than four or five people could squeeze into it, and once there, eating would be difficult. But it seemed important not to eat with the lower grade seamen.

That space, as well as the rest of the mess quarters, was deserted except for three cooks at the far end, who looked up briefly before resuming their quiet conversation, and a fourth, sitting alone, was TJ. His hands were wrapped around a coffee mug, as he stared into the dark liquid, as if searching for something in its depths. Andy grabbed a cup from the counter, half filled it before making his way over to TJ.

Thomas was unaware of him until Andy spoke. "So how's it goin'?"

Startled by the voice, Thomas jerked, then lowered his head, concentrating again upon his cup. "Go away!" he snapped.

Andy did not move. "Those things up there—they getting to you?"

TJ did not reply immediately, but Andy waited. Finally TJ exhaled. "It's Sarah. I'm just wondering if I'll see her again."

"I see." But he didn't.

"Isn't there someone you're worried about not seeing again? Aunt? Uncle? Ex-wife?"

Andy considered but knew there wasn't anyone. It bothered him suddenly, the fact that there wasn't anyone. But he dismissed it and concentrated on TJ. "Who told you a fool thing like us not making it back?" Andy asked, though he knew it was a common subject of conversation around the ship. Rumors about the effects of the object hitting ranged from atomic bombs going off, to their splitting Earth in half, to them bouncing off the atmosphere and disappearing into deep space. "We're all going to see our family and friends." Andy said, hoping he sounded confident.

Thomas slowly sat up, managing a smile. "I know—it's just sometimes I get down; gotta think positive—right?"

"You got it," answered Andy. "Besides, there's reason to believe these things are nothing but air. The radar guy, Slogan, says they don't show up on his screen, and remember, that guy down at the Cape—he said the same thing."

TJ nodded thoughtfully. "Not solid. Yeah, I could buy that."

"You could?"

TJ nodded. "There's something about this you don't know yet—neither do I really, but not being solid could make sense."

"Hey, partner, you're holding out on me. What do you know I don't?"

"Know? Actually, nothing. I'm here to find out answers, same as you. When I do know something, count on me to let you in on it."

Both men were silent for a moment until TJ spoke again. "People in the States are heading toward bomb shelters, you know that? Another thing, the war in the Middle East has stopped flat. One day we're on the brink of nuclear confrontation, the next—nothin'. The whole thing is wacky."

TJ nodded, thinking. Do you think they are just giant clouds of gas?"

Andy thought for a second, perhaps they were. Maybe gigantic fireballs of gas, flung at them from the depths of space. When they hit the ocean—*poof!* Out like a light. "Could be—or maybe something electrical."

Thomas grinned. "Nice try, Andy. Write that in your story and see how long before the next expense check comes." Both men chuckled. Obviously Thomas was regaining some of his old self.

Andy stood up. "Well, let's get back on deck," he said. "Don't want to miss the big show."

TJ nodded. " Okay, I'm with you."

As the two men walked out on deck, the first noticeable thing was the silence. The crew stood mute at their assigned stations, each wearing a life jacket to which many attached crude belts tethering themselves to the ship. The light above, aided by the first hint of dawn, gave an almost midday brightness.

Suddenly a bark from the ship's loudspeakers broke the quiet, startling Andy.

"Attention all decks. Attention all decks. Stand to for a message from the captain."

There was a brief period of silence, interrupted only by the low crackle of the open mike. Finally the captain spoke, his voice deep and steady. His confident tone, in itself, gave a bit of courage to the listening crew. One could not guess at what fear might reside in his heart, if any.

"Gentlemen, the objects are forecast to hit in twenty minutes, oh-five-thirty-five hours, at a point approximately twenty miles off our starboard bow. I want to commend everyone for the courage and dedication to duty you have all shown during these hours. Now, I have some good news for you. Doppler measurements indicate the objects have slowed about twenty percent. We're not clear what this means, but if they continue to slow at this rate, the touchdown will be soft."

Andy heard a ripple of relieved murmurs run through the crew, punctuated by whoops and whistles. Leaning against the railing, he breathed a much-needed sigh of hope. Could it be this was not the end of life on Earth, including his own? He recalled well the briefing he'd attended with TJ given to the officers of the ship three weeks earlier. TJ's friendship with Slogan had earned him a spot with a few others at the event.

Arriving early, they had planted themselves in the rear corner of the quarters, which were typically military, barren would have been an improvement. Aside from a few maps on the wall, a movie screen, the long conference table, and some straight-backed chairs, the room contained nothing else. Andy debated taking one of the chairs, but TJ seemed content to stand and it would be embarrassing if there were not enough to accommodate the navy boys. He sighed, shifted, and waited for the others to arrive. The corn on his left foot was giving him some grief about the metal decks—but by putting most of his weight on the other foot, it was tolerable.

One by one the ship's officers arrived. They did so quietly, speaking in hushed tones, talking mostly about mundane shipboard operations. Andy was amazed at how, even in the face of possible death, these men were capable of discussing day-to-day actions whose fruition they may never expect to see. It had to be the result of years of training, a reflex action that disengaged the temporal emotions, allowing each man to focus upon routine.

Once all officers had gathered, the captain ordered First Officer Butterfield to report.

Butterfield was, as usual, perfectly attired, unlike some of the other officers who showed signs of wear and tear over the past few days. He rose from his chair slowly and in the silence, walked to the front of the room. Butterfield, despite his benign name, was a tough cookie, feared by his fellow officers, though respected. When he spoke, it was with confidence and assumed authority.

"Sir, Washington has confirmed the objects will impact Earth in three days. The size of the objects, number, and the speed of impact, leave no doubt in Washington's mind that the resulting explosion will be equivalent to detonation of several hundred nuclear bombs." His voice was emotionless, delivering his message with the same tone as if reporting on the number of potatoes on board.

The room remained absolutely quiet except for a petty officer's low, "Goodbye, mama."

That was three days ago, and here they were. Remembering the feelings he had then, and the almost palatable emotions of the room, brought a chill to his body. The three days since had passed too slowly. Lifting his binoculars, he squinted to define the images.

The growing light of the objects above was becoming uncomfortable to the naked eye, but Andy found placing yellow cellophane over the lens helped. Though the resulting image was not the clearest, it allowed Andy to see there were indeed multiple objects or crafts. Reports said there were seven, and Andy could just make out each. There was a very large one in the center, triangular in appearance—no, more like a pyramid. Along each of the longer sides of this pyramid, were three similar, but much smaller pyramid-shaped objects, three on each side, making for a total of seven; however, it was difficult to define the six smaller ones because of the combined brightness.

The unmistakable buzz of the deck speakers punctured the quiet. The voice that came was steady, but a bit metallic. "There has been a further reduction in speed of the approaching objects. NASA is now predicting a soft touchdown."

A roar went up among the sailors, as pent-up tension found release. Andy felt his own tension-balloon deflate, leaving him giddy and weak. Smiling at the sailors caught up in their exultation, he raised his glasses again. Watching closely, six of the objects, which seemed to form a loose circle, continued to rush closer, while the seventh, the larger one appeared to stop.

TJ moved beside Andy. "Does it look to you like the big one is sorta hanging back?"

Andy nodded, then turned toward the radar man above them. "Slogan!" he shouted. "Does it seem like the big one is hanging back?"

Slogan continued looking through his own glasses, then answered. "Yeah, for sure."

Now the approaching six smaller objects began to lose brilliance the closer they approached. This time it was Slogan shouting down to see if Andy saw the same thing.

"Yeah. Getting kinda fuzzy!" Andy shouted back. Looking around him at the sea, Andy saw it was now absolutely still, without even the swell. Only the destroyer's slow motion disturbed the arctic water's mirrored surface, its bow producing silk-like watery ribbons on the smooth dark surface.

"Slogan! ever see the sea like this?"

Slogan took a look at the waters fore and aft. "No, never. Weird— water looks like pavement," he shouted, before returning his gaze toward the sky.

Now Andy saw why the brightness diminished. A vapor cloud nearly surrounded the glow. Yet, what he could see of them was assuming shape: Each of the six objects narrowed to a point at the top, their tips pointed toward the stars, while their bases were nearly hidden completely within the vapor cloud. Their size was staggering. Obviously when they hit the water the resulting wave would engulf and swallow the ships. Each of the approaching pyramids was easily 5,000 feet high, with each side of their bases, a few miles wide. They were coming too fast; it would not be a completely soft landing. Instinctively, Andy braced himself.

The descending pyramids plummeted toward the water then, without a ripple or sound, disappeared beneath the water's surface. For a few moments there was absolute silence as stunned sailors stood in shock. The sole remaining pyramid above shone brightly in the sky.

"Did you see that, TJ?" shouted Grady, the helicopter pilot. Grady leaped down the metal gangway in his excitement. "The buggers just disappeared!"

TJ and Andy nodded in silence. Both were still staring at the smooth surface where the crafts had plunged beneath the water.

Grady shook his head. "There's somethin' goin' on here that's weird, I tell you."

TJ, silent until now, snorted. "We just saw some alien stuff come from the heavens and dive into the sea and it dawns on you that something weird is going on?"

"No, no, I mean, besides that."

"Besides that? What could possibly be besides that?"

"How they went into the water: Not a ripple, not a sound. Nothing! That ain't natural. This is too weird for me."

The tenor of the ship's engines increased slightly, the ship's course began to change, and the ship's bow began heading for the spot where the objects disappeared.

"Oh no," sighed Grady, "the skipper's going in for a look. There's gotta be ten ships closer. Why us?"

Slowly the ship's bow crept through the smooth black waters. Suddenly, ahead of them, the waters were beginning to lighten ever so much, as though they were headed into shallow waters under a noon sun. A growing ring of light began emanating from the water as though a huge beam was turned on beneath. The area of water that was lit up was greater than they could see across.

Immediately, the ship's engines died, and the ship turned its bow perpendicular to the light waters. The water's color was changing from a dark, deep blue-black to a lighter blue, then lighter until it was almost white.

Suddenly, with a roaring sound like Niagara Falls, the waters parted. Six spires slowly emerged from the ocean, as tons of water cascaded down the smooth sides, their surfaces casting an even, soft blue glow. Up and up the spires grew from the sea. They were staggering in their size. Skyscrapers emerging from some mysterious abyss of the deep. Higher and higher they grew, the spires turning into pyramid form and hanging over the surrounding ships, dwarfing them.

Andy could see the pyramid's corners were not sharp, but smoothly rounded. As they rose, the lower sides of the triangular spires reached out toward each other until a base emerged, connecting all six. The final shape showed six pyramids, several thousand feet tall, and covering an area one had difficulty seeing across. It seemed to Andy that there might still be as much beneath the water as rose above it. In the center of the six spires was open water, appearing to be reserved for the seventh spire, now overhead.

Aboard ship, aside from an occasional muffled expletive, all remained quiet.

"What is it, guys?" whispered Slogan, his voice betraying some fear.

Both Andy and TJ remained silent. What struck them speechless was not the size or artistry of the huge structures, not the stillness of the waters, or even the bright object still hanging in the sky above—no, it was the realization that life on Earth would never be the same. Institutions, societies, religions—all would have to deal with what had risen from the sea before them now. Here, in the early dawn, was life from the stars. The future of humanity was before them.

Andy closed his eyes briefly then turned to TJ. "You are now looking at either heaven or hell—one of them has come to visit us."

TJ nodded slowly. "I know; it's why I came."

CHAPTER 4

Within the Pyramid

AMID LOW GRUMBLES, Andy drained the last of his coffee. "I don't know if I can stand this anymore. Every day is the same thing—nothing."

Across from him, one of the ship's helicopter pilots, Grady Mitchell, nodded. "Yeah, most I've done is the daily mail run. It's the waiting for something to happen, something you know will, but never does. That's what's driving me nuts. Why don't we get some marines or something and go over there and kick some alien ass?" Grady's youthful voice made him sound younger than his twenty-four years. He had struck up a friendship with TJ and was now included among the small group of friends aboard the destroyer.

"Hmm. I hope you're not thinking of serving in the diplomatic corps when you get outta the navy," smiled Andy. Over Grady's shoulder, Andy saw TJ enter the galley. There was urgency to TJ's step as he quickly approached them and took a seat, excitement glowing from every pore.

"I just heard what the scoop is," he said, quickly swiveling his head to assure himself no one was listening, then leaned closer. "There's a bunch of planes coming to land on the two carriers. Their passengers, that's what we've been waiting for."

"What passengers?" asked Andy.

"Seems whoever is inside those pyramids has invited some humans to visit—and not just a few—thousands. Somehow they contacted most governments, maybe all of the governments, and requested these people. And now they're on the way!" TJ looked around again; still no one was paying attention.

Andy whistled softly. "What's so special about these people?"

TJ shrugged.

"I'd like to see those aliens myself. Why weren't we given the chance to go? After all, we're the press, right? If they are gonna yank so many people, why not us? We can spread the word—whatever the word is— a lot faster than some bigwigs can," complained Andy.

TJ nodded. "Ah, there's the other strange part: These aren't big-wigs. Each of the people going was individually invited—a personal invitation, by name. Can you believe it? Oh they got some big shots in there, but most are just a whole screwball assortment of folks with no apparent connection."

"By name?"

"And here's a super killer: They were invited before those things got here."

"Before? While they were still in space?"

TJ nodded again. "Yep. That means the governments, or at least some of them, knew they weren't going to crash into Earth. They already knew everything would be okay."

"Jerks, not telling us," mumbled Andy. "Probably why all those government agent–types were running around the country, before we left—makes sense. I wondered if it was something to do with the space-ships."

TJ sat back in his chair triumphantly, enjoying the furrowed brows of his small audience.

"Just ordinary folks? Like who?" asked Andy.

"Well, just a whole assortment of people nobody can figure out: There's businessmen, students, teachers, factory workers, you name it. Some screwballs too; they invited that nut you quoted in your first article, what was his name—Trombley?"

"You're kidding. John Trombley?"

"That's the boy."

"I can't believe it. That guy is one screw away from dangerous. Why would aliens travel a zillion miles to meet him?" Andy shook his head slowly. "Who's your source?"

"Well, I can't say."

"I thought we were partners?"

TJ looked around again and leaned in. "Okay. Paul Radner, the night radio chief."

"Radner. Hmm, I don't know him. Is he reliable?"

"I think so, I'm willing to go with him as a source, if I could just come up with a second source."

"Slogan, the radar chief, might be able to help us there. I'm sure he's friends with the radio boys—probably knows the daytime man. That would be a good second source."

As they rose to leave, Grady remained seated. "I'll see you boys around later."

Giving him a wave, the two made their way out in search of Slogan. They found him in the gym trying to make an exclamation-mark physique out of a question-mark body. He told them the name-of-the-day chief in the radio room was Eric Houser. Quickly, they made their way to the radio room located two decks below. Approaching the radio room they found the door locked. To the side was a small window with a Plexiglas section that could be slid open. TJ knocked on the window, and one of the seamen inside opened it.

"Yeah, what d'ya want?" His tone was surly, and Andy felt the hair on his neck rise.

"Is Chief Houser here?"

Wordlessly the seaman shut the window and motioned to someone to his left.

Within moments, a large man well over 6 feet, bent his face to the window. His hair was dark, midnight black and in need of a trim. His blue eyes were the clearest blue Andy had ever seen, except for a tinge of red at the edge. He had the strange feeling he'd met this guy before, but knew that was impossible.

"Yes?" asked Houser.

TJ introduced himself and Andy, then asked if they could have a word with him. The chief allowed a little smile to play with his lips then motioned them to the door on their right. Buzzing the door, he led the pair to a side room, smaller but adequate for a half desk and three side chairs. Motioning to the chairs, he sat down in the government-issue swivel chair. "What can I do for you two?"

Quickly TJ went over the story he'd heard without revealing who had told him, and asked Chief Houser if he knew anything.

Houser reached out and casually pushed his office door shut with his foot. "Maybe I know something," he began. "But first, I got a couple of questions."

"Okay," replied Andy. "Shoot."

"What do you think of these aliens landing?"

Andy and TJ exchanged glances. "Think?"

"Yeah. What do you think they are going to do?"

Andy shrugged, suddenly realizing he hadn't given it any deep thought. It was a story. A way to increase his income. It was a big byline. "I don't know what they are going to do, I guess that's what we are trying to figure out."

"You happy they are here?"

TJ was silent.

"I guess I am," replied Andy. "I've made some bucks off this. Will I be happy tomorrow? I have no idea."

The chief was silent for a moment as he looked at each of them. "Can I confirm that we have a large number of visitors coming to us, and are they headed for the pyramids? Yes. At least that's what the messages have been saying."

Andy slapped his leg. "I knew it!"

"Wait a minute here," said TJ. "That's too easy, chief. Why so willing?"

The chief fixed his gaze on TJ for a moment. Andy could see his jaw muscles working. His gaze at TJ began to reach an embarrassing length when he spoke. "I think people should know."

TJ looked briefly at Andy then back at the chief, who returned his gaze without blinking. "You could probably be court-martialed for telling us what those messages are saying, you know that?"

The chief slowly nodded. "Yeah, I know. But I figure this is the end. There ain't gonna be no navy after this, at least not the navy I know."

"You're willing to risk your stripes to tell us this, to let the world know? Can we use your name?" asked Andy.

The chief shook his head "No. I don't want any part of this connected to my name."

Andy nodded silently, then, "Fair enough," said Andy reaching across to shake his hand, noticing it was cold . TJ did not shake his hand but left, with Andy following. Once out in the companionway Andy tried to give TJ a high five, but TJ did not respond

"Okay," said Andy in exasperation. "What's the problem? This is a great scoop. We got someone in the know to tell us what's going on. And, we got it confirmed by a second source." This was the first real story they'd gotten in the last three days. And they were sure no one else had it.

TJ nodded, managing a small smile. "Yes, I know. I just don't feel good about that guy. Something goofy about him."

"You know, he looked familiar to me, but I don't think I ever met him before. But who cares? We're all goofy at sometime or other."

TJ reluctantly gave Andy his high five.

The remainder of the day was spent in constructing the story using "unnamed sources" and finally sending it to their respective papers with shared bylines. The last of the day was spent checking in with Slogan, and searching the horizon with binoculars, but no planes appeared. It wasn't until the following dawn that radar picked up the approaching planes.

The rapid beating of the helicopter blades woke TJ and Andy at the same instant. They exchanged quick looks then leaped out of their bunks, grabbing their weather gear and stuffing arms and legs as they awkwardly made it out the door into the companionway. Arriving on deck, they saw a long line of twin engine helicopters approaching the aircraft carrier about a mile off their port side. The line of choppers disappeared at the distant eastern horizon. It was an awe-inspiring sight. They would approach the flat top, softly settling down, discharge their passengers, then lift off again, joining a growing line of choppers returning from whence they'd come. Andy guessed it was Japan. Probably they followed the same route as the reporters had in getting out here.

Grady appeared, and from his dress, he was in a hurry to get here: His pants appeared about to drop off with his belt unbuckled. His only other garb was his T-shirt loosely covered by his sea coat.

"Unbelievable," whispered TJ. "I thought maybe they meant a few thousand people, but there's gonna be more than a few thousand at this rate."

Andy nodded. "From here they'll probably chopper them over to the spires."

"Yeah," mused TJ, then turned toward Grady. "I gotta get on the carrier, that's where the action is—that's where the story is now!"

"Talk to the exec…"

"Forget it, waste of breath. Look pal, here's what I'm thinking…"

"Wait a sec," interjected Grady, "Did you already ask for permission?"

"Yeah, already asked. Didn't get squat. Exec says no press is allowed on those carriers," replied TJ.

"So," began Grady, "the plan you are about to lay on me has no permission from anyone, right?"

"It's not really anything that needs permission. See, I don't want to actually walk on the deck and everything. All I want to do is go over with you on the mail run, snap a few pictures from the chopper, and then leave. I'm not technically on the deck. Not actually, physically on the deck."

"Am I suppose to buy that?" smiled Grady.

"Yes."

Grady shook his head and laughed. "Okay, but look, just snap a few pictures, you stay in the chopper, got it?"

"Sure," lied TJ. He hated this, but how else could he do it?

Grady checked his watch. "I leave in twenty minutes. Be at the chopper in ten, okay?"

TJ nodded. "Right, I'll be there."

Grady made his way toward the flight deck as Andy grabbed TJ's arm. "What are you doing? You can't do this. They are gonna lock you up and throw away the key. You have no intention of staying in the chopper, do you?"

TJ turned back toward his friend. "Look, Andy, I got to do this and do it alone. I mean, that's the way it's supposed to be."

"Supposed to be? What kinda crap is that?"

"Look, don't get me wrong. Trust me, this is one thing you don't want to get involved in."

"You got that right." Andy paused. "So what about the story? Remember, you said share and share alike."

TJ considered a moment. "I'll tell you everything when I get back."

Andy nodded, "Okay. What can I do here?"

"You pray?"

Andy was startled by the serious look on TJ's face. "Me? Pray? No. Should I?"

"I'd appreciate it."

Andy nodded slowly, his furrowed brow betraying his doubts.

TJ patted him on the back. "Good man," he said, heading for the chopper. He stopped, turning back to Andy. "Andy, this may not work out, and I might get into some trouble—I mean big trouble."

"Yes, I know. That's what I said!"

"No, I don't mean with the navy—look, I know this sounds a little crazy, but if anything happens to me, well, tell my wife I love her and that she was right."

"Hey, hold on there. This is sounding a little too serious to me. I don't know what you've got in mind, but I think you better rethink it."

It was too late. With a wave TJ turned and disappeared through the companionway, leaving Andy to wonder what his friend had in mind.

TJ made his way toward the helicopter holding the mailbag to his chest. Grady had the blades slowly turning and was motioning toward him to hurry. Jumping in, TJ slipped on earphones similar to Grady's, and heard Grady's voice talking with the bridge, receiving permission to leave. The noise level increased as the chopper lifted off the destroyer's pad.

TJ clutched the bag of mail on his lap, resting his camera, dangling from his neck, on the bag.

Grady's voice came through the headset with a military edge to it. "Remember, TJ, when we land, you can't get out—any pictures you take have to be from right here, understood?"

TJ gave him the thumbs-up response. He felt bad, but this was serious business. Besides, maybe it would turn out that way, after all. It depended upon whether he could get from the helicopter to cover without being stopped. Reaching 500 feet, Grady leveled off, then tilting the chopper, moved forward toward the distant carrier. From this vantage point, TJ could see the enormity of the fleet surrounding the three pyramids. No wonder the war stopped, all the ships were here! He took several pictures and knew they were front-page "sellers." Perhaps not as many ships had been gathered in one location since D-day off Normandy. Grady skillfully brought the chopper into the prescribed landing pattern and received permission to land. Touching down, the blades immediately began to whine as the engine was disengaged. Three men rushed to the helicopter and secured her to the deck, before disappearing as fast as they had arrived. Unbuckling, Grady grabbed the mail sack from TJ. "Remember, it's my butt you're playing with here, pal. Stay put."

TJ nodded, giving Grady the thumbs-up. Grady crouched and ran clear of the blades toward the carrier's superstructure. TJ watched him disappear inside then looked around at the busy deck. No one seemed to be paying the chopper much attention since other big two-bladed choppers were coming and departing in a continuous line. As each landed, twenty to twenty-five people disembarked and were directed toward the entrance. It was obvious they were civilians, though they were dressed alike in blue slacks and blue smocks, which reminded TJ of hospital-like garb. Quickly he snapped several pictures then, unbuckling his belt, TJ stepped down from the chopper and made his way toward the end of a short line of disembarked chopper passengers. He was sure someone would stop him.

Suddenly the roar of an arriving chopper drew the attention of all deck hands. TJ fell into line following the disembarked passengers inside the metal door. Once inside he began to drift back, unsure if following this group was best. The line in front of him turned left down a long corridor, but TJ kept going straight. Several seamen passed him without giving him a second look, which he found encouraging.

"Hey!"

TJ stopped. A chief petty officer came over. He was a bit over-weight with a deeply creviced face. Though not tall, he gave the impression of being a much bigger man than he was. An unlit cigar jutted from one side of his mouth and when he spoke, between teeth gritted to hold it. TJ closed his eyes with resignation.

"What are ya doing here?"

"Well, I…"

"You lost? You better get your ass over to OPS right away, you'll miss your ride."

"Yes, yes you're right…"

"Look, take this companionway straight down that way, down one flight to B deck, then turn left, got it?"

"Yeah, sure—thanks, I guess I got kinda turned around."

"No problem. Just tell the others to stop poking around, you're the third lost puppy I've come across in the last hour. If you people aren't more careful, someone is gonna get hurt." With that he turned and continued down the metal hall.

TJ stood for a moment watching him, then turned around and followed the chief's directions. Finally arriving at B deck, he saw other civilians and began to relax until realizing they all were dressed in iden-tical clothing, carrying knapsack things over their shoulders. TJ approached the group, singling out one man a bit off by himself.

"Pretty exciting, eh?" He ventured as he got near.

The man was carrying a bit of a paunch and needed a shave. He turned toward TJ and looked at him without expression for a moment. "Yeah, exciting. I'd say that was so. Why aren't you in your issued clothes?"

"Got here late, they haven't given me anything yet," replied TJ. "Where did you pick those up you're wearing?"

"At the base. Didn't you go through the base?"

"Ah, sure, but I was late and they rushed me through, said I could get some garb on ship. Do you know where they are handing out the stuff?"

"Don't know, maybe check with one of the guides over that way," he said, nodding toward a distant exit. "Say, is that a camera around your neck?"

"Yeah."

"Thought you couldn't bring any cameras, that's what they told us."

"Oh, well, I learned that too, and I was on my way to turn it in, as a matter of fact."

The man nodded his head slowly. "I see," he said, but TJ could see a look of suspicion growing on his face.

"Well, best get my gear and get back here," said TJ, turning before the man could reply. He carefully measured his steps in an effort to appear purposeful, yet not hurried. TJ could feel his temple pound as he walked at an agonizingly slow pace across the hangar. He was sure someone would shout out a challenge to him with each step he took, but none came. Finally, rounding the corner, he breathed a sigh of relief. It took a few minutes for his heart to slow down. When it finally did, he looked down the metal corridor and saw a restroom, which he headed toward.

Inside the restroom he made for the washbasin and splashed his face with cool water, which made him feel better. Grabbing waiting paper towels he mopped the water and observed his face in the mirror to see if his fear had a look; it didn't. He looked the same, or thought he did. Beyond his reflected face, he could see one of those blue smock things hanging from a hook along with a bag similar to the ones he'd seen them carrying. The owner was obviously in the stall. TJ bent over a little until he could see the toes of the occupant's shoes.

Quickly he looked around and saw he was the only other occupant. Circling slightly, he carefully lifted off the smock and bag and quickly made his way out. In the corridor he slipped on the smock then slipped the bag's strap over his shoulder. A quick look around assured him no one was paying him any attention. He made off down the corridor, away from the large area where the others were gathered. His object was to find another restroom as quickly as possible and adjust his clothing to conform to the others'.

TJ rounded another corner and saw at the far end the sign protruding announcing that this was a "head," the military interpretation of a bathroom. He made for the restroom, breathing a deep sigh when he heard the door close behind him. Several men were in the restroom, but he found an empty stall and opened the bag. As he suspected, inside were two changes of clothes, toiletries, and a second pair of tennis shoes. The robe had full sleeves, which covered his arms, ending midway down his hands. They reminded him of monks' apparel. Undressing, he shoved his used clothes behind the lav along with the camera. Finally, making some last-second adjustments, he walked out of the stall, then slowly exited the restroom, turning toward the meeting area. Halfway down the corridor he saw a Chinese fellow in animated conversation with two security guards. This must be the victim of his crime. TJ casually looked toward the excited man and his two-man audience, then in studied nonchalance continued on.

Once inside the gathering area, TJ looked around.

He jumped as he felt someone tap him on the shoulder.

"Hold on—a little jumpy, huh?" The voice crackled.

TJ turned and saw it was the very same man he'd spoken with the first time.

"I see they gave you your duds."

TJ nodded. "So what's next? Do we just wait?"

"Yeah, not for long though, at least I don't. I'm scheduled to go out soon," he said, then extended his hand. "My name is Bernie Krantz." He held up his name tag attached to his smock. "And you are Cho Chan?" asked Bernie, confusion showing in his voice.

"Cho?" TJ looked down and for the first time saw the name tag. "Yes."

"That's an unusual name for a Midwesterner—well, I mean, for someone who obviously isn't from the East."

"Yes. Yes, I've been told that. Many times, I've been told that."

"Well, Cho, when are you scheduled to go?"

"Well, I think I may have missed my time. The guy I talked to wasn't too clear. Maybe I'll go over with you and see if my name has been read yet."

Bernie nodded, then closed his eyes and breathed deeply. "You know, Cho, I am really excited about this. I mean at first, I was a little nervous. You know, didn't understand what was going on, but now I'm excited. How about you?"

"Yeah, I'm excited. That's for sure."

"Where do you think they are from? I haven't talked to anyone who has a clue. I've heard some speculation that they are from a different galaxy—or maybe a different time."

TJ shook his head slowly. "I'm sorta here to find out where they are from, I've heard some different guesses too, we'll just have to wait and see."

Bernie nodded. A silence hung between the two as each mulled over their private thoughts. Bernie broke the silence. "And I can't figure out why me."

"Any guesses?" asked TJ

"Well, the agents that came for me told me that no one seems to be a churchgoer, and that's about all they can find in common. How about you? You believe in God?"

TJ cleared his throat, then nodded. "Yeah, I do."

"You do? Well, that shoots that theory then. I guess if anything sort of worries me about this, it's that: Why me? I can't figure it out, and no one else can. Why me? Why you? Why anybody here? From what I see, there just doesn't seem to be any connection."

"Really. I didn't know that, sorta assumed everybody had something in common."

Bernie let out a gasp of exasperation. "If they do, it beats me."

"What did you do before this?" asked Bernie.

"Do? I was a reporter."

"Really? That's sorta in common with me. I was in radio. I hosted the morning show. Top-rated in the city," said Bernie, a note of pride creeping into his voice.

"I see, any other media people?"

Bernie shrugged. "Beats me. I haven't found any. Well, what say we head for the transports? I'm supposed to be there soon. You still wanna go with me?"

"Yeah, sure. "

The two made their way between the groupings to a stairwell, leading upward. Reaching deck level, they fell into a line moving very slowly.

Bernie nudged TJ, "We could have waited another hour at the rate this line is moving."

TJ nodded. "Yeah, I don't think you are gonna make your time,"

Bernie nodded, then looked down the long line. "Hey, Cho, look down there. What's going on now?"

TJ looked up the line and saw four uniformed navy personnel with dark blue armbands with "SP" designating shore patrol in blocked white letters. With each person, they would carefully check a list they had.

"Looks like they're looking for someone," ventured Bernie. "Checking IDs I think."

"Really," said TJ, a pang of fear stabbing his stomach. Again he leaned out and looked toward the approaching military police. They were a bit closer now and he could see they were indeed carefully examining the ID cards on each person's chest, then checking the number on their arm. TJ could feel the fear he'd thought he had left behind rising in his loins. If he left the line now it would be a dead giveaway. He waited in silence as the men approached. Finally, they were next to Bernie. One reached over and held Bernie's ID card, then looked carefully at his face, and finally read off the number on Bernie's arm: 5102. The second MP nodded, checked his sheet, and they moved on to TJ.

TJ froze, he couldn't think of what he could do or say. He stood there perfectly still waiting for the inevitable. However, instead of stopping in front of him, they went to the woman next in line, never giving him a glance. TJ remained silent lest they discover their error. Carefully they checked the woman and moved to the next.

"Well, whatever they are looking for, I guess we pass, right?" smiled Bernie.

TJ managed a grin and nodded.

"He didn't even check you, I wonder why? Do you know him?"

"Never saw either of them before." Then turning to Bernie, laughed, "I guess they just know a class act guy when they see him."

Bernie chuckled, "Yeah, right."

The line picked up and slowly the two shuffled out the metal door and down a metal stairway. At the base of the stairs, a seaman was checking names off a list he held. Once again TJ felt his pulse begin to pump. The seaman stopped the line, turned, and swung his arm in a circular motion over his head toward another sailor with paddles, who immediately raised his paddles while facing the chopper. As soon as the last cleared civilian had boarded the chopper, he pointed both paddles directly toward the chopper, then raised them vertically over his head, and began rotating one. The whirl of chopper blades increased with the engine roaring, and the chopper slowly rose off the deck, tilting toward the north, as it made its way toward the pyramids.

"Next," said the sailor, holding his clipboard up again.

The line began to shuffle forward again as another chopper waited. TJ tried not to show his nerves, and smiled pleasantly when it was his turn.

"Chan?" asked the sailor.

"Ah, yeah. I sorta got lost and I was wondering…"

"Oh, here you are. You were supposed to go over a half hour ago!" he said, looking up. Quickly he checked the name badge on TJ's left breast pocket. "Chan? Your first name, Cho?"

TJ smiled. "I know, everybody says the same thing when they see me. I would've been here sooner but I had to stop off at the men's room."

The sailor shook his head slowly. "You civilians, 'restroom.' I would've been there myself if I was about to meet aliens." He laughed and motioned TJ toward the chopper.

Quickly TJ made his way to the chopper and hopped aboard. There was room for perhaps twelve people. Two long benches ran the width of the chopper facing each other. He slid to the far side and Bernie soon took the seat opposite him. Bernie smiled and gave him the thumbs-up sign, which TJ returned. More passengers scrambled on board followed by the attending airman.

"Fasten your seat belts—everybody double-check your seat belts," The aviator had his own belt, which had a long line attached allowing him some freedom around the small cabin. A red light went on followed by a buzzer.

"Okay folks, hang on. Wait until I tell you, before unbuckling when we land," shouted the airman above the rising noise of the blades. The large chopper blades were deafening as they reached their top speed lifting the chopper slowly off the deck. TJ felt the chopper dip slightly forward and to the left and they began to gather speed. He wanted to ask Bernie how he was doing but the deafening sound made talking impossible. Instead, leaning forward to peer out, he watched them rise steadily before leveling off at about 500 feet.

From this height he could see most of the ships of the fleet ringing the pyramids. The triangular structures rose out of the sea to a height above their helicopter's elevation. He could not imagine how the huge pyramids could ever lift off, much less navigate through space. They seemed to have a bluish tint to them, which was clearer as they drew near. Now and then the sun would catch one of the smooth surfaces and reflect dazzling light beams toward them. In the distance, he could see choppers returning to the carriers for more people. How many were they bringing over? It wouldn't surprise him if the number ran into the thousands. He shook his head. It was so unreal.

Within a few minutes they felt the chopper bank to the left and begin to settle. TJ tried to peek out of the window, as did everyone else. He could see they were settling down on the base of the pyramids. The structures rose above him higher than any skyscraper he'd ever seen. They were enormous, much larger than TJ first estimated from the ship. TJ felt the bump of the wheels contacting the pad and immediately heard the whine of the engine as the blades began to throttle down.

"Okay. Unbuckle. This is it," announced the crewman above the din.

The doors slid open on both sides, and they were motioned out amid the deafening crescendo of the other choppers.

Slipping his legs over the edge, TJ hopped down, standing aside until Bernie disembarked. Both followed the small group toward a line of earlier arrivals now awaiting entrance to the pyramid. TJ felt his blood pounding and his hands felt clammy, each step seemed to raise the level of fear he felt. Once out of the deafening sound of the choppers, TJ leaned toward Bernie. "Are you ready for this?"

"Is anybody?"

TJ shook his head. "At least there are a lot of people. They say there's safety in numbers."

The line slowly shuffled forward away from the noise of constant landing and departing choppers. The level platform upon which they stood that acted as a landing field, was larger than TJ first estimated. It easily ran a quarter mile or more with a deep, unblemished, black surface, which was very smooth, giving the impression of marble. But it wasn't. Though the water made the surface glisten and appear slick, it wasn't. In fact, it felt very secure. Above, the walls of the pyramid seemed to be of the same smooth surface. However, while the area beneath their feet was black, the wall above was a deep lagoon blue.

TJ tried to see some evidence of construction technique, but couldn't. There didn't appear to be any visible seams in the monolithic wall. It was as if one piece of the marble-looking substance had been cast or carved and now sat gleaming out of the ocean.

The line ahead finally began turning into an opening. The closer he drew to the opening, the larger it appeared. It was easily several hundred feet across and several stories tall. On either side of the entry were groups of aliens. They all appeared to be about 6 feet tall and of muscular build, though that was hard to tell since each was cloaked in a red robe with either white piping or black piping around the edges and sleeves. The robes were not tied around the waist but dropped in straight folds from their broad shoulders. Each robe was edged with white braid along the hems, around the cuffs and the edges of the collars. They stood with their arms crossed, the long, full sleeves hiding arms and hands. Each had a hood, which was now folded back. By any earthly standard, they would certainly be considered beautiful, with high cheekbones tapering into chiseled square chins and lean cheeks. None were smiling, but their expressions were relaxed, casual, as though watching familiar people pass by.

As TJ and Bernie passed, the one nearest turned his head, his eyes meeting TJ's. TJ felt a cold chill run through his body and heard himself gasp as, for an instant, TJ thought he'd seen him before.

"What's wrong?" asked Bernie.

TJ turned toward Bernie. "Oh nothing, just for a second he looked familiar."

Bernie shook his head. "Familiar. Oh, I doubt that. You got the jitters or something?"

"Maybe," nodded TJ. "I guess I'm a little more nervous than I thought I would be."

"You are? I'm not, should be, but I'm really not. Strange, huh?"

TJ shrugged. He'd given up on what was strange and what wasn't.

After passing through the opening, the group found themselves in the largest room TJ had ever seen—probably as big as some covered football fields. Here the line was spreading out, as more men, these in red robes, were directing the entering group into several lines, each heading for distant exits. Besides the red-robed individuals, there were those with different colors. There were a few with black robes, trimmed in white braid; others with a dappled gray robes. Each had colored braid-work around the hems and sleeves—white, red, black, or gray. Once he caught sight of a white-robed individual. Clearly, these were designations of rank or skill sets.

TJ and Bernie were shuttled into a line, which eventually passed through an exit into a corridor some 30 feet wide, with walls following the shape of its triangular entrance. The walls rose, slowly arching inward until meeting some 30 feet above them. Despite the large walled space, TJ detected no echo from the voices around him, nor did the treading feet make an appreciable sound.

But what interested TJ the most was the light. A soft, blue-white light came from the walls, though no light source was evident. Finally, the hallway turned left, opening into another very large room where thousands of chairs were waiting. All along the way were more robed individuals, mostly red, encouraging and directing people. Finally both he and Bernie found a padded bench and sat down. The room was amazing, not only for its size—accommodating several thousand people, but because one wall, the outside wall, was completely transparent. It was as though there were no barrier there at all. They could see more choppers coming and going in the mist they created, but there was no sound.

TJ looked carefully at the walls and thought he could see pencil-thin lines, but it was difficult to tell at that distance. Whatever technology they were using, it was far beyond the builders on Earth, who would pay a fortune for such an architectural design.

Speakers hidden somewhere in the walls came to life. "Please be seated and relax. It will be a few moments before we are ready to bring you into the auditorium. In the auditorium the leader of this expedition will address you. You will be fed, then there will be another lecture. Finally, you will be shown your quarters. We welcome you as honored guests and if there is anything we may do for you please let one of the attendants in blue robes know. Again, thank you for coming."

As they waited, red-robed men began making their way through the waiting crowd with carts bearing refreshments on them.

Many took advantage of the break to relieve themselves in restrooms that lined the far wall. Finally, after an hour and a half, the group was on the move again, exiting in a different direction leading directly into a large theater capable of seating several thousand. The lines were divided and subdivided until TJ and Bernie found themselves funneled down a row of seats. TJ sat down in the cushioned seat, and was pleasantly surprised with how comfortable it was. There was not a lot of leg room, but it wasn't uncomfortable. He leaned over to Bernie. "Notice anything odd?"

"Such as?"

"Well, these seats, for one. They are perfect—for you and I, for two humans. But these aliens would have a tough time."

"So?"

"Well, look around. This whole auditorium is made to our size, and the room we just were in—all those seats were just our size. In fact, everything I've seen is our size. What about the urinals? Tell me they were at the height for anyone but human males."

"Okay. So?"

TJ let out a small sigh of exasperation. "If the seats and all were built and installed before they came, then they must have known a lot about humans. How would they know what size to build them? How long have they been watching us? Why is it important to contact us now and not years ago?"

"Well, they may not have been here years ago, as you think. Maybe they just started observing recently and built these things, but I get your point."

Bernie stopped speaking as the lights began to fade. It did not become absolutely dark, but the hall was gray. The area behind the stage grew in a soft blue light transforming the flat wall into a screen. Gradually a face began to reveal itself on the screen, filling the entire area 20 feet tall and nearly 40 feet wide. The head was startling in its size as it towered over the assembly motionless. The face was hidden mostly beneath the shadows of a hood that covered his head. His nose though straight, showed signs of an older face. His eyes though hidden within the shadow of his hood, still revealed his eyelids sagging a bit. The most startling thing was his eyes. Peering out they showed a coral blue, with a narrow red ring on the iris' edge. The entire appearance gave mystery yet wisdom.

Finally he spoke, his tone low, yet vibrant, exuding confidence and a quiet, comforting friendliness. It struck TJ that if this creature ever got tired of the alien business, commercials or politics would be a great second career.

"Good day, children," he said, smiling. TJ cast a quick glance at Bernie, who returned the look while raising his eyebrows. Children. The thought made TJ squirm. "My name is Abdon. Perhaps you noticed when you came here a large area of water in the center of our structure. This space is usually occupied by another section. As you know, this section is much larger, and we've left the center area open for it later. It is now still circling Earth. Our supreme leader is there, yet he is with us and aware of all we do. His name is Eli, which means Morning Star, and he will, in his time, join us."

Abdon paused and smiled silently. Even TJ could feel the warmth of it. "You all have been gathered here to help us spread some very good news to all the people upon Earth. You have not been chosen by random, as some have suggested, but have been selected individually, by name, by us, and for a reason. That reason will be made clearer to you as we go along. You can think of yourselves as the chosen ones—which is how we think of you. You are our chosen children, for we have known your names from the beginning.

"We knew your parents, and your parent's grandfathers, and your grandfathers' ancient fathers. We've kept careful track of each of you, and now your time has come. You've been chosen to receive the gifts we are bringing, and in turn give these gifts to others." A ripple ran through the auditorium, if was a low, disquieting murmuring. "And not only gifts, but news that shall change mankind forever. It's news that you will struggle with yourselves—and not until you are able to accept it, embrace it with love and joy, shall you be able to share with others."

His voice had no accent; he spoke perfect English. Yet, many in the audience were not American or English. No one wore headphones, yet all seem to understand the alien perfectly.

Abdon stepped forward a few paces, his face growing in size on the screen. The silence grew, giving electricity to the air. All were in such a state of expectation, that the slightest movement or word might break the spell. Abdon looked carefully, as if searching for something. TJ shifted in his seat, as the alien's eyes appeared to pass over him, hesitate, and then continue on over the audience. Could he actually see him? More importantly, did Abdon know the truth about him?

Finally Abdon took a deep breath. "You see, children, the first thing you should know is we share the same blood." He paused, as though listening to the ripples of voices running through his audience.

TJ's expression did not change, for what the alien was saying was too fantastic. He was shocked. Had he heard correctly? This alien and he shared the same blood?

Abdon continued. "Let me explain," he said. "It is not only that we have the same blood, it's that you are of our blood. You are truly our children."

Now there was an eruption of noise, including from Bernie and TJ.

"Is he saying what I think?" asked Bernie incredulously.

"I guess. Meet Daddy," grumbled TJ. It was getting as weird as he feared.

Finally, Abdon held up his hand and the noise quickly subsided. The alien waited until the hall was absolutely quiet. "I know this is difficult to accept and to understand. Let me explain.

It was absolutely silent.

"Our blood has come down to you through your ancestors. Yes, at one time your ancestors were us. We are your beginnings." He smiled, but the silence continued. "Now, through time, some on Earth have retained more of our genes than others. And those who have retained more of our genes we've invited to come here. You." Once more there was murmuring in the room as some grasped what was being said. The alien waited patiently; the expression on his face was one of complete calm and patience. At last, the murmurs died.

"You see, children, in the beginning your ancestors were not of this planet, but of ours."

"I knew it!" said Bernie. He nudged TJ. "What he's saying makes sense."

TJ looked at him. "It does?"

Abdon continued. "This first session will be short, and I have decided to close with a story. After you have had some time to absorb the truth that this story reveals, I'll return and we will talk some more." Abdon raised clasped hands to his chest and lowered his head as he thought a moment before continuing. "Long ago, there were two lovers. Now, no lovers were happier or as fulfilled as these two. One lover, whose name is Eli, was lord of the kingdom of stars. He was master of all that existed. The woman he loved was named Eve. She was the most beautiful woman in his kingdom.

"Now, much of what Eli ruled, he shared with his subjects for their joy. Some other things he shared only with his lover, and a few he shared with none. Some of what Eli did not share were specific worlds within his kingdom. One world was his favorite. Its beauty was beyond measure and a rare thing had occurred: Life came from it. Eli declared that no one should visit or even look upon this world for he wanted to see how this life would develop.

"Now, after a time, his lover began to covet this world, because it was forbidden and it was beautiful and so rare. 'Why shouldn't I share in this thing?' she asked. 'Are we not lovers? Do we not share our joys?'

"And so, while Eli was away, she and her friends ventured to this world and enjoyed it. She pleasured herself with it, sharing it with her friends. Now, later when Eli returned, he sensed their trust had been violated and he asked, 'Have you broken my law? Have you possessed the forbidden globe, which I set aside?' His lover fell before his feet confessing she had and begged his forgiveness.

"Eli wept, for he loved the woman. Yet, she had broken his law, and it was written all who did must suffer the consequences. 'Though I grieve greatly,' he said, 'you have broken the law and you must be punished.'

"At this, the woman cried, 'Please, can't we forget this has ever happened? I promise I will not do it again!'

"Eli was deeply shaken, but wiping his tears said, 'I cannot. It is the law; however, I will put it to the elders and let them pronounce the sentence, for I cannot. Perhaps they will have mercy.'

"The twenty-four elders came to Eli and then conferred among themselves to see if they could spare Eve, yet satisfy the law. Finally they returned to Eli. 'We know that you love this woman, and that she loves you. But the law is clear. She must die; it is the written word. Her unfaithfulness will spread among our people like a disease.'

"Eli was silent, hanging his head in resignation.

"The elders continued. 'Lord Eli we have found a solution of sorts. By your own words of long ago, what this woman has done requires that she and her friends be put to death. However, we understand, by your own hand you cannot do this. What we suggest is this: Send the woman to this globe that she has violated with her desire. Give her the thing she coveted and it will surely cause her death. For once upon the Earth she will grow old, and her death will be by this globe she coveted.'

"Eli considered carefully what the elders said, knowing there was wisdom in it, and finally agreed.

"Upon hearing the judgment of the elders, the woman begged this would not be done. She pleaded for another chance, but the elders were firm, because the words of the law must not be broken by anyone. When the woman realized there was no mercy, that the sentence would be carried out, her heart began to turn against Eli. She and her friends were taken to that which she had coveted—the world you call Earth.

"Once there her spurned love turned to bitterness, for she knew death was to be the final judgment. She and her friends began to curse the name of her ex-lover, for the sentence was more than they could bear. They told their children a twisted story, so her children also began to curse the name of Eli. Finally one day she said, 'I will take a new love.' She began searching for a new lover but none were as fair and as strong as Eli was, so the woman created a secret love of her own. She told her friends that he would visit her in secret, talk to only her, and claimed he was twice as powerful as Eli and he would be at enmity with Eli.

"Her friends, and children, and the children of her friends rejoiced for the new lover and their children's children rejoiced and thereby the woman's vengeance was satisfied. Her children and her children's children cursed Eli, her first love.

"The people needed a name for their new god, so they called him Bashar, which means Just One. Later this name was changed by different peoples, satisfying their individual needs to have this god as their own."

The alien paused. But no sound came from the audience, including Bernie and TJ. TJ was transfixed. The enormity of the alien's claim drained him of all reaction.

Bernie nudged him and whispered, "Get it? Makes sense, don't it? All the religious mumbo-jumbo. Wow—blows my mind!"

Abdon was speaking again. "You are the children of the children of that woman. You have been deceived all these centuries; but now, we have come to reunite you with the truth, with Eli, and give to you the inheritance that is yours by blood right." He paused, and a quiet smile played across his face. "I know this is difficult for you to gather in all at once. There is so much we have to tell you, teach you, show you, and share. But for now, I am going to stop and allow you to absorb what I have said. There are many of us here to help you with your questions. Please ask; we are willing to help at any time. Welcome to the kingdom of Eli." With that he raised his right hand, palm open, and faded on the screen.

Immediately, lights brightened, and the crescendo of voices with them. Bernie and TJ sat silent, as did some others. Finally TJ closed his eyes. It was worse than he thought. Sarah was right; she had known the truth all this time.

CHAPTER 5

The Deception

OPENING THE DOOR to their assigned room revealed a long hall ending in a living room with a floor-to-ceiling view of the outside. There were doors on either side of the hall, which opened into two bedrooms and a small closet. Further down, on the right, was an arched entrance opening into a small kitchen. The living room at the end, measured 18 feet by 15 feet. The room was fully furnished in conservative, wood and cloth appointments—all showing some measure of artisanship. The walls were painted in pastels and barren except for a painting over the 8-foot couch of a child being read to by an adult, reminiscent of a Rockwell setting.

The most astounding part of the apartment was the outside wall, which was invisible, identical to the one they'd seen earlier. Except for fine lines running the length of the wall here and there, no evidence could be seen of any barrier between them and the outside. There was a slight inward sloping of the wall, which evidenced they were on the outside wall of the pyramid; however, neither had seen any such windows from the outside. Both he and Bernie reached out tentatively to touch the solid surface before truly believing it. Feeling the solid, though invisible, wall was reassuring, since their apartment appeared to be several hundred feet in the air.

The view was spectacular. They could see the military ships surrounding the pyramid. Between the ships and the pyramid, was an area of calm water surrounding the three structures. Beyond the circle of military ships, there were hundreds of ships flying the flags of most of the world's nations.

"See what I mean?" asked TJ. "All of this furniture, the size of the rooms, the dishes—everything is to our size. It's creepy. They didn't just get here, they knew a lot about us before they showed themselves."

"Yeah, well that fits what he was saying. They do know everything about us—you're right, probably been watching us for years and years, back maybe to prehistoric times."

TJ slumped down on the couch facing the window. "So let me get this straight—tell me if I got any of this wrong. A zillion years ago some woman and her friends were banished to this planet to die. They had some kids, and we are the descendents of those children. Right?"

Bernie sat down in the armchair letting a satisfied sigh escape. "Yeah, that's about it."

"So we are aliens."

Bernie snorted. "Ain't it a gas?"

TJ paused for a moment, then looked sternly at Bernie. "Look, you seem like a reasonable fellow. Does any of this seem, well—phony?"

"Phony? What do you mean, exactly?"

"Well, this story he's telling us, I mean, it's pretty far out—don't you think? Doesn't it strike you as a fairy tale?"

Bernie thought for a moment. Shrugging his shoulders he let out a long breath of air between his lips that sounded like a motorboat. "Oh, I suppose it could be. But look, this spaceship and all—this is not phony. Nothing make-believe about it."

"Bernie," said TJ. "May I ask a favor of you?"

"Sure."

"Well, if anything happens to me, could you get word to a friend of mine aboard ship? His name is Andy Moore. He's a reporter with the Washington *Dispatch*. He knows I'm here and I just want him to know I made it and to remember to let Sarah know that she was right."

"Sure. Who's Sarah? What's she right about?"

"That's my wife. What she's right about is personal."

Bernie nodded. "Got a missus at home, eh? Yeah, wish I did sometimes, but now I'm glad I don't. Hey, was there any food in those cupboards?"

TJ shook his head. "Not a bite—and I'm starving."

As though their thoughts were read, a voice spoke from a wall-mounted speaker, startling both men. "Ladies and gentlemen, please proceed to our dining facilities. The number of your floor will indicate which dining area you should go to when you reach the twenty-sixth level. When exiting the transport there will be guides to help you find your way. Please proceed to the dining area now."

Bernie found keys hanging from a clip in the kitchen. "Here's yours," he said, tossing a set to TJ. "Look at this, will you. Our room number is one-seven-five-b-two-forty! Either we are on the one hundred seventy-fifth floor or the two hundred fortieth! Can you believe it?"

"Has to be the one hundred seventy-fifth. I saw the room number was two-forty when we came here. Are you ready?" asked TJ. He did not wait for Bernie's reply but made for the elevator, punching the twenty-sixth level as soon as Bernie had entered. Exiting, they were directed to dining room 175, which revealed itself to be as enormous as everything else was. Several hundred people were filtering down ten serving lines and a few hundred others were eating at tables.

TJ followed Bernie through one line, though which foods were offered, he didn't notice. His thoughts were on anything but eating, despite his feelings of hunger. At the end of the line, Bernie snaked his way through the maze of long tables, each having ten to twelve seats, until finally choosing one at which there were a couple of seats available. TJ followed, setting his tray down and finally taking inventory of what had been placed on it: mashed potatoes that looked real, some kind of steak, salad with a white dressing, rolls, butter, and milk.

The table was silent. Each of the others appeared to be picking at their food while lost in their thoughts. Suddenly a man sitting near the center of the table, threw his fork at his plate, embedding it in the mashed potatoes. "What are we talking about here?" He challenged no one and everyone. He was overweight, but did not appear jolly at the moment. His face had a scowl as he looked around the table. "We're talking aliens, right? Are these guys our ancestors? Is that what's happening here?"

For a moment silence continued, although a few heads gave small nods. It was Bernie who ventured an answer. "We think so," he said, including TJ sitting next to him, much to TJ's surprise. "That's what the guy in the robe said, and I don't see how we can dispute it, right now. After all, they did come in their huge spaceship things—so we know they're from someplace out there," he said, pointing upward. "I gotta say I'm sold."

TJ spoke up. "I don't mind telling you it scares me. I mean, this all looks real friendly and everything, but are they really friendly?"

A woman at the far the end of the table spoke up. "What's this about our being relatives—children?"

"That's exactly what you are." The deep voice from behind startled TJ. Turning, he recognized the alien Abdon. He was quite tall. From his broad shoulders, his red robe dripped to just above the floor. There were several colors on thin piping that circled the sleeve: black, a pale off-white, and a pure white. His hands were clasped in front, with his long sleeves nearly covering them to just above the first knuckle. His face wore a friendly smile and exuded confidence. His deep blue eyes had the same red tinge around the edges he'd seen before. "I hope you don't mind being called children," he continued. "But when you accept in your hearts all that is going to be taught you, then you will understand. Until then, please accept the possibility that you are our children—it's how we have thought of you all these ages."

There was an uncomfortable stirring at the table. TJ and Bernie exchanged quick glances.

Abdon moved slowly to his left a few steps, then stopped. "Let me explain a little," he continued. His voice was calm and his smile had a relaxing effect on everyone except TJ. He was relieved that the alien did not stay behind him. Nevertheless, he had the feeling, each time the alien looked at him, that he knew who TJ was. "Understand, Eli our leader is master of the Elect and counts in his kingdom all of the universe. Earth is unique in the Master's kingdom. When we found Earth, in this lonely corner of the universe, it was just evolving, and it was set aside by Eli much like you would set aside a national park. This was done because Eli wanted it undisturbed so he might observe evolution, as it had never been seen before. He considered it a rare treasure."

"However, a group of the Elect led by Eve, the lover of Eli, was so enamored of the planet that they visited it and had sexual relations with the early men and women, though they were little more than animals. Then, some of those earthly women conceived."

Across from TJ a man drew himself up, mustering the courage he needed, "Now, let me get this straight. We are some kinda nature preserve, with the rest of the universe watching us—sorta like a zoo?"

For a moment Abdon did not answer. His eyes seemed to be measuring his questioner, evaluating. Finally Abdon chuckled, and his smile came easily again.

"I wouldn't say 'zoo.' Earth is not in a cage to be fed every few hours." His lips attempted to smile. "No, it is a very special part of Eli's kingdom—a special treasure to which no harm, or interference was ever intended. Your planet fascinated Eli, for we could watch a unique event, the development of life—the purity of natural evolution. We could do this because the concept of time exists here, therefore evolution can exist.

"But, after the visit of Eve, we couldn't do that any longer. The evolutionary sequence had been broken; the purity of Earth had been violated by the introduction of our blood. We hoped, somehow, we could right that, but we were not able to do so. So we have a new responsibility: to care for our offspring. To bring home the children conceived and give them their inheritance. Do you understand?" Asking the question, he looked slowly around the table. It was the woman who answered.

"In effect, you're saying we are your long-lost relatives?

Abdon nodded. "Exactly."

TJ was startled when Bernie's voice came alive next to him. "What do you mean about time? You said something about time."

"Yes, you see time is not a part of the Elect's natural lives. Time is not uniform in the universe; it varies depending upon where you are. Your day here might be a second, or a millisecond, or a year somewhere else. In our kingdom there is no time. Time is just another characteristic within the universe, like height, distance, weight, and sound. It is a result of physical elements that, once identified, can be manipulated. Time is related to speed; that is, the faster one travels the slower time gets—or conversely, the slower one goes the faster time advances. This can be found even on Earth. If a man lives on the mountain, his time is slower than those who live in the valley." He looked toward a blonde woman seated at the end of the table. "Is this not true, Dr. Welman? You are familiar with physics, can you share with the others, if you believe what I say is correct?"

The startled expression on the woman's face showed her surprise that Abdon knew her name. So was TJ.

"Uh...yes," the doctor responded. "This is a concept Einstein brought up as a consequence of his Theory of Relativity. In fact, some experiments were done with airplanes and chronometers to see if speed could really affect time. And it showed that speed could affect time. A faster speed seems to retard time. Einstein said that if a spaceship were sent out in space, and if it were to go near the speed of light, time would stand still. If the crew were thirty years old when they left, and if they were out in space for a hundred years, when they returned their age would virtually be the same, while everyone they knew on Earth would have died of old age. A more ridiculous example would be, if one lived on the top floor of a skyscraper, the slight increase in the rotation speed would affect time in a very small minuscule way. So, if your man were living on a mountain, his time would run a minuscule bit slower than in the valley. "

Abdon nodded. "Here, yesterday becomes today, and today—tomorrow, but in our world, yesterday is today and tomorrow is today. It's all the same." Again Abdon attempted a smile, but his face resisted. "Some have referred to your God as being the same yesterday, today, and tomorrow. This is true in our society. I believe you will see that your reference to God being thus is actually a reference long ago to Eli. This illusion of time survived in some of the literature of your religions and philosophies. It's not difficult to understand, once the facts are known. I think you will find this to be the case always when we try to separate religious visions and folktales and compare them to fact. Once the facts are known the folktales loose their mystery, their charm, and their attraction."

Bernie shook his head slowly from side to side. He felt a hand pat his back softly. "Don't despair, Mr. Krantz. I know, all of this is overwhelming. But it will make sense to you soon."

Bernie nodded. "But I don't get this about time. You say time moves differently in other places?'

"Exactly. Children, you must understand, the universe's construction is not, as you suspect, with a center and an unknown edge, toward which all objects rush."

"You mean like the Big Bang Theory?"

"Yes and no. The Big Bang did take place; however, the expanding gases achieved equilibrium. The expanding gases acted upon each other to stabilize expansion, and the result was a huge ring of gases; a wispy filament, turning into a loosely organized funnel of widely spaced hydrogen gas molecules through which the evolving stars moved.

"In time, the ring became unstable, folding in upon itself. Today, the universe resembles a hollow rope, which is tied in a loose knot, and through which the stars travel. The movement of the stars inside this hollow rope is not even. There are spaces where the stars move faster, and spaces where the stars move slower. At locations where the rope filament turns, the stars move much faster; and then slower where the star path is long and straight. Picture one of your garden hoses. The water is flowing at a uniform speed through it. Now, put a slight bend in it, and where that bend occurs, the water moves faster. At such a point in the stars, the movement is near the speed of light: time itself stands still, though there is no noticeable change to the people who live there. Conversely, where the stars move slower, time moves very fast— again with no noticeable difference to the people. You live in a space, which moves slower than ours; therefore, time is a real factor in your lives.

"Your scientists have been very good at devising ways to learn more about the universe in which you live. Some of our people think that's due to your being of our heritage." He smiled. "In time, you would have discovered all its secrets, as we have." He paused and walked to the far end of the table away from Bernie and TJ. A crowd was beginning to gather now, and a few people had to step back allowing him to pass.

"For instance," he began again, "you say that all of the universe is still expanding, and that consequently, the distance between galaxies is widening. In reality, the stars are much closer than you suspect, for the ribbons of the universe pass close to each other, but due to the speed of the gases and matter within those ribbons, this fact is distorted to your technology. They are, in fact, passing sideways to you, like two of your freight trains whizzing along in opposite directions. This occurs at such a rate of speed, everything seems to be receding, even those portions approaching you. The combined speed of your paths shifts everything into red spectrum, which indicates—falsely—they are receding."

Dr. Welman spoke up. This time her voice showed confidence, even a hint of arrogance, TJ suspected. "You are talking about what we know as Doppler Effect and Gamma factor. Simply put, it means speed determines our perception of direction and time. What we see as traveling away, may, in fact, be traveling sideways. What we see as a century may be someone else's second."

"Yes, Dr. Welman—exactly. These concepts are not foreign to your people. In time, they would become facts, just as they are with us. It is the special properties of space and time, which we use as confidently as you drive your car's highways."

TJ looked slowly around the table at the faces, which revealed a mixture of reactions. Clearly a few were as confused as he was, but most had that daydreamer look. They were hooked.

Abdon continued. "If the Elect visit here for a long time, our body processes adjust to your time frame, and we begin to age and eventually we would die."

"Like the woman Eve and her friends did?" asked a voice in the crowd.

"Exactly. Time began to affect them and they died. But many lived long lives. There are records of some living almost a thousand years before dying. In fact, their longevity was so impressive, it made its way into your fables."

"Excuse me, sir." Dr. Welman again—she was beginning to annoy TJ. "You've told us so much, I feel like I can't absorb it all. Am I right in saying a lot of this is the interpretation of the story told us earlier, about the two lovers?"

Abdon nodded. "Yes. In the story, the transgressors were sentenced to Earth, which would mean an eventual natural death. As I told you earlier, Earth is a very special place to us. When some of our people ventured here, upsetting the cycle, they contaminated this garden of evolution. Moreover, they had relations with the inhabitants, and the children born were of mixed blood.

"However, those who were confined to Earth did not die quickly, as we thought they would, but aged slowly.

"The exiled woman, whose name was Eve, and the Sons of the Mighty One, Eli, made war against early evolutionary Earth man. They saw that mankind would eventually be a threat to them. Now, they discovered two things: First, their children, conceived in their earlier visit, and born of earthly women, were doing well, although ostracized by the local tribes.

"Second, among themselves, the Elect were unable to reproduce. Now, they sought to change their physical makeup through diet, drinking, bathing, but nothing worked. However, seeing their own children born of earthlings doing very well, they determined through mating the necessary changes could be introduced to ensure they might live on through their offspring.

"So a number of the women earthlings' lives were temporarily spared for breeding, and a new Earth creature was created. It is from these children of the Elect and earthlings that you descend and call yourself, humans.

"Once the new children of the Sons were sufficient to ensure their race would survive, the Sons resumed eliminating their competition on Earth, and all known evolutionary men and women were destroyed. As a result, records on Earth show a space between modern man and pre-historic man. Up until now, it has been unexplained, and they continue to search for the link. The Sons of the Elect are that connection, that link."

There was a rumble among those seated. TJ realized others had gathered around the table so that now their table appeared to be the focus of the room. The alien waited patiently until the group was silent. Then, casting a slow gaze around, he resumed.

"As the generations progressed, the original truth of the Elect was lost. New gods were adopted, which seemed to fit into the needs and fears of the separate tribes that developed. Some were war Gods, such as Indra of the Vedic Aryans, Zeus, the Ares of Homer Greeks, the Yahweh of the Jews; and there were many others: Artemis, Ishtar, Astarte, Anahit, Aphrodite, and so forth. And yet, in all of these new fables, a small part of the truth seems to survive—more in some and less in others."

The gathered guests began muttering among themselves until it became a din of voices. The tall alien waited a moment, until the noise dropped, then raised his hand, quieting the crowd. "I know, to many the truth of this is a shock, but if you give me your attention for a few moments, I can shed some light on this for the worshipers of Balim as well as for the worshipers of Yahweh. In the coming days we will show you how, by the careful records kept by the followers of these gods that Balim was a child of Eli, just as you are, and that Yahweh is simply another name given for Eli."

A voice came from the crowd, somewhere behind TJ; "I just want to be clear on this. You are saying that God, the god of the Jews and Christians and of Islam, is really this Eli?"

Abdon nodded. "Yes, that is exactly what I'm saying. Over the centuries of time the god created by the exiled Eve was a close likeness of Eli, but claimed by Eve to be more powerful that Eli. Balim (or Jesus), son of Yahweh (or Eli), is credited with the healing of people, and of even bringing someone back from the dead. But children, this healing is a normal occurrence, not a miracle. Do not your doctors today do things that would be considered a miracle only a few hundred years ago? We have developed procedures and medicines that are capable of wonderful things. We shall soon give these same healing techniques to you. Please understand, it is not a miracle, simply a product of our advanced society. Balim did not simply wave his hand and command sickness to disappear, he ministered to it from the stars, and the illness was cured.

"Likewise, through the years, the story of Elijah has been expanded and changed so much. Yes, your Elijah was a real person. He was much admired by us. When we saw the efforts of Elijah, and his love of justice and truth, it was decided to bring him to our world so that we could educate him to the whole truth, and learn from him what we can do to bring our children home. A vessel, like the one that brought us, but much smaller, was dispatched to bring him to us. This is recorded in the Jewish manuscript you call Kings. I tell you, Elijah is well today—yes, he still lives."

There was an instant babble of voices and through them a voice behind TJ managed to be heard. "You mean the actual Elijah from the Bible?"

Abdon appeared to chuckle. "Yes," he smiled, "and eventually you will see him. He has come here and is at this very moment in the craft, which still circles Earth. In time, he will join us."

Again the babble increased throughout the room. TJ looked and saw faces from all over the room trying the peer between intervening heads. The more the alien talked, the more frightened TJ found himself becoming. He had to get out of here; this was everything Sarah had said it was, and more. TJ squirmed in his seat as the alien held up his hands for silence, which he instantly received.

"Other examples are the pyramids; crude attempts built to resemble the Elect's spacecraft. The bodies were placed in the pyramids, ready to depart Earth and join the gods in the sky. I could give you many other examples, but you will learn of them in due course. Today begins a wonderful journey for you. Soon, you too shall be not only our children, but also brothers and sisters. I know it disturbs some to hear us call you children, and I apologize, but it's how we have thought and spoken of you all these years.

"We know each of you by name. When you were selected, it was not by random choice. Each of you is well known to us. We have kept track over the centuries of each of the descendants from the original parents. You've been told of this before, many, many years ago during the time of Balim. You were told that all of you were in our book of life, that we numbered the very hairs on your head, that each of you has a secret name, a name given you by the Elect. This name you will learn when you are ready, and it shall be your new name, your eternal name.

"Eli has sent us here to gather his children, just as he promised so many years ago when, through the ill-fated messengers, you were told he would gather the Elect from the uttermost parts of Earth to the uttermost part of heavens. You are the fulfillment of that promise. We bring you health of body and spirit. We give you the universe for your pleasure. We offer you eternal life."

CHAPTER 6

Discovered

"ETERNAL LIFE?" THE voice was small, timid. "Did you say, eternal life?"

Abdon peered through the crowd until he identified the voice, then smiled. "Yes, Mrs. Birch. Recall earlier, I told you time varies." His voice trailed off for a moment as he paused before smiling again. "Children, there is so much, so very much, you have to learn yet. This business of time is so ingrained in your lives; you assume all watches tick at your rate. They do not. Eternal life is not supernatural, it's natural. Now, you can have this too."

The group burst into excited babble, preventing Abdon from continuing. He waited stoically, with no visible emotion upon his exquisitely crafted face, betraying neither impatience nor aggravation. The crowd quieted after a few moments.

"Now, I don't mean to disappoint you, but you are not yet ready for this." He peered about the room, but there was no sound. "Eternal life without a perfect mind and body is unacceptable. After all, we cannot have thousands of imperfect people living forever, possibly infecting others to live a miserable eternal life. Do you understand? That's why we have come. That's why we have gathered you together. It is our job—yours, mine, and all your sisters' and brothers'—to educate and prepare our children for the transition to Forever. And when you have been prepared mentally to accept the truths we bring you, then we will heal your bodies so that they will be ready also for the never-ending future.

"Excuse me, sir," said a young woman standing at the far end of the table, "but what do you mean exactly when you say 'heal our bodies'?"

Abdon nodded. "Eliminating all sickness, ridding the body of any abnormality—restoring the body to a state of perfection. You see, sickness is known here because your blood is contaminated, but once your blood is purified, sickness will disappear and be no more."

"When will you show us this—when will it happen?"

Abdon laughed out loud. "Your clocks have made you impatient." He paused, still smiling. "If you like, I will show you now."

TJ heard a collective gasp and found himself contributing to it.

"There is a man among you here who suffers from a number of illnesses. This man is well known to you, as are his illnesses. His name is Arthur Ramon."

Whispers went through the assembled as many recognized the name of the deputy assistant to the ambassador of France. He'd often been in the news, and was considered an ultra national. Ramon was not a popular man, both for his politics and his personality. The group began to part as Ramon shuffled forward with his familiar cane. His seventy-three years were heavy upon his shoulders as he walked with a slight bend. As a result he faced the floor looking up from beneath a large long nose to see his progress. His face was deeply lined with no clear pattern except for the circle beneath each eye. He had no upper lip and his lower one was turned slightly down at the end. He looked like an old man with an unhappy thought.

Abdon reached out. "Mr. Ramon, I know how much pain you have. Today, we will relieve you of it forever. I take it you would like that."

Ramon smiled, and it was obvious this was not usual, as his face was able only to manage a crooked grin. "Yes, sir, I would like that."

Abdon turned and motioned Ramon to follow. Slowly they made their way out the door into the corridor with the assembled people following them. Outside in the corridor, many others had been watching. The procession made their way to one of the auditoriums. There was no careful seating this time as each made a dash for one of the seats. When they were filled, people sat in the aisles and then along the edges of the auditorium where TJ and Bernie found themselves while many others crowded around the outer doors.

Abdon made his way to the stage with Ramon hobbling behind him. Two aliens brought a seat toward the middle of the platform and Ramon sat. Abdon continued across the stage to a lectern hurriedly placed there for him.

The two aliens with Ramon moved to either side of him in the chair, bent down, and began talking to him, though TJ could not make out the words.

He nudged Bernie. "Can you understand what they are saying?"

Bernie shook his head. "Too low."

"What's happening!" Shouted a female voice a few rows in front of them.

Abdon moved to the lectern. "Mr. Ramon is verbally committing himself to the Elect—to his heritage. He's renouncing his earthly ties, and beliefs, and is also accepting his union with the Elect. You see, children, before the rewards of the Elect may be enjoyed by our children on Earth, they must first renounce earthly things that bind them here, including money, myths, and ancestry. This commitment will begin the healing of your mind and then we can proceed to heal your body."

Silently, the audience watched as the two robed aliens took Ramon's hand and briefly applied a metal patch to it. No indication came from Ramon showing this was either painful or pleasurable. After a few moments, the alien removed the patch, then placed it to Ramon's temple. Still, there was no indication from Ramon. Finally, the aliens stood up and stepped back. There was silence throughout the hall as everyone waited. The absolute silence continued for a long period of time until Ramon finally shouted out loud.

Then he looked at each of the aliens and laughed, flexing his arm and hands. He stood and took a few steps forward, turned left, and walked a few paces before turning and walking back. He leaped, dropping his cane, then leaped again, "I feel wonderful!" he shouted. He clapped his hands, attempted to click his heels, fell down, and jumped back up running over to the nearest alien and kissing the alien's hand. "Thank you, thank you!" he exclaimed.

Slowly at first, then increasingly louder, came applause from the audience until it thundered off the walls as they watched Ramon cavorting about on the stage. Abdon walked over to the excited Ramon and put his arm around him. Ramon looked up at the alien with a grateful smile. Finally, Abdon held up his hand until the applause died. "Who you see here, is the first person of this Earth that has rejoined his ancient family. Welcome Mr. Ramon to the Elect of Eli." Abdon extended his hand, which Ramon took, shaking it with enthusiasm. Applause rocked the hall. Again Ramon kissed Abdon's hand and Abdon patted him on the back. The two aliens that had been with Ramon came forward and, as the applause began to die, they escorted Ramon off the platform.

Abdon returned to the lectern and waited for silence. "I wanted to show you how much accepting your heritage can do for you. The wonderful feelings being enjoyed by Mr. Ramon will be yours too. How is this possible, what is happening? You see, what Mr. Ramon has received is a purification of his blood. There is no surgery needed—that is barbaric. Within each molecule of our blood is the entire perfect DNA, which has an eternal memory of the way our bodies evolved. Once we remove the imperfections within the blood, this molecular memory is freed and health is restored. The only physical thing noticeable is a tiny and painless scar on his hand."

Pausing, Abdon looked silently out upon his audience for a moment. Then raising his open hands even with either side of his face continued, "Let me try to explain in a way in which you will not only understand but can accept. You see, a lot of the myths are really a result of what you were just shown. We, in a sense, have been our worst problem.

"Long ago your ancestors were shown the very same thing you have just witnessed. We told them if we cleansed their blood of Earth's contamination we could restore their health and eternal life. But they were not ready. They did not understand. In fact, they *could* not understand." Again he paused for a moment, staring at the floor while slowly shaking his head. At last he sighed and resumed. "Yet, this simple fact, this healing, was distorted. In time, blood became connected with the concept of sin and with somehow fixing what various cultures considered sin. This blood atonement came to be known in almost all cultures from the very simple to the sophisticated. It led to grotesque things from sacrificing babies, to sacrificing humans; there were terrible things done to fellow humans in the name of pleasing gods and atoning for sin through sacrificial blood. Now this isn't only with primitive cultures which are long forgotten, no, the myths are alive today, promoting the sacrificing of blood, which will make people perfect to be redeemed by their gods."

Abdon stepped from behind the lectern and advanced toward the front of the platform until he reached the edge, then looked down at the front rows. "Can you tell me how this is? Is this logical that you can shed someone's blood and that will make you whole, make you perfect? Can someone explain that to me?" He cast his eyes up toward the back of the auditorium, toward TJ and Bernie. TJ felt fear grip him, then realized it was Bernie that Abdon had chosen to ask. "You. Your name is Bernard Krantz, is that correct?"

TJ was astonished he knew Bernie's name.

"Ah…yes, yes it is."

"Don't worry, Bernard, you are among friends here," said Abdon. A ripple of laughter ran through the auditorium.

Bernie managed a weak smile.

"Now, tell me, Bernard, why is it that people believe such a thing? It isn't logical, is it?"

"No."

"Well, if logic brought you this far in medicine, industry, and exploration why do humans still think this blood thing is true—if it isn't logical? How is it that when dealing with the reality of life, logic is your sword, but when dealing with what cannot be seen, or heard, or touched, logic is treated so shabbily? "

"Well, ah—don't know. Sorta by, well—faith."

"Yes! Exactly, Bernard! " The volume of Abdon's voice roared through the auditorium. "Now, children, let's examine faith. Is this a faith—a trust—in what is real? The stars, Earth, and the water? No, it is in something or someone you cannot touch, hear, smell, or question! How many of Eli's children have been slain, even burned alive, in the name of mystical gods known only by faith? How many have languished in pain, waiting for the air to heal them. Faith, you say?

"It took billions of your Earth years for you to evolve while killing each other to survive —not for myths but for food and water. Countless ancestors of yours are parts of the dust of the universe, having paid the price, so you could conquer all that opposed you, to survive. Yet, you have thrown that away to believe in what—air?" He paused, walking slowly back to the lectern. He resumed, his voice deep and with force behind it. "I have no need of your faith, I have the stars—I have bent them to my will. It is this I bring to you and ask you to accept— not by faith, but by logic, by proof!"

The audience erupted in applause. From the back row, a man stood shouting, "And we are ready to receive!" The applause grew.

Abdon waited until silence claimed the auditorium again. Then, lifting his eyes, asked, "Are you really ready? Can you cast away your deepest reservations and make the transition? I do not ask you for your faith. I want your eyes to see, yours hands to hold, your ears to hear. I want your mind. Do not profane your body, for which so many perished, by speaking of myths."

He turned and walked back toward the small table where the instrument lay that was used on Arthur Ramon. Grasping it, he held it high. "Do you see this?" he said, holding up the metal instrument. In the light its smooth metal glistened. "This came not by chants, or bloody sacrifices, or meditating on the air, praying to clouds in the sky. This came because we snatched it from the bosom of the universe. It was not given to us as a reward; it is a prize of conquest! It came not willingly, but through dedication of countless others, and now, is offered as a gift to you! A gift to enable you to live with a body forever whole, forever healthy!"

The audience broke into applause. As it died a man toward the front stood and waited until it stopped. "I don't mean to insult you, but have you no religions of any kind?"

Abdon looked at him for a moment, gathering his thoughts. "You are not listening." His voice did not rise, but there was an unmistakable tone of impatience. "Religion is a weakness of those who feel unworthy—made to feel unworthy by the very religion they profess. Religion is a system of oppression brought on, and promulgated, by those who wish the spoils of the oppressed. It is a pacifier for the victims of chance, design, or failure.

"Religion is like a virus toward which weak men gravitate, then through which they hold in contempt others who do not share their weaknesses. It is divisive, making select groups superior to other groups. This cannot be allowed. Among the Elect, all are equal, all are deserving, all are allowed, all are worthy. It's the decision of the council that no one will be allowed to receive the benefits of their inheritance, until they renounce all religion!" Abdon's voice rose, echoing through the auditorium.

For a moment the auditorium was stone quiet, until broken by the small voice of a woman. "Excuse me. Does that include the thing with the blood?"

Abdon nodded. "Yes, as you have seen, this is a two-step process. The first step is to stabilize the body's system through the blood. That is what you saw used on the hand. The second stage is to cleanse the blood; that was done at the temple. It is the second treatment that will heal your body. We would like to give both of these to each person on Earth; however, we cannot permit religion, and all of its troubles, to infest the stars. One must come as a whole person, not only in body, but in mind, owing nothing to any mythical creatures or philosophies or political allegiances, but dedicated only to the searching for, and propagation of knowledge—for that is all we have to ensure our lives, happiness, and future. Therefore, we will accomplish the restoration of all our children, in two phases. First, all that renounce allegiance with fables, myths, cults, and sundry religions or political loyalties, may receive the first treatment, which will stabilize their bodies. Your bodies will not deteriorate further. After all others on Earth have renounced, everyone will receive the second, the restoration to perfect health. Then Forever will be yours as whole individuals."

A male voice came from the crowd. "Until all? But there may be some—maybe one—who will not renounce. Are we all condemned because of just one?"

Abdon turned and walked slowly to the front-center of the stage where he stood for a moment staring at the floor. When he looked up, TJ saw for the first time, a look on the face one might call an expression. Perhaps it was sadness.

"We have come a long way to bring you home. We have sacrificed over the years to bring you life—everlasting life. We come here out of love for all our brothers and sisters and wish everyone to come home. But, I fear you may be right. There may be some, for reasons I cannot fathom, who will reject their heritage, who will reject Forever. However, I cannot help you. The law is, all must be as one or none will be allowed."

A low murmur rippled through the crowd.

TJ looked around him. Murmur they should, he concluded. There certainly would be more than a few rejecting this screwball—himself for one, and Sarah for another. He fought a small smile hammering at his lips.

The alien waited a moment then placed his palms together and raised them to his chin as if he were getting ready to pray. He held his hands there for a moment and then, pointing them toward the audience, spoke. "Now, it's not for us to interfere with this. How you overcome this problem is entirely up to you—we cannot interfere. But let me leave you with a thought. Is it not considered a rightful thing to prevent death? To prevent a murder?" He looked slowly around the silent crowd. "Don't you protect your children, your loved ones—indeed society itself—from those who would harm it? In your laws, which you are so fond of making, haven't you many times determined, for the good of all, certain conduct unacceptable; even some warranting death, for the good of the whole? To those who do not agree with the codes of conduct your laws require, don't you rightfully determine they can no longer participate in the society, for the good and safety of all?"

Echoes of agreement rippled through the audience.

Abdon waited, nodding slowly as he did. "And, if one of yours is the cause of an unjustifiable death of another, don't you condemn him as a murderer and judge death as his reward?"

TJ felt a growing alarm at the direction this Abdon fellow was going. Others saw the direction too, as their shuffling and low sounds betrayed.

Abdon raised his hands shoulder high. "But enough for now, rest for a while, we will gather again this afternoon. We have many days ahead of us, all will be revealed to you." With that he turned and exited the stage to the growing sound of a thousand individual conversations behind him.

"Now, that's what I call convincing!" bubbled Bernie.

TJ did not respond but silently followed Bernie down the aisle and then out toward the elevators. It was ten minutes before they were able to enter the elevator and reach their floor. Once inside their apartment, Bernie flung himself on the couch and made murmurs of enjoyment as he stretched out.

TJ opened the empty refrigerator and was surprised to find an assortment of food in it now. "Hey, somebody put a bunch of food in the fridge. Hungry?"

Bernie sat up quickly. "Are you kidding? I'm always hungry." Quickly he came over and did a quick search, finally extracting an apple. "This looks fresh—wonder where they got apples?"

TJ ignored the question and instead posed one himself. "What did you get from the part about our passing laws, for the good of the group?"

"Seems to me he's suggesting we pass laws outlawing anyone who doesn't purify their blood. At least that's my take on it."

TJ leaned against the kitchen sink. "Yeah. Anyone who disagrees with these outer space guys is illegal? Is that what it would be?"

Bernie crunched on his apple for a moment, then stood thinking a moment as he chewed his food. "Yeah, I guess so. Doesn't seem right— maybe we gotta listen to some more."

"I think that is exactly what he is saying. If you do not agree to do what they want, you are declared a menace to society and considered a dangerous person—one maybe akin to a murderer. Therefore, then we will put them to death. Do we get to the point where we execute any-one who disagrees with the space cadets?"

"You don't like them, do you?"

TJ shook his head slowly. "No, I don't. Actually, they scare me. Oh, they are all polite, and courteous, and appear to be our buddies—but I don't buy it. Do you?"

"I don't know what I buy or don't, but look at the facts. They are here from 'out there' somewhere, can't dispute that. They have tech-nology we can only dream about—in fact, it's so far ahead of us, it's beyond our dreams. And here they come and want to share it with us. Think of all the lives that can be saved, all the happiness it can bring." Bernie paused, setting his half-eaten apple on the counter.

"From where I sit, it looks very impressive. Would I be willing to give up some things for that? You bet. Maybe they can take eighty pounds off me with that thingamajig. Would I be angry with those who would want to hang onto the old ways of greed, where only the strong survive? To hell with the weak, poor, sick, uneducated? Abso-lutely. Who are they to hold all the rest back from a future which, up until now, has only been dreamed about?

"They had their chance—a thousand wars, millions and millions of deaths. What did we get? Poverty, sickness, and the strong over the weak—exactly the way it was before. I say 'enough.' They had their chance, now it is time for something different. And these guys—who-ever they are—seem to have a possible answer. I say, 'Let's give them a chance.'" Bernie approached TJ slapping him on the back, almost knock-ing the wind out of him. "And the best part pal, we are in the inner circle. We are going to be the top guys, the number-one sons—what a gas!"

TJ ran his fingers through his hair and was about to respond when the apartment bell rang. It was the first time either heard it, and it played a low melodic tune. Bernie went to the door and opened it. Two of the aliens in red robes with white piping were there.

"Good day, Mr. Krantz. We have come to see Mr. Jenkins, or TJ as his friends call him"

"Sorry, wrong door," said Bernie smiling. "There's just me and Mr. Chan here."

The first alien, who seemed to be the leader of the two, took a small step forward. "No, Mr. Krantz, you are mistaken. The man who is with you here is Mr. Thomas Jenkins, also known as TJ to his friends." He looked past Bernie and directly at TJ. "Isn't that right, Mr. Jenkins?"

TJ felt his insides turn over. His breath suddenly left him and he was only able to nod.

"Really?" asked Bernie, with some astonishment. "Your name is TJ?" He then turned back to the two aliens. "Look I didn't know anything about this—is he some sort of spy or something? Really, I just met him and he told me his name was Cho Chan."

The alien smiled at Bernie "I know, Mr. Krantz. He stole the name tag and clothing back aboard ship."

"I wondered about his name—he sure doesn't look like a Chinese guy."

"Filipino, actually," replied the alien. He then focused once more on TJ. "Come with us, Mr. Jenkins."

Wordlessly TJ allowed the aliens to escort him out the door. He thought about making some kind of explanation to Bernie, but none seemed adequate and so passed silently by him. He heard the door close behind him and the lead alien motioned for him to follow, which TJ did. The aliens seemed taller than before. True, this was the closest he'd actually stood to one. They were easily six-foot-five, probably a little more. TJ felt very small next to them.

He was led down the hall, past the elevators he and Bernie had used, then through a door, to another elevator. He assumed it was a service elevator for the staff—whoever they were. He had never seen any other aliens except the guys in red robes. After entering the elevator, the doors closed and, without a command, the elevator began to descend at a speed that made him feel light, and put his stomach, which already was in bad shape, somewhere around his Adam's apple. The ride seemed interminable, long past the time it would take to reach the water level. TJ surmised they were going below the water, but how far was anyone's guess.

Finally the elevator slowed and the doors opened to a hallway that was much darker than those above and much warmer too. He was preceded out of the elevator by the lead alien and followed by his partner. Turning right, they walked silently down a long corridor. The hall-way seemed endless with no indication on either side of any doorway or other opening. The dark walls were seamless, rising to a height of about 20 feet. It was difficult to see the top because of the dark, but it looked like the walls arched toward the center high above them.

TJ felt a pang of fear growing and attempted to keep it in check. After all, he'd been there only a few hours. How much harm could he have really done? None, absolutely none. Simply seen a couple of lectures, ate a little food—that was it. He would just have to explain how Earth journalists operated. They might be unhappy but that wouldn't be new—welcome to Earth, like it or leave it. Over his career, a number of people and organizations had not been happy with him from time to time. His brow furrowed as he recalled that if Sarah were right, none of that mattered; but she could be wrong. They could be friendly aliens. In the end, they all might get a good laugh out of this. TJ felt better.

At last, stopping at a section of wall, seemingly no different from other sections, the marble suddenly slid open revealing a large door-way. The lead alien entered, with TJ following. The darkly shadowed room was large, perhaps 60 feet by 60 feet with a flat ceiling, which also was some 20 feet high. There was one window in the room, and it revealed an underwater scene. The room was barren, with shadows hiding the far walls.

The lead alien stopped, and TJ almost ran into him before stop-ping himself. For a moment, it was silent, as though they were waiting. Then, from the far end of the room, stepping out of the shadows came three other aliens. This apparently was the cue for TJ's escorts to leave, which they did silently.

TJ stood silent for a long time. Finally, the three aliens took a couple more steps forward, still leaving a good 20 feet between him and them. TJ could see them more clearly now. The two outer ones had black robes with red piping. However, the one in the middle was different. First, he was taller, and more massive. His robe was a pure white and had double rows of red, black, and gray piping on the hems. His collar was all white and trimmed with gold piping. On the cuffs of his sleeves there was white, black, and a pale white piping—the color less-than-white. The hood had been pulled over the top of his head to a point so that the face could not be seen, hidden by the dark shadows of the hood. The shape of the hood over the head seemed oddly shaped, more triangle than round. TJ waited. He could feel fear rising. He could taste it.

The tall alien spoke. The voice was very deep—perhaps the deepest TJ had ever heard. "Mr. Jenkins, why are you here?" His tone told TJ he was not really curious. His voice betrayed tightly controlled anger.

"I am a journalist, and I wanted...see, here on Earth that's my job—the job of a journalist is to find—"

"Silence!" roared the alien; the volume of his voice was almost deafening.

Instinctively TJ stepped back.

"I know why you are here, only you do not know why. You think you have come to expose me—to find me out, to stop me—maybe even destroy me?"

"Oh no, no—I'm just looking for the truth. That is what you want too, right?"

The alien raised his hand, cutting TJ's speech short. For a second, TJ thought the alien was going to strike him. Then he lowered his hand and TJ sensed a smirk twisting the alien's lips hidden in the shadows. "You want the truth? Tell me, Mr. TJ Jenkins, what does the truth say I am?"

"That's what I am here to find out."

"And have you?"

"Well, no." TJ felt himself searching for words. It was so easy when he was alone, or with friends, or at least not in this situation. He felt trapped. Did he have the courage to speak the truth? He cleared his throat. "Well, maybe I do. I'm thinking you aren't from space at all."

"No?" The voice came slowly from the hood.

"No."

The alien clasped his hands behind him and took a few steps toward him, turned, and walked parallel a few steps, all the while not taking his eyes off TJ. "You humans are so easy. How clever you thought you were, slipping on the overalls you stole. I suppose you thought it was a lucky coincidence. So clever, telling the pilot you only wanted to take a picture or two."

"How do you know that?" demanded TJ.

"How do I know? You know the answers to that, don't you? I know everything. Right now, the navy is looking for you. They are worried, yes, very worried about where you are. Soon, they will muster enough courage to ask us—'Have you seen Mr. Jenkins?'" The alien coughed out a laugh.

"What will you say?"

The alien ignored the question, instead folding his arms, paced a few steps to the side and back. "Do you know my name yet?"

"Your name? No, I haven't been told."

"Been told. You disappoint me, Mr. Jenkins. So, tell me, what did you think of our demonstration? I wanted you to see it before we had our little talk here."

"Impressive."

"Really?" He walked a few more steps. "Impressive enough to become one of the Elect? Impressive enough to inherit the stars? Impressive enough to take the pledge?"

TJ was silent for a moment, then mustering his courage raised his head to look directly at the alien. "No." He wanted to say more but his moment of courage fled.

The alien nodded slowly. "So, you and your little wife—Sarah, I believe it is—"

"How do you know my wife's name!" TJ's voice burst out. "You leave my wife out of this!" His voice rose until he was shouting.

Suddenly the alien took a step toward TJ, reached out, and grabbed TJ by the neck, lifting him to his eye level. TJ gasped for air as he struggled to free himself from the vice-grip crushing his neck. He tried prying the hands off, while his flailing feet tried to run. Finally, the alien wordlessly dropped him, turned, and walked toward the sea window.

TJ fell to the floor, nearly unconscious, and heard himself gagging. His throat struggled to pass some air while the pain made his Adam's apple feel like applesauce. For a few moments, he lay on the floor while the alien looked quietly out the window at the placid underwater scene, peaceful with fish lazily swimming by now and then. His back remained toward TJ.

"Don't you think the sea is beautiful, Mr. Jenkins?" His tone was subdued, almost musing. "You know, it is my home now. Oh, I can't claim it as completely mine yet, but I shall one day. And such a lovely home to have, don't you agree?"

TJ struggled to his feet, ignoring the question. He looked first to the tall alien and then toward the other two aliens who hadn't moved or made a sound. They stood there like two statues oblivious to what had happened. TJ rubbed his neck, and the effort hurt.

Finally, the large alien turned back toward him. He smiled. "Yes, Sarah," he began, "I know her well; I'll be visiting her. Did you know that? Does she know that? Did she tell you?"

TJ tried to speak but could not, so simply shook his head. He was sure Sarah did not know this or she would have said something.

The alien continued. "You, Mr. Jenkins, are what some would call a pawn, a feint, a jab. However, you do not know that. No, you think you are a great reporter out to break the biggest story this planet has ever read. You truly don't know what's going on here—you humans are such pitifully stupid creatures. How could you ever aspire to be more than I? It is truly a celestial joke. All of God's heavenly creatures could not defeat me with all of the great authorities and powers of creation, yet you, you dirtball, think you can bring me down." He raised his head, gazing at the ceiling for a moment, then slowly lowered his gaze to TJ. "Tell me, living dirt, tell me of Sarah."

TJ did not speak, not because he intended to protect Sarah, but because he felt the finger of fear reach deep within him, crushing his senses and choking off any words. He simply shook his head slowly.

For a moment, the alien was silent. "I see. Then, let me tell you about her. She knows."

TJ managed to speak. "Knows what?"

"Just as I thought—you're stupid." The alien paused. "I would like to talk to Sarah, Mr. Jenkins, she is a wise woman." The alien's voice softened, it was almost pleasant. "Where is she that I may visit her?"

"Why? What do you want to talk about?"

"Things. Things you are too…that you know nothing about. Where is she?"

"Home."

"Liar!" Roared the alien, the word bursting out with shocking volume. TJ jerked back. It was not only loud, but had a depth and inhuman rasp to it

"She's not at home! If she were, I would not waste my energies on you. She has been hidden. I cannot see where she is, so I must deal with the likes of you. Now, tell me! Where is she!"

The rising volume assaulted TJ's ears, and he felt fear in every cell of his body. Instinctively he raised his hand to cover his throat. How did this creature know Sarah? Why did he want to talk to her? Where was she, if not at home?

"You don't know. I see it now, you do not know. I will not waste my time any longer with you." He paused a second. "You are a journalist, just trying to find out the truth?"

TJ nodded, hopelessly.

"Perhaps you should know the truth. Let me show you the truth." He made a half turn away from TJ, as if to walk out, then snapped around and exploded toward TJ. As he did, his body grew from a height of 7 feet to almost 20, transforming from human into some inhuman form—huge, animalistic, and with a stench that filled the air and TJ's nostrils. His eyes were now mere slits, red, glowing out at TJ, while his body mutated into a prehistoric leather-clad beast with coarse rust-red skin and darkened teeth that could not be contained by his deep brown-black lips curling around them as they protruded out. The long, gray fangs were uneven and curved at the top with occasional drippings of a thick syrup-like fluid from one, and then another. On his head protruded an oddly shaped horn: It curved toward the back. Truly a beast from some long forgotten age.

TJ stepped back, and stepped back again, shrinking from the most frightening creature he'd ever seen. Suddenly, with a deep roar that reverberated off the walls, the beast leaped toward TJ powered by his two great legs. Grabbing TJ with one hand and nearly crushing his shoulder, he lifted him off the floor until his eye was even with TJ's.

TJ's pain sucked in the air while smelling the foul stench of the beast's breath. He looked into the deep red eyes peering intently out of narrow slits in his course skin. For the first time he saw the horror of evil.

He heard a primal scream. It was his own. He wrestled clear of the grasp, falling to the floor, then scrambled back to the wall. It was hopeless, and TJ knew it. Hell was here, and it had come to devour him. The last sounds he ever heard were his own screams.

CHAPTER 7

Missing

THE SOUTHERN OCEAN'S brief summer was yielding to the bitter chill of winter. The wind reached inside his leather jacket prompting Andy to hurry off the deck. Once inside, Andy slipped off his jacket before carefully descending the steep metal steps. Though he'd done it countless times, it still gave him the willies; they were too steep, too narrow. He'd often watched young seamen solve this problem by gliding down, using only their hands on the thin handrails. Perhaps, if he were their age, he'd be doing the same. Perhaps. He found making his way about the ship considerably easier now that he'd learned the maze, and thanks to the continuing calm waters since the aliens plunged into the sea. No longer did he have the appearance of a drunken man, crashing first to the left then right—two steps forward, one back.

At last, stepping over the bulkhead lip, he entered the ship's small galley. Everything was compact aboard the destroyer, and its galley was no exception. Tables, with their benches bolted to the deck in a jigsaw fashion, fit as many seats into the limited space as possible. It was two hours before lunch, the best time to go to the galley. One could actually find a seat without having to squeeze between bodies saying "sorry" repeatedly. Three sailors he recognized from the bridge were seated at two small tables having coffee along with an occasional forkful of pie. After filling a cup half full of dark liquid some called coffee, he made his way over.

"How long we gonna be out here?" they asked as he neared. "It's been almost three months. What's the word?" Some things never changed. They still thought his being a reporter gave him the inside scoop on everything.

"Got me," he replied, as usual.

"Any word from stateside?" asked the second watch helmsman.

Andy shook his head. "Nothing you boys haven't already heard. Doesn't look good though."

There was a low grumbled agreement. They'd seen the satellite news and conditions around the world seemed to be taking a dip. The news of the spacecraft had caused a fissure in society. Slow at first, but growing fast. Government services, day-to-day businesses, professional and personal relationships were under a strain and not holding up well.

"I got a MARS cable from my wife," said the helmsman, referring to the amateur radio operators who passed messages along to servicemen. "She's due real soon. Are the hospitals still working?"

"Last I heard they were," replied Andy.

Without warning, a loud horn sounded in the mess, deafening Andy. He'd only heard it once before, when the objects in the sky were nearing the point of touchdown. Yet, he didn't remember it being so loud.

"Now hear this. Now hear this. All hands to stations. All hands to stations."

Everyone moved at once, except Andy. He had no station. Waiting until the table cleared, he followed the others on deck, half expecting the sight of enemy planes dive-bombing. Instead, he saw choppers rising off the carrier, a quarter mile distant, joining choppers already in the air from the other carrier, the USS *Kennedy,* which had been attached to the task force a month before.

The last of the choppers were still departing as the first wave of returning choppers could be seen in the distance. Obviously the visiting civilians were coming back from those pyramids. TJ would have a story—what a story. He hoped TJ would remember their agreement and give him a piece of it—he promised, after all. Of course, TJ would have to face the music for sneaking aboard the pyramids—but so what?

Everyone knew of TJ's adventure. The man he'd apparently stolen an ID card from had informed the authorities and, within twenty-four hours, everyone was aware. They'd found TJ's cloths and camera in one of the carrier's Heads. The exposed film revealed a few pictures from the chopper, one showing Grady walking toward the carrier's island holding the mailbag. Now Grady was under ship's arrest, and though allowed to wander about the ship, rarely did, preferring to hang out alone on the fantail or spend the time in his bunk. He was a broken man, simply waiting for the assumed judgment.

The returning choppers were now approaching their separate ships. The procedure appeared to be the same as when they left. They would land, disgorge their passengers, and take off, heading back to the pyramids. The din was deafening.

Andy made his way aft searching for Grady.

"Guess the pow-wow's over, eh?" began Andy, finding Grady leaning against the rail.

Grady didn't look up, "Guess."

"Look, Grady, TJ will explain everything—how you didn't know what he was gonna do. You were innocent."

"Yeah sure. They won't buy it, TJ should never have been aboard the chopper to begin with, I shouldn't have let him." Grady rested his head on his arm, which lay atop the railing.

Andy raised his binoculars. "Well, would you look at that? They all got on red bathrobes or something."

He handed the binoculars to Grady who quickly focused on the deck of the carrier. "You're right. What's with that?"

Andy knew he had to get over there. He just had to. Not only to see TJ, but also to get into what was going on. Turning to Grady, "I don't suppose you could take me over there?"

Grady snorted. "Couldn't if I wanted. And I definitely don't want!"

Leaving Grady to his personal miseries, Andy made his way forward toward officers' country. He knew the maze leading to the Information Officer's office by heart now. Rounding the last corner, he was confronted with a host of other reporters who had beaten him there. All he could see of the navy officer were his hands held in the air and appealing for quiet. At last the noise subsided.

"If you all will just give me a chance to be heard, I'll tell you. I've already received a request from the USS *Kennedy* for the press to be flown over at twenty-one hundred hours. There will be a press conference given at twenty-one thirty. Bring your belongings with you. You will be staying on the carrier for eventual return flights to the States."

"What time is twenty-one hundred hours?" asked a voice.

"Nine o'clock at night." The officer's voice betrayed his exasperation at having to deal with these non-navy people for the last six months.

Quickly Andy left to write a short piece then delivered it to the pressroom fax. It was good to file again, a story of real news. The blackout, which the navy had tried to enforce, hadn't worked—as usual. The navy gave up, insisting instead, all stories be filed through the Communication Officer. To his knowledge, neither his, nor any other reporter's story had been censored. However, they had all been background stories—fill really. Now, fresh hard news was here.

After leaving his story to be wired home, he made his way back to the cabin, packed his belongings, and bid farewell to the sardine can–size area someone dared call quarters. He paused when confronted with TJ's bunk. It was still made from the last night he'd slept in it, with his belongings still in the locker. Kneeling beside the locker, Andy opened the lid. Looking for information on TJ, the navy had busted off the latch. He removed those things he knew TJ would want: address book, some unfinished stories, pictures of Sarah, some letters from her, his passport and wallet. Why he hadn't taken his wallet made Andy pause. Why would any man go on a trip without his wallet? He stuffed the assorted items in a plastic bag, along with a change of clothes, then put the bag in his suitcase. He would let the navy deal with the rest. He paused for a second before exiting the cabin. Andy felt like he was almost deserting a friend. Surely, TJ would be returning to the *Kennedy* with the rest. Andy shut the door behind him and made his way amidships where they had been told to assemble for transport over to the carrier.

Before long, two boats, each capable of squeezing fifty or more people in them, did just that. He was lucky to get aboard the first boat. Arriving at the carrier, his group found assigned escorts who led them to an area below decks that appeared normally used to service aircraft.

Now temporary screens blocked off the rear of the bay. Chairs for the press had been arranged in rows facing a single podium in front of the screen. Andy looked at everyone entering, searching for TJ, but he was not there. He asked those around if they'd seen TJ—none had.

At last, several navy officers, followed by a large group of returning visitors, entered the area. Each wore a tunic affair that seemed out of place—almost burlesque in appearance. The robes were made of some light red fabric dropped straight from the shoulders to the just above the floor. They flowed easily in the slight breeze generated by walking. Around the edges of the tunic was a single line of colored piping; some had white while others had black, and pale white, almost gray. Andy looked closely at their faces as they approached the podium. Each seemed solemn, but at ease. None were looking around at the audience; no furtive glances or nervous smiles played over their faces. How they felt before going to the pyramids, Andy didn't know, but if fear was with them then, it wasn't now. They now appeared confident, almost serene with a touch of arrogance in their walk.

Eventually all the representatives stood in front, their attention focused on a navy officer standing behind the podium. The room grew quiet.

"Ladies and gentlemen, you've been invited here by these returning individuals who have, until a short time ago, been guests of our alien visitors. They have a statement to read. Following their statement, I'm informed they will take no questions. Mr. Arthur Ramon is the individual who will give out the statement." Turning, he beckoned to Ramon.

Ramon approached the lectern. He no longer had the cane, halting steps, the slightly bent back, or the stern face. He walked with the agility of a young man, his head held high. "Thank you," he began while looking slowly around the audience. "This is going to be short, and I apologize for that. However, after this conference, a handout will be distributed to you, giving a much more detailed account of the events that have transpired, and will occur in the future.

"As you know, several thousand men and women from around the world were invited, by name, to come to the pyramids to meet our visitors. From the diversity of individuals selected to visit the pyramids, one might suspect the guest list was drawn from a hat; however, I assure you this was not the case. The visitors selected each individual, and similar selections will take place in the future. Over the past days, we have learned a lot about our visitors and much about ourselves. At first, this information was difficult for us to understand and accept. Now, however, we have all seen the proofs, we all rejoice in the truth—as you will also in the future. Over the next six to twelve months, other groups will be following us to the pyramids. We were told that the guest list would eventually number about one hundred forty-four thousand, called the Elect.

"What are some of the things we've learned? We've learned that they are peaceful people. They are gentle, generous, and dedicated to the welfare of all people upon Earth. The one hundred forty-four thousand Elect individuals will act as go-betweens—think of them as facilitators who will help humanity assume their wonderful role in the future." Ramon paused while surveying the room before resuming. "The purpose of this visit by the Followers of Eli is to rescue us from our own follies, which have placed all humankind at risk. In the coming months, everyone will learn what we already have been taught. I assure you it's wonderful news, offering hope and joy to each and every man and woman on the face of Earth."

Again he paused, as though to see if the import of his message was coming across. It was. The area was absolutely still and remained so.

"The aliens—the Brothers, as we are coming to know them—offer not only health to everyone, but can and do offer us a virtually unlimited life span."

Murmurs sprung up immediately from the crowd. Ramon waited until they subsided. "There are going to be some adjustments we'll have to make in order for this to occur. To join the community of the heavens, certain traditions, alliances, and lifestyles will have to be discarded. Nevertheless, when you know the truth, such adjustments will seem almost natural. I won't go into them all now, but I assure you, it will be well worth it for us to receive these gifts. For now, study the plan of the new community of the stars, of which we're about to become a part. Each of the one hundred forty-four thousand has been assigned an area to help shepherd humankind into this new era. They'll make themselves available in every way to assist in what needs to be done." Ramon raised his hand. "See you in the stars," he said, turned, and addressed the navy officer next to him.

The officer stepped forward. "Mr. Ramon has kindly decided to accept a few questions. Please raise your hands, I will call on you. Do not all speak at once, or we'll be forced to end the session." He looked out at the forest of hands that shot up quickly. "You, sir. Please identify yourself and your employment."

"Yes. I'm Henry Aberson with the *Detroit News*. Mr. Ramon, I believe you used the phrase 'eternal life.' Did you actually mean that and, if so, how is that possible?"

Ramon nodded. "I can imagine how it feels hearing such a phrase. I felt the same way when I first heard it. Yes, I meant exactly that, eternal life: life without end. If we are able to conform to the requirements, which have been set out by the Followers of Eli, an eternity of healthy life will be one of their gifts to us—though not the only gift."

Another was selected. "Eve Wills, Jacksonville *Times*. Where did these aliens come from? No one has been able to answer that question."

"That's understandable. I wish I could tell you in precise terms. I will relate to you as it was explained to me. Our galaxy is not, of course, the only object in space. Even with all of the known galaxies and billions upon billions of stars, they account for only a small portion of the total universe: Not only because of the vastness of the visible universe, but also for the billions of unseen stars. If we turn our radio telescopes in any direction, we locate another unseen universe. Thus, it is with the Brothers. They come from another level of space and time. We are, at the same time, a part of their universe and yet excluded from it. I've been informed that precise details will be revealed at the appropriate time to those who join the Elect. Until then, I ask for your patience."

Ramon held up his hand as the crescendo of voices sought his attention. "Ladies and gentlemen, I won't take more questions now. Shortly, the life on our beloved planet is going to change dramatically. Institutions are going to be turned upside down, societies will find themselves unable to hang on to their traditional anchors; governments will undergo metamorphic changes. The effect of all this new knowledge upon human beings everywhere will be traumatic, but take heart; a new and wonderful day is arriving.

"You of the media can help in this change by not employing rhetoric, which has no beneficial effect upon your readers and viewers. It's time to put away the search for sensationalism. Believe me, the truth has more than enough of that. The truths that shall be revealed will require your professional help. I ask you to be kind; let's not purposefully frighten people. This is too important to allow our greed for bylines to take precedence over the sincere need to bring the mass of people into a close relationship with the truths we bring. The stakes are too high," he smiled. "Thank you for your attention." Ramon turned quickly, leading the delegation of robed individuals out the doorway they'd entered.

The reporters burst into frantic questions of how they could file their stories. Quickly, naval officers showed them the area behind the screen, which had been set up with a complex of phones, computers, faxes, and electronics enabling them to file their stories immediately. Andy wrote as fast as he could, and sent his story out. Finally, he walked back along the path he used when arriving, which led him out on deck.

The sea air felt good and helped him to relax. Ramon's announcements had stunned him—not a good thing for a reporter. How he'd even written his story was a wonder. He withdrew from his pocket the stapled sheets of paper that Ramon said would give more details. He'd read them quickly before writing his story, but they seemed almost "storybook.' Space aliens, reeducation seminars, focus groups for neighborhoods. Looking at them a second time did not make them appear any more inviting. There was a hint of Orwell in them, of a fictional story becomes a true nightmare.

His thoughts were interrupted by a female voice from behind. "Excuse me, are you Mr. Andrew Moore?"

Turning, Andy was confronted by a female navy officer. He nodded, crinkling his brow.

"Mr. Moore, I'm Commander Stephanie Collins of Navy Intelligence." She was slightly shorter than Andy, but still tall for a woman—perhaps five nine, with jet-black hair that promised to be long if released from its tight bun. Her angular face was set in a stern, professional, unwavering look. The penetrating gaze from her gray eyes Andy found uncomfortable. "I understand you've been asking about a man named Thomas, is that correct?"

Andy nodded. "Yes, he's a reporter—a friend of mine. Do you know where he is?"

"You say he's a friend of yours. Did he confide in you why he wanted to have access to the aliens?"

"Didn't have to—he's a reporter. He did what reporters do when they want a story bad enough. I didn't know he was going to do it, if I had known a little sooner maybe I could've gone with him, but it happened all so fast. Didn't know it really until…" Andy's voice trailed off.

"You didn't know until Lieutenant Grady told you. Is that right?"

Andy nodded.

"What do you know of Grady's involvement?"

"Nothing. I mean, Grady didn't know Thomas was going to do this either. Grady thought this was just to get a couple of pictures from his chopper—that's what TJ had told him."

"TJ? Oh, of course."

"TJ. That's what most people call Thomas—it's his nickname. So now, where is he? Can I see him?"

Collins stared silently at Andy for a moment then turned toward the railing and placed her hands on top of it while looking out at the sea. When she turned back toward him, Andy could see her features had softened and beauty had claimed her. "That's not possible," she said in a softened voice. "Thomas is dead."

"Dead?"

Collins nodded. "We found his body—or parts of it, about two months ago."

Andy turned and fell against the railing for support. He was stunned. TJ dead. How could this be? Two months ago? "What happened? How did he die? What do you mean, pieces?"

"It's unclear how it happened right now, it's still under investigation. I've been looking into it for the navy. When I learned you were asking about him, I wanted to hear your piece of the puzzle."

"How come I didn't know this sooner—why wasn't it announced?"

"The whole thing was classified until a few days ago. We didn't know what was going on. However, your story confirms what we have been able to put together. Frankly, I still don't know exactly what happened, though I've a feeling there is something more to this. However, as of now, nothing has popped up. The navy is satisfied it was an accident. Anything you could tell me that would help determine what may actually have happened, I'd appreciate it."

"I...I don't know anything, really. Do you know exactly how he died? What kind of accident was he in?"

"Don't know what kind of accident. We found him in the water about quarter of a mile from the pyramids. Actually, we found only his arm—his right arm—and ID'd him through fingerprints."

"Just his arm?"

"Yes, the lab says it's consistent with sharks—or almost consistent. Anyway, that's what they put down and I've no real reason to doubt it."

"What do those alien fellows say happened?"

"They don't know anything. They say that if he tried to get to the pyramids, he never made it. They don't have any record of his coming aboard. Those returning don't recall hearing his name. It's possible he fell into the water before he even left the carrier."

"That's all you know?"

"About all. We found his clothes stuffed behind a toilet, he stole a set of clothing from an Oriental guy. He just disappeared until we found what we found in the water."

"You said, 'almost consistent with a shark.' What do you mean?"

Collins turned, resting her back against the rail, and folding her arms. "Well, as I hear it, there were no actual shark bite marks, but the way the flesh had been ripped from the arm, indicates it probably was a shark—or perhaps a propeller."

"A propeller." For a moment, Andy was silent. "Don't believe it, TJ gone." Andy rubbed the top of his head. "I've got his personal effects, the navy went through them and brought them back, do you want them?

"Yes, and I'll see that they are sent to his widow."

"I'll check around and see if anyone else knows anything. If they do I'll be sure to get back to you."

Collins turned, holding out her hand. "I'd appreciate that."

Andy nodded. "Will you do the same for me? TJ was a friend of mine."

Collins nodded. "Sure."

Andy gave her his card, hoping she meant it. "By the way, you've notified his wife?"

"I didn't personally, but the navy did. She knows."

Over the next few days Andy didn't think about the Commander, or of TJ, or of anything aboard ship, his thoughts were ever more on home. All the reporters were becoming increasingly anxious to get back on land now that the story was moving away from them. With the departure of each planeload of red-robed Elect, there was an urge to run and jump on board.

Andy tried to get rid of some of his tension by running laps on the hangar deck when it was allowed. It was while running he spotted Commander Collins again. She was waiting for him. This time more informally dressed in her own pair of sweats and her hair was not in a bun but in a long braid that trailed down her back. When he reached her, the pair shook hands.

"Feeling fit now?" she smiled.

This was the first time Andy remembered seeing her smile. He hoped it would not be the last. Her full lips framed beautiful white teeth exuding a warmth he found beguiling.

Andy returned the grin. "Not feeling, not looking." He toweled off his wet hair. "Looks like you're about to get a little fit yourself."

Stephanie nodded. "I stopped you because I've got some more information on your friend, Thomas."

"And?"

"Turns out, someone did remember seeing him at the pyramids. One of the people invited was named Krantz, Bernie Krantz. TJ ever mention that name to you?"

Andy thought a moment then shook his head. "Don't think I've ever heard the name."

"Umm. I understand he used to have some kind of radio show. He was asking around about a guy he met and lost track of. I guess they sorta struck up a conversation. Anyway, he was asking around about him

"He did make it to the pyramids?"

"Apparently. But the strange part of this is, when the navy looked up Krantz to confirm it, he stiffed them." Collins began a relaxed jog and Andy joined her.

"Stiffed them? What do you mean?"

"Claimed he didn't know what they were talking about. Said he never heard of the name Thomas."

"So he lied."

"Yes. But why?"

"Obvious. Somebody—meaning the aliens—got to him. Something went on at the pyramids they are trying to hide. If this guy Bernie Krantz knew he came aboard, so did the aliens. TJ made it aboard, talked to Krantz, and whomever else we don't know, then turned up missing. Now, both the aliens and Krantz say they don't know anything—never heard of TJ. That tells me we might not be talking accident. I mean, if we were, there would be no reason to deny that he made it there. In fact, they probably knew a good examination of the body would show it was no accident."

Collins stopped running and placed a hand on Andy's shoulder. "Hold on now. Let's not go off the deep end. Maybe they just don't want any complications. Having someone turn up dead, who was last seen with the aliens, would be a complication. It could well have been an accident, and the aliens just want to sweep it under the rug, or spaceship in this case, so it doesn't interfere with something they feel is a critical situation."

"And what will be the navy's conclusion?"

"The same, that he died of unknown causes, most likely lost overboard."

"I see. Even though he probably didn't. You're gonna let them just pretend it was some kinda accident they never knew about, that they never knew TJ?"

"Look." An official tone crept into Stephanie's voice. "This TJ fellow is dead. I am sorry about that. However, I have no proof anything shady went on, in fact, everything does point to an accident—including the coroner's report. So maybe those aliens knew about it, maybe they didn't. It doesn't change anything."

Andy breathed deeply, exhaling slowly, then nodded. "I suppose. However, you didn't think it was an accident, that's the impression I got when we talked before. What's your reason for thinking that if there's no indication it was anything else?"

Stephanie wiped her face slowly with her towel. "I wish I knew. Something doesn't seem right—and don't say women's intuition.'" She smiled. "It's just one of those cases where I feel I'm missing a key piece, but I don't know what it is."

Andy nodded. "Maybe I'll get in touch with his wife later, see if there's anything I can do."

"Do you know his wife?"

"Yes, and no. I really was a friend of TJ's and I knew her through him."

"Odd, but I can't get her out of my mind. She keeps popping up every time I think about this, and even sometimes when I don't."

"I know what you mean, I've been thinking about her too, it's why I want to contact her when I get back. Oh, wait—something just occurred to me," said Andy. "Just before TJ got on that chopper, he said something to me. Actually, they were his last words to me. He said, 'If I don't make it back, tell Sarah she was right.'"

"His wife was right? About what?"

Andy shrugged and felt foolish. "I guess it sounds pretty stupid. But I got the feeling that TJ knew something about the aliens he didn't tell me."

"Like?"

Andy shook his head slowly.

"But you think he knew something that got him killed?"

"Yes," said Andy, slowly at the thought. "Yes, I do. I guess it's the way he said it as much as what he said." Andy let out a sigh. "I'm grasping at straws here, trying to explain the unexplainable. I've just got a feeling in my gut that the aliens were involved in it."

To Andy's surprise, Stephanie nodded. "I think you're right, but I can't figure it out either. However, someone else will have to worry about it. I'm leaving the navy."

"You are? I thought once a navy officer reached Commander they were in for life."

Stephanie smiled. "So did I. However, things have changed—at least for me they have. Ever since this alien business, I have had the urge to get out, as though something was pulling me," she laughed. "I don't know why I'm telling you, guess I'm trying it out, seeing how it sounds."

Andy extended his hand. "Sounds good to me and best of luck in whatever career you're headed toward."

Stephanie shook his hand. "Thanks, I'll probably need it. And good luck to you. I think we are all going to need a little luck real soon," she said and resumed her jogging.

Andy was tired of running. He was tired of everything: Tired of this ship, tired of the aliens, tired of navy food. He put his towel around his neck and began a slow walk. Within a few days he would be leaving this ship and starting a new adventure. He should be excited, and he was, until learning of TJ. Had the aliens killed him? Was it an accident? Was TJ the first of many deaths? Andy was suddenly too mentally fatigued to think or care. It was time for a long, hot shower.

CHAPTER 8

Old Friends

SPRING WAS LATE: El-something, somewhere out in the Pacific, was either too high or too low—who cared? It was cold, wet, and miserable. This late in May should be a time for picnics and lemonade, rather than boots and hot chocolate; not that he indulged in either. It wasn't only the weather making Andy's mood foul—it was the train. They'd just cut scheduled service to Washington in half, due to a lack of engineers, and talk was it might be halved again. Great. Now, it would be hours between trains. Not only that. When they did come, they were filthy. When they'd last been cleaned was anyone's guess.

The only things left working were the taxicabs, and arriving in Washington, he hailed one, taking it to the hotel. There he planned on checking in and then visiting his old friend Robert, if he was still mixing drinks. Andy had known Robert for a number of years, both before and after Andy gave up drinking. In all that time, he couldn't remember ever knowing Robert's last name. He was just always behind the bar.

The taxi ride through the nation's capital was depressing. Normally it was a bit dirty, but now it was filthy. Papers were flying about everywhere as cars passed. Trash cans stood by the curbs overflowing, with bags stacked around them. The smell was not good, but dogs and cats seemed to enjoy it.

"You know there's a premium on fares now," stated the driver over his shoulder.

"A what?"

"Premium. They charge a fuel premium of three bucks a fare now."

"Never heard of such a thing!" However, as he said it, Andy remembered something about just such a fee being charged also in New York. Gas stations were getting fewer and fewer and the prices were reflecting it. One gallon of gas now was eight dollars and increasing weekly.

"Yeah, can't find gas and when we do, it's outta sight."

Andy grunted. He had his own problems. Why had the newspaper called him in? Moreover, why hadn't Jim Morgan called him? After all, Jim was his boss.

Finally, the taxi pulled up in front of the hotel and Andy fished for the money, careful to hand it to the driver with his left hand. The driver accepted the money with his left hand, and for a moment both exchanged glances. It was becoming uncomfortable, even dangerous, for those who hadn't received the Elect's Mark on their right hand.

Stepping out of the cab he gripped his collar tightly while looking upward at the grayness. It was no longer raining but the sky promised more.

Through a thin spot in the clouds Andy could make out the reflection of the seventh pyramid, which constantly hung in the sky. It was like the eye of Big Brother, and he was disliking it more and more.

Once inside the hotel, Andy was appalled at the condition of the lobby. Wastebaskets overflowed, carpets were badly in need of a vacuuming—and if not that, at least a pickup of the random crap lying around. He walked by the desk where there was no evidence anyone was tending it. He made for the bar and Robert.

There he found the light was low as usual, but now it was more a result of burned-out bulbs than design. There were no customers but he could see the top of Robert's head behind the bar. Robert stood up as he heard someone enter.

"Hey there, stranger. Don't see you much anymore," greeted Robert.

"Hey, yourself. Got something black and hot I can drink?"

"How about tar?"

"Sounds like your coffee."

Robert chuckled as he poured a cup. "So what brings you to the big city, and how come I ain't seen you?"

Andy took the cup and searched for sugar.

"If you're looking for sugar, forget it. We don't have any—in fact, we don't have much of anything. They shut down the restaurant last night—plum ran outta food. "

"Incredible. I tell you it's all going to hell."

"You got that right. Are you a lefty or not?"

Andy smiled and nodded.

"Me too," smiled Robert, indicating he too had not received the tattoo from the aliens. "Lefty" was now a common phrase, a private way of establishing who had not received their mark. Nevertheless, one had to be careful.

"I don't like to come to the city much anymore—looks like a garbage can was dumped from the sky. At least in the suburbs they have a few services still going. Tough to get gas, though, and you have to know which stations are still open."

"So I hear."

"Why you here today?" asked Robert.

"Got called in. Dunno why."

Robert groaned.

"What's that supposed to mean?"

"Nothing. But I don't think it's good news."

"Why?" challenged Andy.

"I noticed your column's been missing, and I don't see any other stuff by you."

Andy nodded. "What are you doing, trying to cheer me up?" But Andy knew Robert was right. The paper had given his stuff the cold shoulder, and for the past three weeks, nothing of his had been printed. He'd tried to call his editor, but was always put off. Yes, Robert was right, this was not good news. "Yeah, I think you might be right. I better get over there and let Morgan chew on me for a while. He won't be happy until he gets whatever it is out of his system."

He left Robert wiping down the bar, as though it needed it. At first, he was going to take a cab, but decided to walk. It was close enough, and he needed the exercise.

As he walked, he could sense the difference in the city. He felt cities, like people, had a heartbeat, a certain rhythm to them: noise levels changing with the hour, people moving slowly or quickly at different times of the day, along with traffic. In addition, restaurants had their individual, special smells, which wafted and swirled together in a delicious mix and stirred in with the sounds of different clientele at certain times with certain noises. All of this merged in the back of one's mind, never noticed, yet a part of the palette used to paint each day. However, now it was different. There were fewer colors on the palette—a drab dullness to the city. The noises were muted, the traffic less, the dirt more, and few smells other than occasional garbage. Things were different. If this was a time of great new beginnings, they were starting on a messy note.

Pushing the doors of the newspaper open, he entered the familiar building. Here there was a difference also. First, there were fewer people around. He'd heard this was true throughout the city. People were leaving jobs and migrating back to their roots, or just hibernating, giving up. Second, he had to try three elevators before he found one that worked. Entering the city room, he found people he didn't recognize occupying a handful of desks. Not that he knew everyone who worked at the paper, but he was somewhat familiar with which desks had which faces, and now the faces were different and younger.

Rounding the corner to the national newsroom, Andy came to an abrupt halt. Someone was at his desk—not that he ever used it. In fact, he couldn't remember the last time he'd actually sat at it; but still, it was his. One shouldn't use the desk of a senior reporter without permission—it was impertinent, to say the least. Andy approached the young man sitting at the desk engrossed in his computer screen. He was about to interrupt him when the nameplate caught his eye: Ron Whitholt. For a moment, Andy stood still, frozen; he could feel the cold filtering through his bones. He'd been replaced.

"Yes?" the nameplate asked.

"Uh, nothing, just thinking." Andy turned and headed for Jim Morgan's office. Reaching it, he opened the door without knocking, as usual. The stranger at the desk looked up in surprise.

"What th—who are you? Don't you ever come in here without knocking!"

"Who are you!" retorted Andy.

"I happen to be the editor of this paper, Eugene Styles, and if you don't leave immediately, I'll call security."

"Editor? You're the editor? Where's Morgan?"

"Morgan? Morgan doesn't work here anymore—retired last week. Now, get out!"

"But I work here—my name is Moore, Andy Moore. And what's this 'retirement' crap. Morgan wouldn't retire now—ten years from now!"

"Moore, Smoore—I don't care who—wait—Moore? Oh yeah, Andy Moore, you did the coverage at the touchdown." Styles rose from his chair and came slowly around to the front on his desk, leaning against it and folding his arms slowly in front. "Look, Andy, things have changed. Morgan wasn't in the mainstream lately. I'm sure if you knew him, he was a bit on the religious fanatic side, right?"

Andy nodded. "Yes, but I don't think he was on the fanatic side—at least I didn't see that."

"Yeah, well the powers that be retired him. Plus the economics have changed. Don't know how to put this really, but we're cutting payroll and have to take you off salary. The paper is cutting back everywhere, plus we want to go in a new direction. We want our paper to be out in front here, a partner with the Brothers. The owners want the paper to be a helping hand in merging the culture of our city with that of the Brothers. After all, who could deny we're going to have a cultural change? And we want to be part of it." Putting his hands in his pockets, Styles walked behind his desk and sat down again. "Now, I know your pieces were good in the beginning…"

"In the beginning…?"

"…But now your pieces have the wrong slant. You seem to be suspicious of the Brothers, even casting doubt upon them. Frankly, some feel you are anti-Brother. In fact, your last five or six pieces we just couldn't run, too confrontational. Now we're not just up and firing you, not at all," he smiled. "We still want you to write, on a freelance basis. You know, get out, see what's happening in the world, and recognize the wonderful future this whole thing could mean for all of us. Sorta get a new perspective on how the aliens are benefiting us. Then write some stories reflecting that view. I hope that we can use some of them. I'm sorry to break the news to you like this, but that's the way it is."

Andy stood for a long moment in silence. "So that's it. I break the biggest story this paper, or any paper on the face of the Earth, ever had—and you're canning me."

"Now, we aren't firing you, I told you that. We want you to reposition yourself into the new frame of mind—be part of our new look."

"Is that what you call it, 'the new framework—the new look'? Sounds to me like you don't want reporters, just people who suck up to those alien jerks!"

"I'm sorry you feel that way." Styles' voice deepened and there was an edge to it. "Now, please excuse me, I'm very busy, as you can see we're trying to put out a paper with only half the people we used to do it with." He didn't wait for Andy to respond, but began pecking away at his keyboard.

Andy stood facing Styles, his face filled with changing emotions. After a minute, Styles looked up. "Mr. Moore, please leave. I don't want to call security, but I will if you force me."

Silently Andy turned and exited, closing the door quietly behind. He didn't have enough feeling left to slam it—an oversight he later regretted. Slowly, he made his way back to the front door. Here he was, back where he was before those alien things showed up, going to write for nickels and dimes on speculation. 'Course, he'd made a lot of money since, so he didn't have to count his nickels anymore. Still. And what about Jim Morgan retiring? Morgan wouldn't have left the paper unless it was boots first. Taking a deep breath, Andy walked to the curb and hailed a cab. He was too spent to walk back to the hotel. Giving the destination to the driver, Andy slumped back. Life was changing.

Arriving at the hotel, he walked slowly through the accumulated trash toward the bar. For the first time in years, he wanted a drink. He looked around and saw only one other person in the lobby, a well-dressed manager behind the formerly vacant desk, who nodded. Andy returned the nod. So many people had given up working Andy was surprised anyone still did. Apparently, it was all in anticipation of the day when this world would be history and the Brothers would lift them to their rightful place among the royalty of the universe. Stopping work was a phenomenon generally associated with the lower paying jobs. Bank presidents were still going to work, but tellers and janitors were not. There was a lot of talk about future utopias and forevers; but to-day and tomorrow were the pits. Society was going through a metamorphosis with ominous fallout. It seemed more ill-tempered, like an expectant woman sick of being pregnant.

Entering the bar, Andy saw Robert at the far end. The only patrons were three men engaged in a low conversation and oblivious to anyone else. He walked past them, and took his usual end seat across from Robert. Robert flashed his usual big smile and leaned on the bar. He was always impeccably dressed, his uniform pressed, and he wore his familiar white gloves.

"Well, Andy, how did it go?"

Andy snorted. "You are looking at an unemployment statistic."

Robert nodded solemnly. "I thought so. A lot of people—even those willing to work, are getting laid off lately."

"For God's sake, Robert, what's going on here? The whole city seems headed for the trash bin, including this hotel. It makes me sick. Gimme a whisky and water."

"No! I ain't giving you anything like that, and don't ask again. Just 'cause the city's falling apart don't mean you have to."

"Well, gimme some coffee then, I need something to drink. So what's happening? Why is everybody giving up?"

"Hey, they're all getting ready to hop some spaceship and bounce around the stars."

"And you're not?" asked Andy stirring his sugarless coffee.

"Nope. You?"

Andy snorted, "I haven't even given it a thought. This is all so screwy—unreal."

"It's real, all right. Heard the desk manager turn in a guy to some vigilantes this morning in the lobby 'cause he didn't have one of those tattoos on his right hand. They're checking now, you know. Some of the fanatics are taking the law into their own hands."

"The law? Take what law into their hands? There's no law you have to have a tattoo!"

"Gonna be, real soon. It was on the tube today. Passed the House and Senate by voice vote and is being sent to the president tomorrow."

"Damn."

"Yeah, and get this: They are starting to issue ID cards. You're gonna need these ID cards to get money outta banks, get groceries, get a newspaper subscription—everything."

"And when's that supposed to happen?"

Robert shrugged his shoulders. "By the way things are going, I'll bet it'll happen soon. Enough of that. What are you gonna do tonight? Go back home or spend it at the Trash Hotel?"

"Oh, guess I'll get a room, and make your life miserable tonight."

"Well, you better hurry, they only got two hundred thirty vacancies," grinned Robert.

"Guess I should. I'll be right back."

At the desk, the neatly attired manager greeted him from behind the counter. Andy recognized him as the same manager who had stopped him in the lobby and was going to kick him out because there wasn't enough credit left on his card. He wondered if the manager remembered too.

"I'd like a room."

"Certainly, sir. Would you be wanting a single or double?"

"Single."

"Very good," replied the manager, turning, and studying the board behind him, as though there were some question of vacancy. "I believe room two-oh-five would be very nice for you. It's a double, but of course we don't charge extra for that. Have you stayed with us before? You seem familiar."

"Oh yes, from time to time."

"Sign here, please."

Andy drew the card to him and began filling it out.

"I see you don't have your mark yet," the manager mused.

Andy felt himself tense, but his voice was casual in reply. "Oh. Yeah, you mean the tattoo. No, I'm going tomorrow to get it."

"I see. It's going to be the law, you know."

"Yes. So I've been told. There," he said, handing the card back, "that should do it."

The manager glanced at the register, then processed the credit card. Finally, he handed the card back. "You know these things are going to be obsolete too," he said, waving the credit card. Soon everyone is gonna have to have a Buyer Card."

"Yes. I know."

Andy picked up his key and put the credit card away, well aware of the manager's steady gaze.

"Have a great night," volunteered Andy as he walked away.

The desk manager nodded, but remained silent, as he studied Andy.

Returning to the bar, he told Robert about the strange behavior of the desk manager.

"Yes," said Robert, "I should have gotten the key for you. Perhaps it's best you stay here for a while just to see if he called anybody."

"Call? Who would he call?"

"Oh. He's one of the fanatics, and he has buddies who are too. They think it's up to them personally to cleanse the Earth of Bible Scum—that's what they call them, that or BS-ers."

"I'm not a Bible kinda guy. Well, I am—but not really, not fanatical."

"You are, you aren't—which is it?"

"Well, I believe in everything, but I guess I just don't get the big picture."

"I see. For some reason I think maybe you will become a thumper."

Andy smiled. "Not likely. I'm not a BS-er."

"Don't matter, they just use that term for anyone who ain't got the mark yet."

"Okay, so he makes the call, then what?"

"They come and haul you away—where, I don't know."

Andy nodded. He suddenly liked the idea of going home much better than staying here, but felt foolish about it.

Robert retrieved a fresh cup of coffee and a deck of cards. Andy owed Robert 452 dollars in cribbage debts so far—a debt accumulated over the past ten years, which Andy had no intention of paying, nor Robert any desire to collect. Andy was certain his luck would change, but in ten years, it hadn't. Slowly, Robert shuffled the deck and began dealing.

"How do I get one of those Buyer Cards? You got any applications here?"

"You don't understand, friend. You gotta go down and apply in person, and you had better have a tattoo before you go, too. Unless you're a member of the flock, you don't get a card. Once you get that tattoo and card you aren't an American anymore, or a New Yorker, or Irish, or Jewish, or Methodist, or Catholic—you aren't even a human being anymore, you're one of them: a Brother, one of the Elect."

Andy remained silent as he considered Robert's words and his cards. Both sucked.

"He's one." The loud voice startled Andy. It came from the drunk at the other end of the bar; the words were slurred but understandable.

"Now, Henry, I think it's time we headed to the room," said one of his companions.

"I ain't goin'—I wanna know why he wants my li'l girl to die!"

Andy, looking toward the commotion, suddenly realized he was the subject of the man's remarks.

"Yeah, you—you're killin' my little girl!"

Andy looked away, as though he didn't hear, trying instead to concentrate on his cards. Perhaps he should leave. The last thing he needed was some drunk harassing him.

He felt someone grab his arm. Instinctively he tried to pull away, but the drunk had a vice-grip. "See!" he yelled at his friends. "I told ya! I saw when he walked by."

Beer breath washed over Andy. One of the drunk's friends, a middle-aged man in a wrinkled suit that hadn't been cleaned lately, approached with an apologetic look toward Andy. "Come on now," he said to the drunk, "this doesn't do any good."

"You're a killer!" yelled the drunk, his veins pulsing beneath his forehead. "Why ain't you done it yet—why?"

Finally, Andy succeeded in wrenching his arm loose as the sobbing man's friends pulled him back, and began leading him toward the door. One of his companions hung back.

"Sorry about that. He's pretty busted up about his daughter."

"I don't even know his daughter—I don't know him. What's wrong with his daughter?"

"She has leukemia—they say she only has six months left. He wasn't raging against you personally, but he saw that you didn't have the mark of the Brothers yet. They won't give out that healing stuff until everyone has the mark."

Andy turned his hand over, revealing its smooth unblemished surface. With exaggerated casualness, he shoved it into his pocket. "I just haven't got around to it yet."

"I know, lots haven't. But I tell you, if I was you, I'd get it right away. Sure make life a lot easier. Well, sorry again," he said, giving a small wave as he followed his friends out the door.

Andy turned to Robert. "Can you believe that?"

"Yeah, I can. I've seen it before, and probably gonna see it a lot more."

"So where do I go to get that mark?"

"City Hall, for one. You gonna get it?"

Andy thought a moment. For the first time, he really did think about it. Eventually, he looked at Robert and shook his head. "No."

"Why?"

"I don't know. I get a bad feeling thinking about it." And he did. "You?"

Robert smiled. "No, not me. I don't plan on zipping around the universe. Figure I'll just work here until they carry me out in a box."

Andy nodded. "Guess I don't like these bums coming here, and requiring me to think one way or another just to get their approval—it's un-American," he chuckled.

Robert grinned. "I guess."

Picking up his cards again, Andy looked them over. Perhaps this was his lucky night. It could be. But it wasn't. The two men played well past midnight with only an occasional interruption when Robert served a rare drink to a customer. Finally, Andy stretched. "Well, I guess I'm gonna head up," he announced.

Robert nodded as he added up Andy's new debt. "You know you owe me five hundred ten dollars and fifty cents? I think you should consider paying it since we will have to use space money soon, and I don't think the exchange rate is too good."

"You consider it, I'm goin' to bed."

Robert nodded. "Yeah, guess it's safe to go up now. I haven't seen anyone that didn't belong going past the door."

Andy shook Robert's hand and made for his room. Slipping the card through the lock he hesitated a moment before opening the door. Robert had made him spooky. Andy gently shoved the door open waiting until it had swung to the wall before entering, and then only far enough to reach the light switch. Flicking it on revealed an empty room. Entering, he closed the door, bolted it, and attached the chain. Pausing a moment, he took the straight-back chair from the dresser and slipped it under the doorknob. He was nervous, without real cause, and he felt a little foolish, but still, something made him very uneasy.

The room he'd been given was a typical upper-rung motel room. Two double beds had their heads against one wall, separated by a small nightstand. A picture window looked out on the street below where Andy saw only slight traffic. He drew the drapes shut. Against the window were two comfortable-looking armchairs, which turned out not to be as comfortable as they appeared. Across from the beds, a long dresser with a mirror hung above it on one end, and a TV on the other.

He flopped down, grabbing the remote from the nightstand, and clicked on the television. It was always the same on every station: aliens, aliens, and aliens—what to do, why they are here, what it means. Even the commercials were alien-friendly. Perfumes used to be intoxicating, or sexy, now they were potions from the stars, eternally fragrant, or secrets of the novas. He used to hate commercials; now he detested them. Andy raised the remote to turn it off, when a face he recognized came on the screen. It was John Trombley, the weirdo.

There he was, in living color. However, now John was looking better. He was leaner, in fact, he was healthy looking. His eyes no longer darted around as though something was about to eat him. He was talking in even, self-assured tones, even carrying a tone of authority. Not only was he talking confidently, but people were actually listening. Didn't they know this guy was a fruitcake? Pulling back, the camera revealed Trombley dressed in a red robe thing with white piping—so he had a position now. Why not? Trombley was crazy and this whole thing was Loony Tunes. Seeing Trombley in red, he was sure the aliens were dangerous. Andy turned up the sound.

Trombley gazed around the auditorium, sizing up the crowd. His gaze was slow and intent. At last, he raised his hand and the crowd quieted almost instantly.

"Since the beginning of recorded history, we thought we were God's created beings: special, unique, destined to rule, first this planet—next the stars. However, we are not unique. We aren't even superior. We are the offspring of a race of beings whose powers we've only dreamed about, and whose accomplishments the science fiction writers haven't caught up to yet. Moreover, they've come to share it with us—not as benevolent gifts bestowed upon inferior beings, but as equal brothers and sisters, entitling us to all they have without question or doubt."

First, a ripple then a growing crescendo of applause swept over the assembled, ending in a standing ovation.

Trombley held up his hands to quiet the crowd. "What are we asked to give them in return for all that they have offered us? Do they want our gold, our money, or our jewels? Do they ask us to bow down before them as lowly servants? No! No, none of that! All they ask is that we accept what is being freely offered. Simply receive."

Trombley moved a few steps to his left, paused, then raising his left hand to his chin, appeared to ponder a moment. "There is something they need though, our trust. Yes that's it, really: our trust. Our friends are only asking us to unite as one people so that we may receive our inheritance as a united people. They are asking us to cast aside all labels we have come to affix to one another, denoting where we were born, or how, or what political entity ruled over us, or what religion we followed, or which social class or caste was our fate. They ask that we come together, as brothers and sisters, which we certainly are. Come together as one, speaking as one. Casting aside all things that have separated us from one another. We cannot do this unless we are able to throw these labels aside, until we are willing to discard all the baggage that comes with those labels. No more Englishmen, or Americans, or

Chinese. No more Christian, or Jewish, or Hindu. There should be no more Buddhists, Transcendental Meditators, Jews, Catholics, Christians, Islam, or devil worship. The truth has arrived. It is the truth and only the truth that we should serve. We are a part of that truth; enjoy it, and immerse yourself in the wonderfulness of your restored heritage."

Trombley paused for a moment and the silence was complete. Andy was impressed. Is this the Trombley he knew? Surely not, he'd been taking speech vitamins. He was now super tongue.

"Now some," continued Trombley, "have asked if the Visitors are Gods. Let me say this, there are no gods as you may think of them; that is, no spiritual entity sitting up in some heaven keeping watch over all his created beings and dishing out judgments in an ongoing battle with a supposed devil." Trombley paused for a moment, framing what he wanted to say. "In a sense, we—you and I, the Brothers, are gods. We rule the universe. Our leader is referred to by his people as being the First and the Last. One of the truths we are attempting to reveal to you, is the awesome truth of your heritage. It is us that others of the universe refer to as gods. And why not? We have the technology, which they only dream of having, and many don't even know how to dream that far ahead. For too long you, your brothers, and your sisters have been confined to the physical space of this Earth, and to the intellectual confines of folklore. Now, the Elect shall open your consciousness to all that awaits you. When finally this is accomplished, when the truths of life and the universe are accepted by your minds, then there will be rejoicing among you and your brothers and sisters, as has not been seen since the beginning of time. When that happens, and you assume your rightful positions, then some shall indeed think of you as gods. I tell you...."

Andy clicked the TV off. Jerk. It wasn't the first time he'd heard such things, nor would it be the last, he assumed. The whole thing sounded too good to be true. Every time he heard that gibberish, something inside of him squirmed. However, these ideas were having a great effect upon everyday life, for sure. Not only were people giving up their jobs and social responsibilities; but they were also starting to go after those institutions and people that did not, claiming they lacked commitment and devotion to the new order of the Elect. And what was with those robes? Different colors with those stripes of colored embroidery. It was all just too weird.

Putting down the remote, he stretched. Though it wasn't that late, he was tired. Actually, he was exhausted, and without warning sleep crept up and embraced him.

CHAPTER 9

New Times

LITTLE MORE THAN dark shadows beneath the gnarled oak, the two stood silently holding hands. They were ready. Jerry could feel a growing excitement mixing with feelings of hatred as he gazed across the road. The lone streetlight struggled to reveal, but succeeded only weakly in giving stark, distorted definition. The church's steeple, bathed in the light, seemed taller than it was, the church smaller. Once it had seemed so big and wonder-filled. Yes, once so wonderful, but now so forbidding, cold, and condemning.

Snatches of memories raced in Jerry's head of a young boy running down the hallway toward his mother, clutching a treasured drawing. He'd colored the manger orange, the grass blue, and the lambs yellow. Thinking back, he could almost feel his mother scooping him up in her arms, making wonderful noises while reviewing in glowing terms his artistic endeavors. He'd liked church; his friends were there, his family was there, and so was Reverend McDonald. McDonald had been too difficult to say so he called him "Reverend McDee" as all the other kids did. Jerry could always count on a kind word, or pat on the head, from Reverend McDee. That is, until that particular day. Jerry felt flush as his anger began to grow again. He felt a squeeze on his hand and he returned it. Finally, he'd found someone who understood him, someone who was offended as he by the events of that day, as ready as he to exact punishment.

Jerry wondered where the reverend was now. How was he handling the truths the aliens were giving them? Maybe he felt like the ass Jerry knew he was. How did the ol' reverend feel knowing he'd wasted his entire life on something that was a figment of someone's imagination? Did he feel like the fool he was? Did he cry? Did he beg forgiveness for the things he'd done in the name of a stupid myth? Like the things he'd said to Jerry? Things that hurt him so much because he loved Reverend McDee and his disapproval felt like a hot piece of steel running through his body. Did the reverend remember? Whether or not he did, Jerry certainly did. It was why he was here. Tonight they would destroy what the reverend loved so much.

Jerry took a deep breath and closed his eyes as the pictures of that day came back: his coming to church after school. His teacher had given him a note that Reverend McDee wanted Jerry to stop by. The reverend must have heard him come through the side door for he leaned out of the office doorway as Jerry came down the hall.

"Hi, Jerry, m'boy," he said, as usual.

"Yes, you wanted to see me?"

"Yes, Jerry. Come on in," he said, motioning. "Say, you want a soft drink or something?"

Jerry climbed on the straight-back chair facing the reverend's desk and shook his head. "No."

However, instead of going behind the desk, Reverend McDee chose his overstuffed chair, to Jerry's right, and sat down heavily in it. The chair had been a birthday gift from the congregation three years earlier. It was beginning to show a little age. Reverend McDee's ample body was destroying the springs so it now had a concave seat. For a moment, the reverend drummed his fingers on one of the chair's worn arms, and the long silence caused Jerry to feel uncomfortable. It was obvious Reverend McDee was searching for words.

"Jerry, I got a call from Mrs. Ferny." Once more, he paused, folding his hands beneath his chin. "Jerry, she tells me you and her boy, Martin, have been doing something you shouldn't."

Jerry's heart stopped. Martin had told. Jerry could feel his breath coming in short, silent gasps, and his hands turning cold.

"Is this true, son?"

Jerry couldn't speak, but he nodded.

"Why, Jerry?"

Finally, he found his voice "We didn't mean anything. We were just sorta foolin' around."

Reverend McDee nodded slowly. "I understand, son, but Mr. and Mrs. Ferny are very upset. They called me this morning and called your parents too."

Jerry felt fear coursing through his body, a cold flash followed by a hot one. He felt ill. His parents. His intestines were turning to liquid. Not because of his mother, but his father. What would he say? He couldn't bear to have his father angry with him.

"Jerry, your father called me and asked me to speak to you today after school. To sorta find out what's behind this. You say you were just fooling around, is that right?"

"Yes," he replied, looking at the floor.

"Jerry, there are some things we just don't fool around about. This is one of them; this thing is not what makes your parents, or I, happy. Something like this is not right. Now, I don't think it was your fault, I think that the devil just tricked you. What do you think?"

"Uh-huh."

Reverend McDee nodded, then smiled and put his arm around Jerry. "Let's put this behind us, okay? You won't do this again?"

"No," said Jerry, shaking his head slowly and continuing to look at the floor.

"Good boy."

Remembering this instinctively made Jerry's hand tighten around John's again. It was the first time he could recall feeling shame. This, John understood, he always did. He'd been through similar times too. Now, it wasn't shame he felt, but anger: All those years of hiding and feeling afraid someone would find out, tell, or ridicule. Tonight would be their revenge for all those times spent in hiding.

He stepped out from under the tree and John followed. Quickly they crossed the street toward the wall surrounding the church. The wall had been built years ago as added security for the church, though few came anymore. Maybe the 6-foot wall deterred people, but it wouldn't Jerry. He led John around the side toward the rear of the church where the wall lowered to 4 feet. Here, it was not hard to scramble over and onto the inner grounds. Jerry took a moment to look around at the playground where he'd spent so many hours, years ago. It was almost the same. Even the worn depressions in the ground beneath each swing seat seemed the same. Yet, it all looked so different. Had he remembered wrong? The swings were so much smaller now, even crude—but in his mind he remembered them as so daring, death-defying in their challenge to swing standing up.

He heard John land on the ground behind him. Motioning, he led him to the side entrance door. It was locked, as he knew it would be; but the small window on the left had a pane, which used to be loose. Tentatively, he pushed and jiggled the windowpane until finally feeling it give. Some things never change. With a few more encouraging pushes, it was dislodged. Removing the pane, Jerry reached up and undid the latch, allowing the window to be raised. However, getting through the raised window turned out to be more difficult than he remembered as a boy—but he pushed himself. As with everything else, it seemed his memory was trying to fit today's realities into yesterday's facts. Finally, managing to squeeze through the small window, he fell to the dark tile floor of the hallway.

It took a few seconds for his eyes to adjust and find his way to the door, but he did, and opened it for John. "What now?" John asked, closing the door behind him.

"Follow me," said Jerry, making his way down the dark hall. He could see much better now as they made their way down the tiled corridor toward the muted glow of an Exit sign. "Up these stairs," he said.

Quickly they ascended, then through a door, finally arriving at the sanctuary. The glow from the streetlight shown through the large church windows, creating a surreal scene inside with long, dark shadows dripping over neat rows of pews. Jerry stopped a moment, looking across the open area of the sanctuary searching, counting the rows, and stopping at the seats where his mother and father always sat. He sat down in his old seat while John stood still, waiting. Jerry was silent. It had been years since he'd been back here. It all seemed not quite right. It wasn't exactly like the picture he had in his mind. Everything seemed so much bigger then, and now the church revealed itself as small, very small. He could hear Reverend McDee in his mind preaching, raising his finger every time he said the word "God," then pointing dramatically at his foot when he said "devil."

"You gonna sit there all night, or are we gonna do the deed?" asked John, walking slowly forward.

"I was just thinking, I'll bet they have no more than ten people here on a Sunday now."

"I'd be surprised if anyone came, I mean—what's the point?"

"Yeah, what's the point?" echoed Jerry. "Can you imagine how these jerks felt when they first heard there was no God? Blows my mind." Jerry smiled. "I bet some wanted to jump right up there and kick the preacher's ass."

John smiled. "So is McDee or Mickey D, or whatever his name was, still the preacher you think?"

"Nah, I heard he retired a few years ago, maybe dead now. Don't know. Hope he's not though, I'd like to think that he opened the newspaper one day and read 'God Doesn't Exist, You Idiot!' Jerry laughed, and John joined in. "Well, these jerks sure did a number on me—now let's do a number on them!"

"Amen, amen," laughed John, waving his hands in the air.

Jerry walked down the blue carpeted aisle toward the altar worn in the middle by years of faithful feet. Ascending two steps to the altar, Jerry made one sweeping motion, flinging everything to the floor with loud crashes echoing off the shadowed walls. "You know, John,…" said Jerry, pointing to a large cross above and slightly behind the altar. It was larger than life, carefully carved out of oak, and polished. Each end was capped with polished brass fittings that reflected even the weak light from the window. In addition, a brass plate shaped as a narrow scroll was attached to the top of the cross proclaiming in Hebrew "Kings of the Jews."

"They called this thing the way to God. Yeah, they hammered that into me every Sunday when I was a kid. They also said 'love is God.' If love is God, I guess that makes us priests, eh?" He laughed, then quickly took out his penknife, and carved J-E-R-K-S in large letters on the altar top.

John hopped up on the altar and leaning toward the cross, began tugging. Jerry watched as his friend finally gained a firm hold and he heard a groan from the wall. As a boy, the cross was the prettiest part of the church to Jerry. Behind it were hidden lights that, when lit, made a halo around the cross. The lights would catch the brass fitting and they would seem to glow. He always thought that was neat. It was especially pretty on Christmas Eve when, during the candlelight service, all the lights were turned off except for those behind the cross and each parishioner held a lit candle. That was neat too.

Another groan came; this one was much louder as John succeeded in pulling loose the bolts. Quickly, Jerry hopped on the altar and added his efforts. The bolts resisted, but finally yielded with a last, long groan. With one final tug, the cross fell straight down, hitting the altar's edge; the brass scroll broke in half as it hit square upon the altar. The two men pushed the cross up against the wall where it tilted to the left, hung for a moment as if undecided what to do, then crashed on an angle, narrowly missing the altar this time.

John and Jerry needlessly leaped from the altar to avoid the possible impact.

"Whew! Great!" shouted John, holding up his hand to receive a high five, which Jerry gave enthusiastically. "I told you this was gonna be fun. Here, let's bust it up!"

Jerry hesitated. "No, no let's keep it. I wanna use it for some special occasion,"

"Special occasion, like what?"

"Dunno, but I got a feeling there might be something," said Jerry bending over the fallen cross. "Look here, the metal scroll is broken in half." He reached out and touched the jagged edge of the scroll. It hung by one nail at an angle. "You know what that says?" he asked John pointing to the metal scroll.

"No clue."

"King of the Jews—well that's what it used to say before it got broken. Don't know what it says now, probably just 'King.'"

The two hauled the tall, heavy, brass-tipped cross away from the altar.

"Okay, now what?"

"I got an idea," said Jerry. "Gimme your lighter."

CHAPTER 10

Sarah

ANDY AWOKE WITH a start, listening. He paused, wondering if he'd imagined it. Again, the knock came, three times, softly. Scrambling out of bed, he felt his heart pounding. Had they come for him in the night? Had Robert been right about the desk clerk?

Carefully he approached the door, trying not to make a sound, and looked through the peephole. Those viewing holes were no good; it revealed a slightly distorted man with an oval face that tended to look one way then the other. Nevertheless, it was only one face, meaning he was alone, which calmed Andy a bit. Fixing the chain, he opened the door a crack.

"Excuse me," the stranger began, in a hushed voice. "Are you Andy Moore?"

"Yeah. So?"

"May I come in?"

"No. Why?"

"My name is Jeff Lange. I'm here at the request of Sarah Jenkins—TJ's wife. You knew TJ Jenkins?"

"I did. Just a sec." Andy undid the chain and opened the door. As Lange passed him, Andy peeked out in the hall; it was empty.

Lange was about the same age as TJ. But his thirty-five years had not been as kind TJ's. Lange's hair was retreating from a forehead that showed deep crevices from too much sun. He also had literally no eyebrows. TJ thought he'd never before seen a man with no eyebrows. Lange quickly surveyed the room, turned, and waited until Andy closed the door. "Sarah sent me here to get you—or that is, to try and convince you to come and visit us."

"Us? I don't understand."

Lange nodded. "The 'why' of it may be a little difficult to answer. I understand you knew Sarah's husband TJ pretty well?"

"Yeah, I knew TJ. I knew him for many years, professionally. While we were at the pyramids, we got to be pretty good friends."

"Did he impress you as a religious man?"

Andy nodded. "Sure, anyone who knew TJ also knew he was into God."

"Yes, he was. In fact, that's the reason he was there. He demanded that assignment to the landing because he believed these so-called aliens weren't what they appeared, and his objective was to see if he was right, and if so, expose them."

"Expose them?"

"Do you think of these creatures as, what—aliens?"

"Sure."

"Are you sure that's the case? TJ wasn't."

"He didn't think they were aliens?" asked Andy in disbelief. "But they came in spaceships, for God's sake."

"Nevertheless."

Andy walked to the window that looked out and down upon the street below, now dark and almost deserted, with only an occasional car passing by. A year ago the street would have been very busy with a mix of cars, cabs, occasional busses, and always a police siren sounding somewhere. He stood thinking, trying to relate what this man was implying to his conversations with TJ. Was this what TJ meant by his last words to him? Was he going in to expose the aliens? It didn't seem possible. Turning back he said, "That doesn't make a lot of sense," he began. "I don't mean to denigrate TJ's memory—he was a good man—but look at the obvious. They came down in some kinda spaceship; the whole world saw that. I saw it myself, in person. Believe me, there weren't any wires attached to those babies—they were huge. Don't tell me you think they're some kinda spies, maybe from Russia or something. Why, the Russians have trouble getting money together for cab fare these days, let alone something like this."

"No, not the Russians." His tone was neither confrontational nor antagonistic.

"You think this is a fake—some kind of gigantic masquerade?"

"Exactly."

Andy snorted. "Just where do you think they're from?"

"Hell."

Andy was silent for a moment staring at Lange, but Lange remained calm, returning Andy's look with quiet confidence. Seeing Andy at a loss for words, Lange continued. "Are you a religious man?"

Andy shook his head, then sat on the bed.

"Let me ask you something," said Lange. "Do you remember the location where the ships came down?"

"Sure, of course. I told you, I was there."

"I mean the location on the map?"

Andy thought a moment. "Yes, it was sixty-six degrees south and east six degrees."

"Exactly. If you put them together, that's six-six-six. Does that mean anything to you?"

Andy was silent for a moment, then shaking his head said, "that's just coincidence. That doesn't mean they are from the devil."

"Well, let me put it this way: Do you believe there is a God?"

"Yeah, sure."

Lange nodded. "Since it was Sarah who sent me here, I'm surprised you aren't a religious man, a Christian. I assumed you were."

"Hold on. I wanna make sure I got this straight. You're saying those aliens aren't really aliens—people from another planet. You're saying they're from hell—the Bible kinda hell?"

"Yes."

"Now, if they're from hell, that means you think they're demons, fallen angels."

"Exactly! Masquerading as aliens."

Andy rubbed the top of his head. Was this man nuts? Did he have a crazy man in his room? "How do you know this?"

"Sarah told us."

"Sarah told you? What does Sarah know? She's a housewife! You're talking like she's some kinda mystic. TJ never mentioned he was married to a know-it-all psychic." Andy thought for a moment. "I guess from the way he always spoke about her, TJ thought she was something special but…"

"We don't consider Sarah either a mystic, or psychic. We believe she is a prophet."

"A prophet, like in the Bible?"

"I know, this is all so new to you, and I can imagine how this must sound coming out of the blue. Sarah doesn't consider herself a prophet— refuses to let anyone use the word. She says she believes the Spirit speaks to her and she accepts it on faith. I do accept what she says, and I accept it on faith also." Lange took the chair from the hallway and straddled it. "Sarah knew the spaceships would appear long before they did. She knew exactly where they were going to land, and what would happen." Lange smiled. "I know how you feel, believe me. She told us these things nearly a year before they happened. We all thought, or at least I did, 'She's gone off the deep end.' However, it happened exactly as she said it would. She knows."

Andy thought for a moment. "I always meant to write her and express my condolences about TJ, you know. I even went out where TJ used to live, but the house was all locked up, grass turned into weeds. Looks like someone broke into the place too. I wondered where she went."

"Now you can see her," argued Lange. "And there's a second reason too. You're in danger here. You must leave. If not with me, then by yourself. The longer we stay here the closer we get to danger."

Andy felt a pang in his stomach. "Danger? I'm in danger?" Immediately he remembered Robert's concern again.

"You are. I must leave now; will you come with me? If you value your life, you will."

Andy hesitated a moment, then nodded.

"Good. Don't pack, we'll give you anything you need."

"Okay, but I have to take a few things." Quickly Andy swooped up his computer, overnight bag, and a couple of clothing articles. He met Lange at the door. He was already peeking through a cracked opening.

He looked at Andy, nodded and the two silently went into the hall heading for the elevators. Halfway down the corridor, they heard the bell announce an approaching elevator car.

"Here," whispered Lange, ducking inside a small space carved out of the hallway for vending machines. With some effort, Lange squeezed behind the Coke dispenser while Andy, following Lange's lead, squeezed beside the chips. He could see out into the hall from a small opening between the machine and wall. Leading the group was the desk clerk he'd seen earlier. In his hand was a room pass-card and following him were four large men. The first had nothing in his hands; however, the two that followed had what appeared to be small bats, and the last, a revolver. Andy felt himself tense.

The hotel clerk stopped in front of Andy's room, and waited until each of the men positioned themselves in a well-practiced arrangement on either side of the door, then slowly the card was passed through the slot. Upon hearing the click of the lock, he threw open the door and stepped back as the four men dashed inside. Andy could hear the bathroom door being flung open, as well as some things being thrown around, then there was silence for a few moments, ending when the leader exited into the hall and addressed the hotel clerk. "Not here. You didn't see him leave at all?"

"No. He didn't leave, at least not through the front door."

"Well, he ain't been gone long," chimed in an emerging third man, "the bedcover is still warm. My guess is he just left."

The leader motioned the others to follow. He headed for the stairs, and Andy could hear their rapid decent. He waited until their sounds faded before peeking out from behind the machine.

Lange was already out, peering down the hallway. Seeing Andy, he motioned him to follow and quietly they followed the men down the stairs for two floors before Lange held up his hand. Andy stopped as Lange opened the door into the hallway beyond. Satisfied, he motioned Andy to follow into the empty corridor. "Down here, there's a skywalk over to the bank building. I used it once-upon-a-time when I worked there and came here for lunch." He half walked, half ran to the sky bridge and then over it to the bank building beyond. Though it was called the "Bank Building," it no longer housed a bank, but was renovated into shops and office suites. Even at this late hour, there were a few people inside patronizing the two bars inhabiting the building.

Lange led him down a flight of stairs, then to one of the six glass elevators, which descended into the lobby below. Emerging from the elevator Lange struck a slow, almost lazy pace leading toward the entrance facing the Linden street parking area. Andy tried to mimic his pace and style.

Finally, emerging from a sliding glass entrance door that emptied them into the parking lot, they stopped and looked around. Seeing a four-door Ford several rows away, Lange waved. Immediately, the car's headlights came on and it began moving toward them.

"We've given them the slip, I guess. But you never know." He barely finished the words, when two of their pursuers burst from the adjoining building and immediately saw them.

The car had almost reached them, but neither man waited as they ran toward it. The driver, in anticipation, leaned over and popped the passenger door open as the car approached. Lange reached the car first, taking the rear door while Andy, only a step behind, dove into the open front door. The driver didn't wait for the door to close or Andy to drag his feet inside, but immediately sped up, only just missing their two pursuers who jumped back to avoid being hit.

As Andy retrieved his legs and managed closing the door, he heard Lange shout from the rear, "He's got a gun, stay down!"

A shot rang out and glass exploded into the car. Shards of broken glass rained upon Andy, but he had his head buried between his legs. No second shot came as the car zigzagged its way out of the parking lot onto the street.

For a moment, Andy remained tense, in anticipation of more gunfire, but when none came, carefully brushed the broken glass from his hair, and sat up. "What is going on? Why are they shooting at us?"

Lange ignored his question and continued to look out the broken rear window.

Andy looked at the driver and was shocked to see Stephanie Collins, her gaze firmly fixed on the road ahead. "Anything?" She snapped.

"Not yet," came Lange's response. "Wait, yes—it's them. They're coming after us!"

Stephanie did not hesitate but threw the car into a sharp right turn. Andy could hear the shrill protest of the tires as he grabbed the door's armrest, preventing himself from being thrown into Stephanie's lap. The car fishtailed on the edge of a spin, but Stephanie fought it. As she instantly applied the gas, the car leaped ahead, pinning Andy against the seat. Turning, he watched out the back with Lange. Suddenly, two headlights turned down the same street. The weaving lights reflected the driver's own control problems. Andy thought they looked closer. "They look closer, don't they?" he asked.

Neither of his car-mates responded.

"Stay off the expressway," snapped Lange. "These guys have more speed than us."

At this time of night with the few cars ahead of them, Stephanie was able to weave between the traffic they overtook without sacrificing speed. Approaching a corner, Stephanie took her foot off the accelerator while putting the car into a complete sideways slide as she whipped the wheel to the right. Andy was thankful no cars were coming the other way as their slide took them well into the other lane. Again, Stephanie timed her handling perfectly, preventing the car from fishtailing.

The car settled down in time for Stephanie to fling it into a hard left turn. This time the slide of the car took it across the centerline despite screeching efforts by the tires. Andy felt them hit a parked car broadside, but they bounced off as Stephanie punched the gas again and the car accelerated.

Suddenly, she jammed on the brakes flinging both Andy and Lange forward. Andy had time to put his arm in front of his face as he felt the hard impact of the windshield and a searing pain in his chest as it hit the dashboard. Stephanie flipped the wheel to the left at the last instant as Andy looked up to see they were headed full speed into a small automatic car wash. Instead of the entrance to the car wash being blocked by a door, it had a wooden gate in front.

The gate proved no obstacle as Stephanie shattered it, driving the car into the depths of the car wash. The sprayers and brushes bounced loudly and heavily off the car denting the hood and cracking the wind-shield. At last, the car came to a halt in the middle of the track. Large brushes surrounded them, while on the hood of the car lay some broken metal parts that may have come from a spraying unit. For a few moments nothing was said, no one moved. Finally Lange tried to open his door. Despite a groaning protest it yielded, but no more than a foot or so. However, it was enough space for Lange to squeeze through, which he did. Quickly, he disappeared between the brushes.

"That was quite a ride there. Where did you learn to drive like that?"

For a moment, Stephanie said nothing as she took a couple of deep breaths. "My daddy owned a dirt track in North Carolina. He let me drive on it. Then later, I raced for a few years. You okay?"

"I think so," replied Andy, massaging his arm. "Think maybe I hit the dash there a little hard. What's this all about?"

"If you ask me, it's about you."

"Me?"

"Yeah, I never saw them so anxious to get someone as you. Usually they are lazy and would never put themselves into danger. Tonight they were possessed, I think"

"Yeah, they sure seemed intent."

"When I say possessed, I mean it literally."

"You know these guys? Sounds like you've had experience with them before."

"Not them in particular. I just lump them all in the same category, they all pretty much act the same—except for tonight."

"You mean the chase."

"Um hmm. You must be as important as Sarah thinks." She smiled.

"I don't understand. Why do you say that?"

"Never mind, Sarah will explain it all. I don't really understand too much myself." She laughed suddenly and Andy reacted with a grin. "Surprised to see me here?" she asked.

"Yes. Surprised would put it mildly. Last time I saw you, I thought you were headed out for parts unknown, maybe the business world. But your coming here would have been my last guess."

Stephanie laughed, but was interrupted by Lange's rapping on her window. She tried to get the window down, but it wouldn't budge, so she pushed the creased door open far enough to allow her to exit. Andy did the same on his side, before rounding the front of the car to join them.

"First, no sign of those goons. Second, I got us another car."

"Another car?" asked Stephanie "How did you...you stole it!"

A look of exasperation crossed Lange's face, but when he spoke, it didn't show. "Yes. I think God might understand this, don't you?"

"I suppose."

"You got a problem with it?" asked Lange of Andy.

"Me? No, not me. Let's get outta here."

The three made their way out to the driveway where an older Ford Escort waited with the engine running.

"As a car thief, you suck," volunteered Sarah. "Does this thing run?"

Lange didn't smile. "Get in quick. I wanna get out of here as soon as possible."

This time Lange took the wheel and Stephanie the copilot seat, as Andy crawled in the backseat, which was filled with ancient McDonald's wrappers, Kentucky Fried Chicken boxes, Taco Bell bags, as well as discarded coke and coffee cups. "Whoever owned this piece of junk ate regularly," grumbled Andy.

Lange pulled out and drove carefully toward the expressway, which he took north, advertised as the way to Washington, D.C. After a few moments, Lange broke the silence.

"Back there you wanted to know what was going on."

"Yeah, and nobody talked to me."

"Yes, well, we were a little distracted. I must say you aren't what I expected."

"And what was that?"

"Well, I suppose I expected to see a Bible thumper who breathed fire and brimstone."

Andy chuckled. "Well, sorry to disappoint you, but I'm nowhere close to that."

Lange nodded. "Yeah, so I guessed." He smiled.

Stephanie turned around, facing him. "Why do you think Sarah sent us to get you?"

"I haven't a clue, really. Why would you think I would be a Bible thumper?"

"Fair enough, but first let me ask you a question. What do you think is going on in the world today?"

"The aliens, of course. That's the only thing happening really, and it's getting scary. I really don't understand it. Now I'm told they aren't aliens at all, but some kinda demons."

"What if I told you a war was going on right now, and we were right in the middle of it?"

"War?"

"Yes. We're in the midst, have been for several thousand years, of a spiritual war being fought all around us. Now, this spiritual war has entered into the physical world, our everyday reality."

"Go on."

Lange took over. "Satan is revealing his hand and doesn't care who knows it. I've seen a lot of things happen, some of them resulting in the deaths of my friends. Every day now is like living in a shooting gallery, and Christians and Jews are the clay pigeons. I used to make this drive almost every weekend without a care in the world. I don't anymore. I drive like my life depends upon every mile I cross—and it does, and now so does yours."

"It does?"

"Yes. If Satan doesn't want you to get where I'm taking you, this will not be a simple journey. If I'm a little quiet, it's 'cause I want to concentrate on what I'm doing here. I don't want any accidents, if you know what I mean."

Andy didn't, nor did he want to. "Okay, let's say that's happening. What's that got to do with the alien guys?"

"You don't understand, do you?" asked Stephanie. "The so-called aliens aren't men from outer space, Andy. They truly are demons from hell disguised as Beings of Light bringing to us all the promises we ever hoped to receive. All we have to do is renounce God. These beings are trying to take us to hell, literally."

Andy was silent. Both Stephanie and Lange allowed the silence to continue, affording Andy a chance to digest what they'd said.

"I don't know what to say," ventured Andy after a while. "I mean, I believe in God and the Bible and Jesus and all that, but this is so— different. I gotta tell you I'm no fanatic, not by a long shot."

"No kidding," said Lange with a chuckle. "Don't go thinking you have to believe anything. We don't expect to convert you, or have you believe us, having just heard it. It will take a while maybe. It did with me."

Andy nodded. "Where we going?" he asked.

"Not allowed to tell you where we're going eventually, but first, we're going to a cabin I have. I wanna pick up a couple of things. I figure now's the best time—don't think I'll be coming back. It'll only take a minute," said Lange.

Lange exited the expressway onto a two-lane highway, which soon became a dirt country road. All the while, Andy could see they were approaching the distant hills. Finally, Lange took a right onto another dirt road leading directly into the approaching hills. A half hour later, he slowed and turned onto a private drive guarded by a mailbox, skill-fully dodging between numerous potholes. A cabin, nearly concealed in the trees, came into view after rounding a final curve. Andy could see a light filtering through the leaves.

Abruptly Lange brought the car to a halt, turning off the head-lights. "Company," he said flatly, as much to himself as anyone else.

"Who? Do you know them?" asked Andy.

Lange didn't respond, but sat several seconds considering before slowly inching the old Ford forward. Another car, with a large cross strapped to its roof, revealed itself parked next to the house. Lange relaxed. "It's my son."

"What's that on the top of it?" asked Andy.

"No clue, sorta looks like a cross," he said, then added a moment later, "It is a cross.'

"Your son is religious?" asked Stephanie.

Lange pulled next to the Bronco. "No. No, not by a long shot."

"Does he live here? I thought you and your son didn't get along too well," said Stephanie.

"I haven't seen him for quite a while. The last time I did see him he seemed all right, but just not connected to me somehow."

Getting out of the car Lange looked carefully around, then motioned the others to follow him as he made his way to the wood-planked, slightly ajar, front door. Cautiously they entered the dimly lit cabin. At first, it seemed deserted. A modest fireplace on the back wall faced them, and on each side of the hearth was a door. To their left was the living room, to the right, the kitchen. The light above the kitchen sink dimly illuminated most of the cabin. Lange stepped forward into the living area.

From the left, came a voice out of the dark shadows. "Well, well, if it ain't Daddykins."

Lange turned. "Hello, Jerry."

Behind Jerry, John emerged, making his way to the sink where, leaning against it, he folded his arms. Jerry sauntered forward. Instinctively, Andy did not like him.

"What brings you up here? Is this your hiding place, Daddykins?"

The hairs on Andy's neck were standing. Jerry's tone was cheap, taunting, and menacing.

"No, I came by to get a couple of things, that's all. What's with the cross?"

Jerry snorted, smiled, and turned to his companion. They both shared a short laugh. "Well, Daddykins, I paid the church a visit earlier."

"Really? Our church—oh no, Jerry, you didn't."

Jerry laughed. "Yeah. Paid our respects, and we got a little souvenir." He laughed again, and John joined him.

Lange remained silent, shaking his head slowly.

"Hey, John," continued Jerry, " wanna bet none of them has received the vaccination mark?"

"Is that what they are calling it now—the Mark?" asked his father. "Look, Jerry, I didn't come up here to fight with you. I'm just gonna get a couple of things and leave—you and your friend are welcome to stay here, if you want, and for as long as you want."

Jerry mimicked his father, "You and your friend can stay here," he whined. "You still don't get it, Daddykins. You don't tell me what to do anymore, not now, or ever." His voice raised in volume as he spoke. "You don't count anymore, understand? You and all your Bible-thumping friends are all big zeros!" Jerry moved forward, approaching his father.

"You're what's holding everything up. You and your garbage," he said, nodding toward Andy and Stephanie, "you and your holier-than-thou buddies." Jerry shoved his face toward his father, who instinctively took a step backward. "Yeah, you knew everything. Looking down at me, telling me I was garbage."

"Jerry, I never said anything like that, and didn't think it either!"

"Shut up! Yes, you all thought it. I know it. But now I'm not, now I'm not!" The young man stepped back, nearly bumping into Andy, but seemed not to notice. "Now I hold all the cards, now I'm with the right people—and you're not. How's it feel to know, all the garbage you were spewing out was just a bunch of crap?"

"It isn't garbage, Jerry. I'm still a Christian and I'll continue to be one."

Jerry reached inside his shirt, and pulling out a gun, he pointed it at his father, while waving it slowly. "I'm not gonna listen to that crap anymore—understand?"

The room was absolutely quiet. Andy exchanged glances with Stephanie. Clearly, if the wrong word was said, or move made, someone was going to get hurt.

"Now, Jerry, we've had our differences…"

"Differences? Telling me I was goin' to hell, call that a little difference?"

"I never said such a thing."

"Shut up! I knew what you were thinkin'—and that's as good as saying it. All you Bible thumpers are the same! Well, I'm not going to hell; I'm goin' to the stars! You hear that? I'm going to the stars! You're the one going to hell! And I'm the one that's gonna send you!"

Andy saw Jerry raise the gun, and the hammer starting to pull back, and he lashed out at Jerry's arm, hitting it. A thunderous roar filled the cabin as Andy's grip tightened on Jerry's sleeve, forcing it downward. Another roar echoed. There was a shout of pain from Lange. The force of Andy's attack propelled both men forward and down, both hitting the floor heavily near where Lange now lay. Andy saw the gun fall out of Jerry's hand to his left and skid across the floor toward his buddy John.

John reached to retrieve the gun, but Stephanie jumped in front of him instantly, delivering a karate kick to John's groin. With a cry of pain, he fell to his knees, but began to rise again. Stephanie whirled on her left foot, striking John in the chest with a lethal right foot. John flew back against the wall, the air fleeing his lungs as he collapsed and withered on the floor.

Andy rolled to his left, away from Jerry, grabbing the gun, and quickly pointed it at Jerry who froze as the barrel came level with his line of sight. Jerry remained motionless, first staring at the gun, and then raising his eyes to focus on Andy's face. Andy had not seen such a look of intense rage from any other human being.

Across the room, John crawled to the front door, then slowly stood up, motioning to Jerry. When he spoke, his voice was strained. "Come on man, let's go. Forget 'em." With that, he stumbled out the door.

For another moment Jerry did not move, then slowly straightened up. Silently he raised his finger toward Andy, jabbing it wordlessly at him as he slowly backed out the door. Andy followed him to the door, took aim at the retreating men, finally raising the barrel to the sky, fired twice, then returned inside as the sound of spinning tires in the gravel echoed from outside. He found Stephanie cradling Lange's head. His chest was covered in blood, which oozed onto the floor. Andy kneeled, took Lange's hand, and looked at Stephanie. Her eyes told him Lange was dying.

"Where's the phone, I'll call for help," he said.

Lange managed to grab Andy's arm. "No. I'm beyond that." His voice was weak, and there was a definite rattle to his lungs.

"If I don't get you help, you're gonna die," protested Andy.

Lange slowly shook his head. "Listen. You got to leave here, now. Stephanie knows the way. You gotta go. They know you're here now. Gotta go."

"Okay we'll go, but let me at least call an ambulance first."

Lange attempted a smile, but failed while a small stream of blood dripped from between his lips. "Why?" He shook his head slowly, this time his bloodied lips succeeded in turning upward. "Go."

Andy hesitated, looking to Stephanie then to Lange.

"He's right. We have to go," she said, as she lay Lange's head on a makeshift pillow.

Andy nodded. Reaching down he put the gun in his belt. He turned back to say goodbye, but Lange's eyes were closed. Kneeling, Andy put his ear to Lange's nose, then placed his fingers on the side of Lange's neck to find a pulse.

"Dead?" asked Stephanie

Andy nodded, as he reached over to Lange's coat, retrieving the car keys.

Outside, night had wrapped its dark cloak around the sky. Stephanie stood gazing up with unseeing eyes. Andy put his arm around her. Immediately she turned, burying her face in his chest and Andy could feel the silent sobs. The two stood there for a few moments until Stephanie stood back and wiped her eyes.

"Better?" asked Andy.

Stephanie nodded.

Getting behind the wheel, Andy drove down the narrow dirt driveway toward the county road.

"Careful here," said Stephanie, her voice betraying none of the weakness of a few moments ago.

"Right," replied Andy, slowing the car to a crawl and turning the headlights off. Both tried to see ahead in the dark for the two men possibly waiting for them. "Anything?" asked Andy.

Stephanie shook her head. Gunning the engine, the car leaped forward, spinning its wheels in the dirt driveway and then upon the gravel county road. The car almost got away from Andy as he turned toward the state highway, but he managed to control it. There was no sign of the two young men.

It wasn't long until they reached Highway 85 and, at Stephanie's direction, Andy turned left.

"How long we got to go?" Andy asked

"'Bout an hour or so."

For the next thirty minutes, both were quiet, lost in their private thoughts until Andy broke the silence. "You gonna be all right?"

Stephanie looked over, "Yes. I'm fine. He's in a better place now. For him this entire struggle is over. We don't need to mourn him, really. We should envy him."

"You never told me how you got from the ship to Sarah's."

"The Lord works in mysterious ways, you know."

"So I've heard."

"TJ's disappearance bothered me. Something wasn't right. The more I thought about it, the more I wanted to search for answers. I called his wife to see if she had anything that would shed any light on this. I introduced myself as Commander Collins, and said I had a couple of questions if she didn't mind. I felt a little ill at ease 'cause I didn't know how she'd take my call—you know, what state she was in and everything. However, instead of weeping or being angry, she was very kind, she told me the navy already informed her and she was expecting my call—asked me if my name was Stephanie. I hadn't told her my first name up to this point."

"No. Really, and she knew it? You're putting me on."

"I swear. Well, you can imagine how shocked I was that she knew my name. Then she asked me if I was going to come and see her, and when. Well, it suddenly seemed like a good idea. I'd already given my resignation letter and was at a loss to what I was going to do anyway; and I suddenly wanted to meet this woman who knew my name outta the blue."

"So how did you think she knew?"

"Didn't have a clue, I thought maybe ESP or something. I didn't know it had anything to do with God, or that Sarah even knew God. I'd discovered through my investigation that TJ was a religious man, and I suppose I assumed his wife would be also, but I didn't actually know."

"So you went to see her."

"Yes. They were waiting for me. I swear to you, they were waiting for me. They had come back to her house to pack the rest of their things, and get me. They had their cars and two vans all packed up and they were sitting around waiting for me, 'cause Sarah told them I would be there—and she told them I would be coming with them. So they waited."

"And you went with them?"

"Yes. Sarah asked me if I was a Christian, and I told her yes. She told me that she had a dream about me and that in the dream I was going to join the group and leave with them for the cabin."

"Incredible. I don't think I would go based on someone's dream, or premonition."

"Then why are you here now?" asked Stephanie.

Andy thought a moment. "You know, you're right. I don't have much better reason than you. I'm here 'cause Sarah sent some guy to get me. This is weird."

Stephanie laughed. "Face it, you're gonna be another Sarah Groupie like the rest of us."

"Well," smiled Andy. "We'll see about that. So this dream she had about you coming, what else did it say?"

Stephanie was silent for a moment. "Well, some other stuff—maybe I'll tell you about it someday."

"Oh, sounds mysterious—spooky."

Stephanie did not smile. "No, it's not spooky. Not mysterious. Not weird. I think it's holy. If I didn't think that, I wouldn't be here today with you."

The two drifted back into silence for another thirty minutes until Stephanie spoke as they rounded a lazy curve in the road. "Pull into the gas station that's up here. They've sold us gas before without ID. Let's get some coffee and hope they do sell us gas. I need to take over the driving here too, we're getting close."

Andy pulled into a large gas station that was part grocery store. It was brightly lit and seemed out of place in its isolation. Inside, he asked for fifty dollars of gas and was relieved when the attendant rang it up without question. Evidently, the word on identification had not reached here yet. Andy grabbed two coffees and after handing them to Stephanie, pumped the 6 gallons of gas.

With Stephanie behind the wheel, they pulled out of the station in the same direction as before, but she was constantly checking the rear-view mirror and peering into each driveway they passed. Finally, after several miles, she turned onto a dirt road, made a U-turn, stopped the car, and turned out the lights.

"What's up?" asked Andy.

"We always do this to see if anyone is following. Sometimes I sit here half an hour."

"Great," mumbled Andy, suddenly very grateful for the hot coffee. He was tired and hoped where they were going had at least one soft bed for him.

After waiting fifteen minutes, Stephanie started the car. She pulled out on the highway turning in the direction from which they'd just come. After five minutes, she made a right hand turn down a two-lane asphalt road, which began immediately climbing, first into the foot-hills, and then the tall smoky mountains. The road eventually placed them on the outside of a mountain on a road carved out of the granite slopes. Only a waist-high guardrail separated them from open space as they wound around one mountain and then another. Andy felt his ears popping as they ascended, while watching in the distant lights of the countryside, few in number now that the night was aging.

At last, Stephanie turned on a narrow road, not much more than a path off to their left, and immediately began a steep climb for a quarter mile before leveling off and then descending into a small dark valley where only a few weak lights shone about a mile away.

"This it?"

"Yes. Those lights are from the main house."

A few minutes later, Stephanie parked in front of the house and two men waiting in front of the cabin greeted her warmly. A third made his way over to Andy and opened the door. "Welcome," he said, extending his hand. "Trip here okay?"

Andy grasped the firm hand, "Well, not too good, but I'll let Stephanie fill you in on that."

The group headed for the house, whose windows were curtained, preventing all but a little light from escaping. Inside, Andy allowing a few seconds for his eyes to adjust to the light, found the house much larger inside than it had appeared outside. They'd entered the main room running the entire length of the structure, about 70 feet, with the width looking about 30. Several long tables covered a wood floor. All of the tables were occupied with faces running the gamut of expressions from smiling to scowling. It was clear to Andy he was being sized up.

Above him, a cathedral ceiling ran the width of the room; however, there was a banister walkway running the length of the rear wall with a second floor showing doors, which Andy assumed were additional bedrooms.

"So where's Jeff Lange?" asked one of the men.

Stephanie looked at the floor a moment before answering. "He's dead."

A collective gasp ran through the room.

"His son Jerry shot him at his cabin. He went there to pick up a few things and we ran into his son and another guy. They had a gun." Stephanie paused for a moment, collecting herself. "It was terrible."

A smallish woman with red hair done up in a bun, approached Stephanie and taking her hands, looked into her eyes silently, then stroked Stephanie's cheek. Stephanie lowered her head and began to cry quietly. Drawing her close, the woman stood there a few moments rocking her slowly side to side until finally Stephanie straightened up.

"I'm okay."

The woman kissed her on the cheek and then moved her attention onto Andy. She approached him and startled him with an embrace. "It's good to see you, Andy."

Andy smiled. "Hello, Sarah." Andy almost didn't recognize her, and if it had not been for the red hair, he may not have. This was not the woman he remembered. She had been shy, diminutive, and almost mousy. Now she appeared a bit taller than her 5 feet 4 inches, certainly more confident, and with strength that leaped out at him. Her oval face was devoid of any makeup, and needed none. Long full eyebrows tapered gracefully slightly beyond her soft green eyes.

"Yes," she smiled, "we've all been waiting here for you to come. I'm sorry the trip was not a good one. We will all miss Jeff Lange. He was a good and decent man, but we'll not shed too many tears, for we will join him soon. He is where we all want to be eventually, right?"

"In heaven?"

"Yes."

"Well, I'm hoping for that. That's for sure."

Sarah nodded, then turned and asked for attention. She introduced Andy and many came forward shaking his hand, welcoming him to the camp: Some were lawyers, others doctors, homemakers, mechanics, and bus drivers. There wasn't any pattern to the occupations, nor the areas from which they came. Some were local, and had known Sarah and TJ, yet others hadn't known either before the aliens had come. They'd arrived here much like Andy had. Someone had come for them. And, for their own reasons, they joined the group. After introductions were over, many left while a few stayed, engaging in private conversations.

"Andy, make yourself at home, and I'll be back in a minute," Sarah said.

"Here, sit with us and have some coffee." The voice belonged to a man about his own age, seated with two other men and one woman, but Andy couldn't remember their names as he shook their hands.

"I'm Dave Clawson," the first man said. " I know how you feel, we all do. Trying to learn all the names, and faces—plus trying to figure this place out." He laughed.

Andy pulled a chair over to the table. A woman, later introduced to him as Clawson's wife, brought over a cup of coffee, a welcome sight. "Thank you, believe me, I need this."

Clawson shook his head slowly from side to side. "Jeff dead. I just can't believe it; and he was shot by his own son?"

Andy nodded. "His son went into a rage the more he talked and all of a sudden had a gun in his hand. When I saw the gun, I knew we were in big trouble, so did Stephanie. After it was all over, I brought it along." He pulled the gun from his waistband. "I think we're gonna need it."

Clawson seemed to shrink back, before reaching over for the gun. "May I have it, please?"

"Sure." Andy handed it to him, trying to remember how one was supposed to do that, safely.

"Sarah!" Clawson barked. "Got a gun here."

Sarah came over and Clawson handed it to her. She motioned to another man who took the gun. "You know where to put it, right?" she asked. The man nodded and disappeared.

"I should tell you Andy, we don't allow guns, or anything like that around here."

"I can see why—accidents. But how will we know when we should get them?"

"Get them? You won't. I mean, we don't plan on getting the guns," Sarah replied.

Andy was silent for a second. "But isn't that why you came here, to defend yourselves—you know, strength in numbers?"

Clawson shook his head. "We didn't come here to live together, we came to die together."

"Die?" Andy's voice squeaked. "You're here to die? Am I supposed to die too?" This last question he addressed to Sarah.

Sarah stepped forward putting her hand on Andy's arm. "Why don't you and I go for a little walk? I think I better explain some things."

Andy followed her into the cool, cloudless evening. Above, the reflection of the large alien ship seemed brighter than usual casting shadows on the ground. Neither Andy nor Sarah looked at it.

Andy didn't wait for his walking partner to start. He had something he'd wanted to say to her since coming off the ship. "Sarah," he began, "I'm real sorry about TJ. I regret there wasn't something I could have done to stop him, and I'm sorry I didn't write you. I do need to tell you something though, and I'm so happy I've got the opportunity to do so. TJ gave me a message for you."

Sarah stopped short.

"He said if he didn't come back to tell you, you're right."

Sarah silently lowered her eyes to the ground, remaining silent for a few moments, then asked, "Did he say anything else?"

"That he loved you."

Andy heard her take a long slow breath. When she looked up, there were no tears in her eyes, instead she smiled. "Thank you. I wish I'd been wrong."

"Me too."

The two continued for a few paces in silence.

"Let me ask you a question, why did you send Lange for me? Did you have a premonition or something?"

Sarah laughed. "No, now don't you start with all this talk about me seeing in the future and all that. I got a message from someone that you might be in trouble; in addition, I felt a need to bring you here…"

"Someone told you I was in trouble. Who?"

"Sorry Andy, I can't tell you. We have friends around who sorta keep an eye out for us and for others. Aside from that, I felt you should come here. Now, if you're going to ask me why I felt you should come here, the answer is, I don't know. And my question is, do you?"

"Do I?" The question surprised Andy. "Sarah, I had no intention of coming when Jeff Lange knocked on my door. I don't know why I'm here; other than I wanted to tell you what TJ said to me before going over to those pyramids. But, I must say, I feel very good that I'm here. I was just rescued from some nasty people. That's all I know."

"I see." There was a hint of disappointment in Sarah's voice.

"Does there have to be a reason? Didn't you just send someone to help me escape? That seems reason enough to me."

"Perhaps, but I think there is more. I just don't know yet."

"I don't understand."

"I know. Let me explain. Some around here call me a prophet, a gifted one, or a seer. I don't subscribe to any of those titles; however, about five years ago, I do believe God started speaking to me."

"He spoke to you? You heard him?"

"No, no I didn't hear him—no burning bush. Nevertheless, God does speak, in his own way, to many. It began in small ways, concerning everyday things: premonitions, coincidence, and feelings about things. At first, I thought it was amusing, but no more. I certainly didn't think it was God. More like coincidence or luck, I didn't recognize what was happening. Then, one night I had a dream I was reading a newspaper. I saw the headlines; it concerned a train accident that happened in Florida. I remember reading a part of the story about how many people were hurt, and where the accident happened, as well as what time and why. The next morning I told Tommy about the dream, it seemed so real that I wanted to share it. Two days later, I saw the exact same headline in our morning newspaper. When I showed Tommy the headlines, he swore. I think it was the first and last time I ever heard him swear." Sarah paused.

"The headline was exactly the same as in your dream?"

Sarah nodded. "The headlines, the look of the front page, the time it happened, everything."

"Incredible."

"After that, I began having those kinds of dreams about once a month. Other times, I wouldn't be dreaming, I'd just suddenly know something. Then, about two years ago, I had a dream about the future. And, not just once, the same dream went on for a week, each night picking up where the last night's left off. I saw pyramids come down from the sky, and people coming out. Each one had two faces, one in the front and one in the back. The one in front was beautiful, but the one in the back was ugly, distorted, grotesque, and wickedly half human/half beast. I knew in my dream they were demons from hell. I saw great men as well as ordinary people from all corners of Earth in a valley and on the surrounding hills kneel and worship these demon aliens. And the demons opened their mouths and devoured them all."

"You knew they were coming. That's what TJ meant when he said you were right."

"Yes. At the time, I spoke to Tommy, and the two of us decided we should tell our church. I did. I don't think many, if any, believed me. In fact some were outright hostile. It wasn't until those things up there came that some I'd told realized what I said was true. Some of them are here now.

"I still have those dreams, but not as often. Sometimes, I know what they mean, most of the time I don't. The same is true with you. I dreamed about you. I saw you. You were in a small room, a bedroom—the bedroom you will sleep in tonight. A white horse came and you got on it. The horse spoke and said, 'It's going to be a rough ride, hang onto me.' You got on the horse, grasping his mane with both hands, and the horse began to run."

"Horses," said Andy slowly. "I don't get it. I don't know anything about horses—never rode one. You have horses here?"

"No," smiled Sarah, "the white horse is a symbol. It's the symbol of God's word. When you read more in the Bible, you'll see it used."

Andy felt cold goose bumps on his arms. "That's scary. So I'm here, now what?"

"I don't know, and I guess you don't either. Be patient, it'll come in its proper time. I can tell you this, and of this I'm confident, your being here is very important. Satan sent out his men to kill you, but they killed Jeff Lange instead. If Satan wants you dead, it must be because you're going to do something against him. Now, for the time being, you and the rest of us are safe here. God is hiding us here, for the time being. But I must tell you, in time, Satan will find us and when he does, he will kill us."

"Doesn't that scare you? Why don't you do something about it? Build up some defenses, set some patrols. I can tell you from my army experience, this place could be well defended if you positioned your people on those bluffs up there. Plus, the only reasonable access is that road—and you can see them coming a long time before they get here."

"You make the mistake of thinking that our fight here is a physical one. It is not. I could bring in heavy weapons and a thousand men and still we would die. Here is where we shall die. I know it, and have known it for a long time. However, I don't ask you to accept this. I don't ask you to stay if you feel led not to remain, nor do I ask any of the others. We will all do what we feel God leads us to do."

For a few moments, they walked silently. "I'm sorry but I just don't get it. Maybe when I've been here a little while I'll understand. Is this a dream you saw?"

"No. I just know."

"I see." Andy's voice was quiet. "Sarah, why don't you think of yourself as a prophet? I thought the test of a prophet was that if what was said came true, then he was a prophet. You seem to have passed that test."

Sarah shook her head slowly. "No, I won't allow such a label to be put on me. I'm simply a woman who, by faith, understands what God wants me to say or do, though usually not the 'why' of it. Nevertheless, I do it. I'm no different from any other servant of God doing what they feel led to do."

For a moment, Andy was silent. "You think I'm somebody special, I don't think so. I'm not a Holy Roller. I think that maybe my coming here is a mistake. I mean, I believe in God and everything, but I'm not what you'd call a churchgoing man. Everyone I've met so far seems to be really into it, religion I mean."

Instead of responding, Sarah motioned Andy to follow her and she crossed over to a worn path leading behind the main house. In the night's light, Andy could see they'd arrived at a small flower garden.

"This is my garden," she began, "I think of it as God's bouquet every time I work in it or walk past."

In the unforgiving reflected light of the night, the colors of various flowers were dulled.

"Tell me, Andy, which of these flowers do you think is the star of the garden, of this bouquet?"

"I have no idea," replied Andy, shrugging. "Hard to tell at night, I guess those in the back might be the prettiest—they would be the stars, I guess." He pointed to the roses in the rear.

Sarah nodded. "You may be right, you may be wrong, it's hard to say. Some days, when the roses are in full bloom, I would agree, but then they fade, and the marigolds, or petunias, or nasturtiums spring into flower and take over the beauty of the garden. But there's something else here most people overlook." She kneeled down pointing to a green plant that looked like a weed. "The greens."

"Greens?"

"Yes, see here?" she asked, pointing to a particular group of low green plants among the flowers. "Some of the plants here never bloom, that's not their job. Their job is just to be green. Their job, in this bouquet, is to highlight those that do bloom. Because of the greens, the beauty of the garden is so much more than it would be without them." Sarah stepped back a few paces with Andy following. "Now, from back here, the entire garden—the entire bouquet—merges into one presentation of beauty. Each section of flowers, blooming in its own time, each flower highlighted by its greens, all contribute to the beauty and purpose of the garden. Who can say which is the most important plant?"

"Yeah, I guess so."

"Let me show you something," Sarah said, stepping forward to the garden and bending down. Cradling a bare green stem between her middle and index finger, she said, "See this? It looks like part of the greenery; some might even call it a weed. It sorta sits here among the ferns, actually a little hidden by them. From a few steps away, one might not even notice it as an individual plant. However Andy, this is a baby rose. This baby sorta reminds me of you."

"It does?"

"Yes, kinda hidden among the greenery. It's plain, a little knobby."

"Knobby?"

Sarah smiled. "In a few weeks, it will be larger, and then one morning, burst into bloom."

Andy nodded, patiently.

Sarah stood up. "I wanted you to see this, because I think it shows that, in God's bouquet of people, there are some viewed as beautiful and some not. A lot depends upon what time of day, or what season."

"I can see that."

"Now, that baby rose and you are similar. You may not think yourself pretty in God's eyes, but God sees you as already beautiful. In time, the right time, you'll bloom."

"I don't know about that," grinned Andy. "I hope He's got lotsa fertilizer."

Sarah smiled and began walking, leading him from the cabin toward two black silhouetted buildings.

"You think I'll become like a Bible-thumping guy?"

"I don't know. In the garden, some flowers shout their beauty—they're sorta like the Bible thumpers, as you call them. Maybe you're a different flower, a quiet bloom. What does it matter, as long as you're part of the garden, all are essential to the bouquet. God will show you what your tasks are."

Andy nodded silently, as he thought, "Bunch of crap."

Sarah remained quiet.

"So," began Andy, "you think I should wait here until that happens, until I know what I'm supposed to do. Or, maybe, he'll send another dream and tell you what is supposed to happen. You think that might happen?"

Sarah shook her head. "As to whether you should stay here or not, I don't know, and I wouldn't want to influence you one way or the other. Maybe what you have to do is right here, or maybe it isn't. That's a decision you'll make on your own, for you own reasons. As to whether God will give me another dream about you, well, I don't know that either."

"For a prophet you don't know too much."

Sarah laughed; it was an easy one, tumbling out unhindered. "No truer words were ever said. All I do is repeat what I believe I'm shown. Usually I have no idea what it means. I do think God has much to teach you in a short time, and it may not be easy for you to understand, but understand you will, in time."

"Okay. Let's say these aliens aren't creatures from some other world, they are demons—I don't get it. Why the big masquerade?"

Sarah was silent for a moment. "You've asked the million-dollar question—and I have the two million answer." She smiled. "But before I tell you, let me ask a couple of questions. You want to know why the big masquerade because it doesn't make any sense, right?"

"Yeah, right. It doesn't."

"Yes. And that's where you make your first mistake. You think that this is a logical battle between Good and Evil, fought within the confines of human logic between Almighty God and Satan, right?"

"Well…I…"

"This is a battle being waged between two spiritual forces each using the weapons of choice. Satan's choice is logic. God's choice is faith. The two are like oil and water, they never seem to match up, never seem to validate the other in our puny human-logic driven minds. Personally, I think at some point they do, but that point is far beyond our comprehension. Right now we are stuck with human logic and it's human logic that Satan is using to defeat us, to romance us away from the truth."

"So logic is evil—is that what you're saying?"

"No, no! Not at all. God invented logic for us to use in order to function. I don't think he ever meant it to be the sole determinant of how we make decisions, of how we live. Logic is a poor substitute for faith. It's like we tied our fortune to a wagon when God had a jet all ready for us to use. When you read the Bible through, which you will, examine how God works His will. Search out the basis of his relationship with us. Was it logical for Moses to lead his people into the wilderness where there was scant food? For them to take forty years to make a trip of a few weeks? Was it logical for David to stand up to Goliath? Look at these and countless other stories of God's relationship to man and all will show that they are stories designed to demonstrate the power and reliability of faith, and the fallibility of human logic."

"So when I say to myself, 'this doesn't make sense,' you're telling me I'm on the right track?"

Sarah laughed at Andy's expression. "That's right, that's exactly right. It takes practice, but learning to deny the human logic of this world is the first step in our walk with Christ."

Sarah stopped walking and pointed to someone approaching them down the path. It was Stephanie. "I'll let Stephanie show you the cabin where you'll be staying. Inside, you'll find a hallway off the main great room. About halfway down, on your left, is a door with your name on it. Think about what I said, Andy, and the more you consider it, the more you will accept it for the truth it is."

Andy smiled; Sarah was really a remarkable person. "Yes, I will think about it. By the way, the door has my name on it?"

Sarah nodded. "Yes, I asked Dave to make it a few days ago."

Andy grinned again. "Naturally."

"Well, goodnight. It's good to have you here, Andy," she said, shaking his hand. Then she turned and began walking back to the main house.

"I see you and Sarah have gotten reacquainted," said Stephanie as she neared.

Andy nodded. "She's a remarkable person."

Stephanie nodded. "Come on, I'll walk you to your cabin. I brought you a present—sort of a 'welcome' present," she said, lifting her hand and the book it held.

"A Bible?" asked Andy, a little taken aback.

"Yes, I think you should take some time to read it. After all, we are in the middle of a battle foretold by it for two thousand years."

Andy nodded, "Yes, I think I would like to do that. I'm not ignorant of the Bible, you know. I've read parts of it from time to time, but I've never really studied it, I mean, read it from cover to cover."

"Well, I think this would be an excellent time to start," smiled Stephanie.

"When are you gonna tell me the other half of the dream Sarah told you about?"

Stephanie was silent as they walked. Then, running her fingers through her hair, brushing strands from her eyes, she cleared her throat, " Well, I guess it's a bit embarrassing. The other part said there was a man coming soon who was lost, found by us, but not himself, who was chosen for a task I was to help with and that I would die with him." Stephanie paused and looked at Andy quickly. "When Sarah told us you needed to be picked up, I asked her if she thought you might be that man, and she told me she did."

"Wow. I'm lost, found by others, but not myself. And you are going to die with me? Are you sure about that part?"

Stephanie nodded.

"Well, then, I hope you are old and gray when you kick the bucket."

Stephanie laughed. "Yes, I hope so too, but Sarah didn't say." She stopped walking and pointed to the first cabin a few feet away. "Here's your quarters, it's nice seeing you again, and welcome to our little retreat. The adventure is just beginning." She smiled and shook his hand before leaving.

Andy watched her walk away for a few moments while rubbing his chin. This thing was getting curiouser and curiouser.

CHAPTER 11

Captured

THE SUMMER ENDED with soft lazy rain, cool drops bringing relief from the hotter-than-usual summer days. Andy spent these rainy hours lingering in his room reading the Bible Stephanie had given him. He discovered the last book, *Revelations,* confusing, to say the least. He found these days of reading adventures having a slow, yet marked effect upon him. He began to understand the book he was reading was more than a collection of unrelated stories, it was an instruction manual to the world of faith. The concept "faith," this mysterious, elusive word that had changed heaven and hell, seemed to leak out of every page. He began to find it as a new and exciting concept he never really understood and didn't now. Though still rough around the edges, he was changing.

Yet, despite the differences, which should be bringing peace to his soul, he found himself cast into a quandary of uncertainty. Something was causing an uneasy feeling within him, and he didn't like it. He felt himself evolving, and it frightened him. What would it require of him in the future? He didn't like uncertainty, and these new feelings brought along with them an unsure feeling about himself and his future. He was not, by nature, an adventuresome soul—yet this was an unknown adventure he was beginning. He felt uneasy about it. Religions always dealt with martyrs—which worried him a lot.

But it wasn't only the unknown future that plagued him, there was something else—or someone else: Stephanie. She was complicated—perhaps too complicated for him to understand. At one time, she was laughing and playful, with a sharp sense of humor. Other times she was quiet, serene, lost within her thoughts. At one time she would appear as a vulnerable small girl in some ways, yet in another, the navy officer: aloof, analytical, commanding. He found the dichotomy confusing, unpredictable, and well, worrisome. Still, he found himself growing fond of all her varied hues. That worried him too.

How did his life accumulate so many worries? He considered himself a very simple man, and he liked only simple problems. These were not. Andy stretched, looking out his small window that allowed sunlight during the day and the maddening, reflective light of the spacecraft overhead at night. Now, as the sun settled in the west, a thin veil of clouds captured its red rays, lighting up a fiery display of flames whose elongated tongues stretched eastward into the darkening blues and blacks of the approaching night. Andy got up reluctantly and put on his jacket. It was time for the sunset gathering.

It even had a name: Last Day Watch. Though all knew the name, no one ever used it. Sarah didn't like it. They simply referred to it as the Sunset Gathering, or Sunset. Each evening most everyone could be found on the sloping hillside in front of the main cabin. From here, they had a clear view of the mountain across the valley, and most importantly, the winding ribbon of mountain road skirting the mountain's edges. Eventually the ribbon of road led to them. It was the road Andy and Stephanie had traveled when he first came. Sitting here after sunset was more than a pleasant ritual, it was a vigil. They were all waiting to see what might be coming up the road. Andy learned that when their time came, Sarah had said they would see a caravan of lights coming up this mountain road at sunset.

Andy joined them tonight, not to wait for the lights so much, as for the beautiful view of the valley and mountains beneath them, bathing in the red hues of sunset. In the summer, couples stood holding hands or lay on the grass, while the sun went seeking someone else's dawn. It was the best and worst time of the day. Until the sun fully set and darkness covered them, there was a sense of nervous expectation; but once the dark was deep and no headlights appeared across the valley, a feeling of euphoria would reign. There was song and laughter. It appeared to Andy a strange juxtaposition. On one hand, they were waiting with anticipation for the end to come, and on the other, rejoicing when it didn't.

Tonight, as most nights now, there was a nip to the evening air and many wore sweaters. Andy sat alone enjoying the others and the beauty of the evening. Suddenly Andy felt someone behind him. Turning he saw Stephanie.

"Got a minute?" she asked

"Sure," replied Andy, motioning her to sit.

"Hear anything more from Sarah?" asked Stephanie. She hadn't spoken to him about anything other than mundane day-to-day things in the months he'd been there. Everyone including her left him alone, almost careful not to engage in any deep conversations. She could see it was beginning to bug Andy.

"No, not really—I assume you mean specifically about my future?"

"Yes."

"Nope," Andy said. "Nothing. In fact, I was just sitting here thinking the opposite—how the future, or even the present, doesn't appear to intrude here. It surprises me how little circumstances of the world seem to influence the daily lives here. It's as though we are on some grand vacation trip in the mountains. No talk about the aliens, of what they were going to do or not do, or how the rest of the world is faring. It's as if the rest of the world didn't exist. Most conversations I run into are built around the vegetables they hope to harvest and preserve. Repairs in the camp. Gas. Supplies. Everything except the most fundamental thing we all share: aliens."

Stephanie took a deep, relaxed breath. "Yes. Can you blame them? I don't care how one prepares for death, or what one's views of it are, death is still a scary thing. Sorta like going to the dentist."

Andy chuckled. "You musta had a really, really bad experience with the tooth fairy."

Suddenly a voice shouted from the cabin. "Come here—something's up on the tube!"

Once inside the crowded cabin, they saw a special broadcast was beginning. Normally, the TV was not turned on except at night for the news—the one time during the day the outer world was allowed in the camp. Tonight an alien, one they'd not seen before, was on screen. He was big, much bigger than others they'd seen, with a robe of slightly different color combinations, deep red with a white hem. There was gold around the edges and a white collar. He stood with his arms folded while another alien by his side, smaller in stature, was speaking. His voice was resonant, with a tone betraying authority. He was in the middle of his speech.

"…In these cases, signs and wonders seem to be the only answer," he said. "In fact, isn't that how your religions allegedly got started? Therefore, now we will show you a sign—a wonder. Watch the night skies tonight." With those words, the image faded and the talking heads came back to drone on, repeating what had just been said, as though no one else had been listening.

The group around the TV did not wait, but immediately went outside into the clear night. Above, the alien spacecraft hung in the cool, cloudless evening. Stephanie grabbed a blanket wrapping it around her. The group waited for the better part of an hour, and then suddenly from the southern sky, low on the horizon, and streaking in a north-easterly direction, roared a giant fireball meteor. Then it was gone, followed a few seconds later by a sonic boom that shattered the front window of the cabin.

For a moment, all were frozen, then as if of one mind, they rushed back to the cabin. Andy and Stephanie squeezed in with the others, moments before the TV game show was interrupted again. This time the newscaster was visibly shaken, shouting that a meteor of unusual size hit midway between Europe and the United States. The impact was such that people in New York saw the explosion. The size of the impact was not global; however, a large tidal wave was expected and was, at that very moment, rushing toward both Europe and the United States. The program switched to the University of Maryland where a man was being interviewed. The interview was chaotic, with questions coming from all sides and no one waiting for the answer.

"Please. Please!" the man shouted. "I will tell you, if you will allow me. This tidal wave will hit our East Coast in about an hour and twenty minutes. From the size of impact, we have determined the height of this wave will exceed one hundred feet." His statement was answered with shouts from all sides—then, suddenly the program was interrupted by the image of the same alien who had spoken earlier. For a moment, he looked without expression into the camera. His intense dark blue eyes seemed to be penetrating through the camera lens into their very room. His unwavering stare made Andy uncomfortable. Finally, a small smile played across his face.

"You see your scientists are at a loss. What to do? What to do? As I speak, a gigantic tidal wave is speeding its way toward both Europe and the U.S. There is no escape from it. Flight is hopeless. This meteor is not the sign I wanted to show you. No, what I want to show you is this: Your best minds have arrived at the unalterable conclusion that within minutes thousands of people will die. They say it is a fact. I say it is not. Already we have taken steps to alter the wave—no tidal wave will hit the coast of any nation."

In the room Andy looked around, and saw the others were doing the same.

Again the alien spoke. "We are working what many would call a miracle right now. However, we don't call it a miracle, we call it science and it can be yours too. Come join us. Be part of a future with rewards beyond your dreams."

Andy felt someone touch his right shoulder. It was Sarah and she motioned him to follow her outside. With Sarah leading, they walked until out of earshot from the cabin. Finally she stopped and faced Andy.

"Andy, I have a favor to ask of you," she said.

"Sure."

"You remember Robert, the bartender at the hotel?"

"Yes, Robert. You know him?"

"Yes, I do. He needs someone to come and bring him here."

"He's one of you?

"Yes, remember I told you someone called me about you needing help?"

"It was Robert?"

Sarah nodded. "Robert has been a good friend of ours for a long time. Now he needs our help."

"Why doesn't he just drive himself out here? No car?"

"He has a car, but he doesn't know where we are. He's never been here. In fact, I've never met Robert. I have no idea what he looks like. You do."

"I see. So you need someone to bring him here? Sure, I'll go get him."

"It could be risky. Every day it gets more dangerous for people of faith. Here we are hidden from the Eli, the evil one, but out there, you must be very careful."

"I see. I wondered why he hadn't come for you yet. He doesn't know where we are, right?"

"Exactly. We've been hidden here from his view, but that will change one day. Now, about this trip. I should tell you I don't have good feelings about going into the city. I don't have good feelings at all. You have been there before and someone may recognize you. Nevertheless, Robert has been a loyal friend and has helped saved many people. Those people have moved on, and now you are the only one here who has actually met him, and knows what he looks like."

"I understand. I feel obligated to go after him."

Sarah smiled, but it was without joy. "Yes, I was certain you would feel that way. I've already spoken to Stephanie about going with you. She is very familiar with routes and has been out on several rescue missions. With her military awareness, I think you have an edge. In fact, she's on the way over to the garage to get the car now. Come, I'll walk you there."

"I feel I should be saying something to prevent Stephanie from going, since it might be dangerous, but I've seen her in action and I think maybe I'm the weak link here." Andy smiled. "Should I be concerned that you don't have good feelings about this?"

"Yes, I think you should. I'll tell you what I feel and you can make of it what you will. I sense this will not go well, yet, that it's necessary. Somehow, this trip is very important, a major piece to the puzzle of our destiny and of yours. I think you'll have to make some important decisions. Therefore, I tell you this: all that you must require of yourself is that the decisions you make rest easy with your soul."

"I see," he said slowly. "Perhaps Stephanie shouldn't go, after all. I can find my way into the city and to the hotel. I don't need Stephanie for that."

"No, I want someone to go with you and Stephanie is that person."

Reaching the garage area, he found the car was already pulled out and running with Stephanie in the driver's seat, waiting. She smiled as Andy opened the passenger door. "So a new adventure begins."

Andy's brow crinkled. "I'm not sure I'm as happy as you seem to be."

Saying goodbye to Sarah, they headed out toward the city and found few cars on the road. These days gas was too precious to waste on trivial trips and cars were usually bedded down after work.

"I was told he's at the same hotel where we picked you up at—that right?"

"Yes, same one."

"What's with that hotel, why so popular?"

"He works there." Andy's answers were short. His mind was still on Sarah's warnings.

Stephanie didn't answer, and the two drifted into a long silence lasting most of the way into town. Finally, Stephanie turned the corner allowing them to enter the rear of the hotel. Andy could see the door where they escaped last time a hundred feet or so away. Near to it was the rear entrance of the hotel. Stephanie pulled into the parking lot searching out a space next to the road and several hundred feet from the hotel entrance. She backed into the parking space, which allowed them to see the entrance, then turned off the lights but not the motor.

"I think maybe we should watch for a little while, just to see."

Andy grunted.

They waited for half an hour. Finally Andy stirred. "I think it's time to go."

Stephanie turned the lights on and slowly drove to a space near the door where she parked and turned the motor off.

"Okay, I won't be long," said Andy.

"I'm going with you."

"No. Best you wait here with the car."

"I'm coming along," she said, opening her door before Andy could reply.

Letting out a long sigh of exasperation, he walked with her through the hotel doors. Andy led the way into the bar. It was deserted and the lights were out. Only enough light found its way into the bar to allow walking in safely. Andy looked at Stephanie and shrugged his shoulders. "This is where he works, he's the bartender here."

"Bar's closed for sure, now what?"

Andy hesitated. He didn't want to go to the desk and ask, certainly after the incident when he last visited here. "He's probably in his room, told me he stays in a room in the hotel. The room number was his lucky number for the lottery, but I can't remember it—oh wait, one-two-two-five-five, that's it. One-two-two-five-five."

"I doubt there's a room number that high." responded Stephanie

"The last five he doubles when playing. The room is one-two-two-five."

Quickly he and Sarah went to the elevators and up to the twelfth floor. Robert's room was down the hall and then to the left, second door.

Softly Andy knocked on the door. He gave the knockity-knock-knock rap. They waited a few moments before hearing the security chain unlatch, and slowly the door opened. Robert's eyes darted between Andy and Stephanie.

"Hey, how ya doin', buddy?" asked Andy in a half whisper as he entered the room.

Robert was silent. His face was unsmiling and bruised. There was a large, recent welt on his left cheek, and a cut on his forehead. He preceded Andy and Stephanie through the narrow hall into the bedroom.

"Hey, why so glum? We've come to take you out of this."

A strange voice came from behind, "I'm sure you have, Mr. Moore." Both he and Stephanie whipped around. Standing in the doorway was a uniformed police officer, and behind him, men in plain clothes. "We've been waiting for you quite a while."

"Who are you?" demanded Andy.

"I am the region consul, and I've come to take you to the regional director. "

"On what charge?"

"A felony warrant issued by the regional director himself."

Instead of replying, Andy turned and looked at Robert.

The look on Robert's face told of his inner anguish. "I'm sorry, Andy. They made me do it; I didn't have a choice. You don't understand, they can make anyone do anything, Andy, anyone do anything." There was desperation in Robert's voice.

"It's okay, Robert, I understand. So," said Andy, turning back to the officer, "what now?"

"The three of you will come with us. That's all you need to know."

Quietly Andy, Stephanie, and Robert exited the room to find several other officers waiting. They were told to face the wall. Then each was approached and had their hands pulled behind their back. Andy could feel the hard metal handcuffs against his wrists.

Suddenly there was a commotion to his right. He saw Robert turn and grapple with one of the sheriffs. A shot rang out, nearly deafening in its report. Robert turned slowly toward Andy. A look of surprise was frozen on his face. He tried to speak but collapsed on the floor.

"You didn't have to kill him, he was unarmed!" shouted Andy.

"Shut your face!" shouted one officer who wore two stripes. "Or I'll put a bullet in you too. Your kind doesn't deserve to live!"

Andy looked at Stephanie, who pursed her lips, giving a look imploring Andy to settle down, which he did. They were taken out of the hotel lobby where a number of guests had gathered in response to the police cars outside and the gunshot.

Placed inside the police cruiser, they were driven in silence to the Dunlop Towers, located downtown. Once the twin towers were part of a large office building housing the sheriff's department on the bottom three floors—as well as two different insurance companies, and one of the city offices, along with an assortment of other businesses on the upper floors. Now it was completely occupied by the regional director and his offices.

Inside the building Stephanie and Andy were taken by elevator to the lower level, where instead of being processed, they were placed in a holding cell together, and their handcuffs were removed. All this was done with minimal communication. Both remained silent until left alone in the cell.

"Any bright ideas?" asked Stephanie after checking to see if they were truly alone.

Andy shook his head. "Just play out the string, I guess. We'll see what develops."

"They didn't have to shoot that man."

Andy shook his head slowly, "No, they didn't. Robert was a good man. Wonder what possessed him to do what he did?"

"Desperation, I guess."

"Well, that's about where I am now."

"Right," agreed Stephanie, "Let's be ready for our opportunity. Be ready at a moment's notice to do whatever needs to be done to get out of here. I'm very sorry about Robert. You two were friends?"

Andy nodded. "Yes, I'd known him for many years. Used to stay at that hotel when I was in town. We developed a good friendship. I'll miss him. Right now, though, we gotta think about ourselves. I saw only three guards here: The two that processed us, and the one turnkey outside the door."

"Yeah, well, I'm sure there are more," answered Stephanie.

"That's a problem we'll have to deal with later, first we need to get out of this cell and I'm thinking our best chance is to try and take the two guards, then go for the turnkey."

Stephanie nodded. "We'll play this by ear, but no stupid moves or we'll both end up like Robert."

Suddenly, the sounds of approaching feet and then four guards appeared at their cell, and the cell door was opened. The lead guard wordlessly motioned them outside the cell saying simply, "Follow me."

"Where to?" demanded Andy.

"You'll find out," came the curt reply. The guard turned, leading the way. No cuffs were used, which surprised both Andy and Stephanie.

Andy glanced quickly at Stephanie, then followed. The lead guard and another walked in front, followed by the other two. From the way they were being led, Andy felt they were being guided as guests rather than prisoners. They were taken to an elevator and then up several floors, where they exited into a waiting room of someone important; lavish chairs surrounded the room along walls bearing artwork that wasn't cheap. Nor was the carpeting that adorned the room. On the far side, a woman was seated behind a desk. She rose as the four exited the elevator, then disappeared behind two large double doors leading to someone's office.

The lead guard stopped, holding up his hand for them to stop also, which they did. The four stood silently for several minutes until the woman emerged again, this time holding open the door.

"The Regional Director will see you now."

The guards accompanied them to the door, then halted, allowing Andy and Stephanie to enter alone. The door was closed silently behind them, and for a minute, there was absolute silence. The large office appeared deserted. Walls on either side of the entrance door were actually long bookshelves, though only half full. A large ornate desk with an equally large chair faced them along with the backs of two large armchairs facing the desk. Behind the desk were several French doors opening onto a large patio area on the roof of the building.

Besides the desk and the chairs facing the desk, the only other pieces of furniture in the room were a Lazy Boy recliner off to their left, facing a large screen television. Not at all what Andy would have expected from a highly placed administrator in the New World government.

"Mister Moore and Ms. Collins?" The voice came from the balcony behind the large desk. Andy and Stephanie walked toward the sound, through the French doors, onto the sunlit balcony.

"Yes, that's right," said Andy when they were on the balcony, which opened up to an impressive view. The city could be seen, as well as some of the near-suburbs. Andy saw a portly man standing by the wall. He was middle-aged, with a round body and thinning hair. He stood with hands on hips and wore a slight smile. "Come here, have a seat," he said with a friendly voice and a smile, motioning toward a round table with four padded chairs around it. He took one chair and Andy and Stephanie followed. "My name is Bernard Krantz, my friends—

when I had friends—called me Bernie. I'm the regional director. I'm deeply sorry to hear about your friend's unfortunate death. I assure you, I had no intention of harming him, or you either."

"There was no need to shoot him, to murder him," replied Andy, keeping his tone even and under control.

"You are absolutely right, and the deputy who did that will be severely punished, I assure you."

"Why are we here? Are we going to be marked?"

Bernie looked around, then leaned closer. "No, and when you speak please lower your voice. My office is bugged, as is every room in the building. Out here on the balcony there aren't any bugs, we can talk; however, let's keep our voices low in case the mikes in the office pick something up."

Andy exchanged glances with Stephanie.

"I know, I know," continued Bernie. "Sounds goofy, but I need your help."

"With what?" asked Andy, a note of suspicion in his voice.

"I want you to help me escape."

"Escape? From what? You don't need our help, just walk out the door."

Bernie glanced nervously around. "Please, keep your voice down. You don't understand—I know how they work. They know everything. There's nowhere I could hide that they wouldn't find me. Every day I wake up feeling trapped. I can't take it anymore. What they are having me do is no less than murder. I'm a part of a holocaust greater than that of World War II. But I can't stop it, I can't. I'm just riding a wave that will drown us all soon. I want out. You won't believe this, but I'm a Bible-believing man."

"You're right, I don't believe that," said Andy.

"Well, no one would confuse me with a fanatic Christian, but I believe in God. Thought I didn't for a long time, but the longer this goes on, the more I do. This is something straight out of hell. Believe me, I know—I'm part of it."

"I don't know what to say," ventured Stephanie softly after some silence. "When did all of this come to you?"

"It didn't all come to me in one swoop. It's been slow, over a period of time. Things I see and have to do. I remember some of the things my mother taught me—now, she was a Bible lady if ever there was one. But I just shoved it all aside, thought it was a bunch of stories made up by old people to comfort other old people and scare kids.

Silence fell over the three again as Andy and Stephanie digested what the regional director said. The director waited patiently.

At last Andy broke the silence. "Let me get this straight." You, the most powerful man of the eastern half of this state, who has everything he could want just by asking, with the power to do anything with anybody at anytime, you say you want out. Is that right?

Bernie nodded

"I don't buy it. Why do you want out? Why didn't it occur to you not to get in?"

Bernie held up his hand imploring Andy to speak quietly. "I understand how this may sound to you, but it's true. I was caught up in this. I had no idea what it would involve. At first, I thought it was great. I was the same as everyone else in believing their story. It seemed so logical. And, I admit it, I was thrilled when I was chosen." Bernie paused and looked past Andy toward his office for a moment, holding up a finger to silence. Then, when satisfied, continued. "But then they started talking crazy stuff, at least I thought it sounded crazy. You know, like we gotta get everybody to worship the aliens and make them gods of some kind, and then we are all gods too. We just gotta tidy up the planet by exterminating all the Jews, Christians, and Muslims."

"Is that what they plan on doing, exterminating them?"

Bernie nodded. "There's no way to make the faithful convert or get them to deny their faith. Sure, some do, but I think their association with the church must have been pretty shallow. I'm talking about millions and millions who are true believers. They will never convert, so the plan is to exterminate them all."

Andy looked at Stephanie who was shaking her head. "And how do you feel about that?" asked Stephanie.

"I don't want to be a part of that. I can't be a part of this any longer."

Andy rose and walked a few paces away, turned, and retraced his steps. "Look, I think we need some time to think about what you've said."

"Of course you do. I have to return you to your cells though. It would look very suspicious if I were to release you, or give you guest quarters. However, I assure you, orders will be given to treat you well and supply any need you may have."

"Thank you."

Bernie called for the guards and Stephanie and Andy were soon back in the semi-dark and somewhat humid cell. The two sat in silence for a long time. Finally Andy went to the cell door and shouted for the guard, who came immediately. His attitude evidenced he'd been told to treat them well.

"Is it possible to have a radio?"

"A radio? I will see," said the guard hurrying off, only to reappear in a few minutes with a small clock radio.

Andy thanked him. He turned the radio on, cranking up the volume. He scooted over to sit next to Stephanie. "I'm sure these cells are bugged, but the radio should cover our conversation."

Stephanie nodded.

"Give me your take on this Bernie fellow."

"It's crazy. Do you believe him?"

"I don't know. One side says, 'No way, Jose'; the other side keeps reminding me that it could be possible. He would be a great help to the camp. He knows so much about the aliens and their operations."

"Yes, he would be a great coup for sure. I'm sure with his help we could save a lot of suffering."

"Still, I don't know," said Andy slowly. "This could all just be a fake, a clever plan for us to reveal where Sarah and the group are located."

"Exactly," said Stephanie "and if there was a way to do it, this would be it."

"So what do we do. Say no?"

"That's my vote."

"Course, if we do say no, it will probably mean our death," said Andy.

"Yes. I don't like that part of the plan."

"No," said Andy, then pausing for a moment before resuming. "How about this? We agree to take him. Then somewhere between here and there we dump him and make our get-away?"

Stephanie sat a moment thinking. "Sounds good, also simple. Maybe too simple."

"Yeah, well sometimes the simplest is the best."

"Let's hope so. I say let's think about it a little while and see. If we feel that's the best plan we can come up with, we do it."

Andy nodded, moving over to turn the radio's volume down. For a few moments both were quiet, lost in private thoughts. "Steph?" said Andy, finally.

"Yeah?"

"Is Robert in heaven right now?"

"I think so. Some say he will sleep until the Rapture, but I think that the dead in Christ live now in heaven. They watch us and are interceding for us, I think."

"Really. So you think Robert is watching over us right now?"

"Possibly. I think a lot of people, and angels, watch over us. But don't go asking me in-depth questions—how, what, why, when. I just don't know."

For a few moments the cell was given over to just the soft sounds of the radio.

"Steph?"

"Yeah?"

"I'm glad I met you."

"I'm glad I met you too and don't call me Steph."

"No, I mean really glad. You are a wonderful person and I wish I were younger. You'd have to beat me away with a stick."

The soft music played, violins echoing off the cell walls.

"I wouldn't need a stick, I'm trained."

"Oh, yeah."

"And who says I'd beat you away?"

CHAPTER 12

I See You

TWO HOURS LATER the sounds of a key against metal echoed down the corridor followed by the approaching sound of boots. Two guards arrived, and both appeared to be in a friendly frame of mind.

"The regional director instructed that we were to give you the best treatment and food." He signaled the barred door to be opened, walking in as soon as it was. "See, we have here hot dogs, hamburgers, French fries, and coffee—is there anything else you would like?"

"Yes," said Stephanie. "A woman's bathroom and some privacy."

For a second the guard seemed embarrassed, but recovered. "Oh yes, of course, please follow me."

Andy attacked his plate and was surprised at how good the food tasted. Minutes later Stephanie returned and Andy reached over and turned up the radio volume.

"So what's your decision?" he asked.

"On dumping him?"

Andy nodded.

"I think it's the way to go. The best of two worlds: We get outta here and we lose him."

"Agreed. So someplace between here and the camp we need to pull over for something and then get him outta the car. We'll just have to wait for the right time."

Stephanie mumbled her agreement while devouring the last of her hamburger.

The guard returned announcing that the director wanted to see them. They were led on the same path as originally taken and found the director on the porch again, only this time he seemed decidedly more nervous.

"Have you thought it over?"

Andy looked at Stephanie first. "Yes. We've decided to help you escape. But have you a plan to get us out of here?"

Bernie was enthusiastic. "Yes, yes I do. I have a van waiting for us down in the garage. I will be taking you. My story is, you have decided to cooperate and you are going to lead me to some hideaway for rebels—" Bernie stopped, seeing the expressions on his guests' faces. "Sounds too real? Oh it's just a ruse to explain why I'm taking you outta here. Besides, no one will question me, but it's always best to be prepared. Any questions?"

Andy and Stephanie shook their heads, then Andy held up his index finger. "You're just leaving, without any goodbyes, bringing nothing but the clothes on your back?"

Bernie smiled "Well, no, not quite. I packed a couple of suitcases last night and they are in the van."

"Oh, okay, we're ready if you are."

"Fine. Now, walk in front of me, and I'll tell you where to go. Make sure your demeanor is solemn, and don't walk too fast."

Making their way out into the hall, the three went down the elevator and into the lobby. Far from being challenged, or even asked where they were going, the influence of the regional director was such that people stepped aside, soldiers saluted, and a few civilians even bowed. From the lobby, they went down two flights of stairs to the underground parking garage. In a parking space reserved for him sat the director's van. They were getting in when a voice came from behind.

"Director, sir."

Bernie turned, smiling. "Hello, colonel, how are you?"

"Fine, thank you, Director. Aren't these the two prisoners I saw taken in here last night?"

"Yes," said Bernie; his voice was very relaxed. "You're right, they were brought in last night."

"Are you sure you should be going alone with them anywhere, sir?"

"Oh, not to worry, colonel, they have decided to help and are leading me now to some information that will enable us to round up quite a few rebels."

The colonel nodded slowly, looking over both Andy and Stephanie. "I don't think it's a good idea for you to be with them alone, sir."

"I appreciate your concern, but everything is in hand," said Bernie, turning back toward the van, but the colonel's voice stopped him.

"Sir, I insist I come along, for your protection." He patted his side arm.

For a moment Bernie hesitated. "But I am well armed." Bernie pulled a forty-five caliber pistol from beneath his cloak.

"Nonetheless, sir, I insist. It is, in fact, in the orders that no member of the Brethren should be alone with rebels at any time."

Bernie sighed and said, "Very well colonel, come sit in the back with me and we will let these two drive."

The four climbed into the van and were soon on the expressway headed north. Andy did not look at Stephanie fearing he might betray something with his face, but wished he knew what she was thinking. What of their plan? What of Bernie's plan? They traveled in silence.

Bernie leaned forward as they approached the Route 21 exit. "Take this exit north," he said, calmly.

Andy nodded. Once on Route 21, Bernie seemed to be looking for something as he sat forward in the rear seat examining each road they passed. Finally, he commanded they turn onto a gravel side road, and soon after directed them onto a narrow gravel trail that could have been someone's long driveway, though there was no house in sight.

"Stop here," stated Bernie. Andy brought the van to a halt and upon Bernie's command all four got out. Andy saw that Bernie's gun was drawn, as was the colonel's.

"What now, Director?" said the colonel over his shoulder to Bernie as he kept his gun focused on Andy and Stephanie.

Bernie approached them, his gun also pointed in Andy's direction. "This," he responded, slowly redirecting the gun to the rear of the colonel's head and pulling the trigger.

The gun roared, hurling its lethal hot lead into the colonel's head, exploding the left temple, and flinging blood to the side and front.

Andy and Stephanie jumped back instinctively when blood landed on their clothes. Stephanie gave a short scream, then became silent.

The colonel's head flew sideways and for a second he remained standing with his right arm pointed at an angle to the ground. His own gun slowly released from his hand, and he collapsed soundlessly in a heap.

Moments passed before anyone said anything. Bernie broke the silence. "I regret that I had to do that, but there was no choice. He was dead from the moment I could not talk him out of coming."

"Couldn't we have just dropped him off?" asked Stephanie.

"No. They would have found us sooner than you think. They are all connected, you see. There may not be a telephone handy, but they are able to communicate. Not clearly, but enough that they can figure things out fairly quickly." Bernie shoved the revolver beneath his robe's pocket and motioned his traveling companions back toward the car. "We have to go now, no telling how long we'll have."

Andy turned to Bernie. "I will have to have that gun."

"Of course," replied Bernie as he offered the revolver.

"Thank you," said Andy. "Excuse us for a few seconds, I need to talk to Stephanie." He and Stephanie walked a few paces out of earshot. "What's up?" asked Stephanie.

"I'm wondering if we are doing the right thing."

"You mean dumping him?"

Andy nodded. "After what he just did, seems like he might be sincere."

Stephanie nodded. "True. But, so what?"

"He would be a great asset to our little family. He knows the aliens frontward and backward. He'd be able to let us know how they think, what to look out for, and who knows what else? He's been to those pyramids, and with his position—well, I just think he might be of great value to us."

Stephanie paused thoughtfully. "If you recall, that's what I said before."

"Do you think Sarah would agree?"

Stephanie was quiet for a moment. "I think she would."

"Okay then, he comes with us."

Stephanie nodded. They returned to Bernie wordlessly motioning him into the car. It didn't take long until they were on the road to the camp. Nearing the mountain road to the camp, Stephanie used Bernie's cell phone to make the call. When someone answered, she kept the message very short, "Tell mom we'll be home soon." After disconnecting, she did not return the cell phone to Bernie. "Sorry, can't have this where we are going."

"I understand."

Andy followed the routine, driving past their road to see if anyone was following, then returning. Finally, an hour after sunset, they arrived at the cabin in the dark.

"Looks like we have a welcoming committee," said Andy as they pulled up to the main cabin. It was difficult to tell, but all indications were that everyone was waiting for them. As the three emerged from the car, two men approached Bernie.

"Please follow us, Director." Then, looking over Andy's way added, "Andy, we need you to come too."

Andy gave a quick look at Stephanie, who shrugged her shoulders. The small group went to the cabin, and into one of the two main-floor bedrooms. As Andy entered the room, he was surprised to see every bit of furniture had been removed except for three straight-back chairs that lined the wall to his left. Next to the chairs, a door led to a connecting room, and to his right, on the far opposite wall, was a set of rings newly attached to the wall approximately 7 feet from the floor.

Sarah was sitting in one of the straight-back chairs; the others were vacant. Besides Sarah, in the room were the two escorts, himself, and against the far wall opposite Sarah, four men standing.

Andy approached Sarah. "Sarah, about Robert. He—"

"I know," she interrupted without looking at him, but continuing to focus upon Bernie.

The two escorts stopped, remaining close to the director, their hands thumbed inside their front slacks. Everyone was quiet. Bernie's director's robe hung in large folds from his shoulders ending four inches from the floor. He stood with his arms in front, hands clasped, and appeared relaxed.

Sarah rose from her chair, clasping her hands behind her. "You have arrived," she said softly, but there was no smile. Instead, she appeared tense, almost strained.

Bernie smiled "Yes, thank God—I didn't really think we'd make it, but we did—though it wasn't without problems. I'll let Andy and Stephanie fill you in on that!"

Sarah approached Bernie closer and leaned forward, looking into his eyes for a few moments. Seemingly satisfied, she straightened up and stepped back a few paces.

She placed her hands together as if praying, but instead rested the tips of her clasped fingers beneath her chin. "I say again, I know that you have arrived."

"I apologize, Sarah, but I don't understand what it is you want me to say, yes I'm here." Bernie's voice showed his confusion, and he looked toward Andy for some direction.

"Mr. Krantz, please remain quiet," said Sarah, a note of slight irritation showing in her voice. Again, she spoke to Bernie. "I am speaking to you, and I command you to answer!" Sarah's voice rose as she spoke.

Suddenly, there was a low growl from Bernie as he lowered his head. His brown eyes took on a dull red cast and, though they were half hidden by his brow, looked up at Sarah. His mouth dropped open and saliva dripped from his lips. Again, the deep growl came from him. Finally, he spoke; his voice had a deep gravel-rasp, and was filled with contempt.

"I found you, Sarah." Suddenly, Bernie's face broke into a wicked smile and he roared with laughter. The volume was almost too much for Andy to bear. As quickly as his laughter started, it ended. He lowered his face, peering up with a look of hatred toward Sarah. "Yes, I found you. You hid for a long time, but I found you. You didn't think I would find you, did you? But I did."

Sarah had not moved, nor had her expression changed. "Yes, you found us, and we are ready."

Bernie seemed in a daze. He stood swaying while his red eyes rolled up. His voice was low and kept repeating, "I found you, Sarah. I found you." He would then croak with a half laugh and repeat the words again.

Sarah nodded to the men along the wall who then approached Bernie and grabbed him from behind. Immediately, Bernie began struggling and his strength was surprising.

"Help them!" shouted Sarah.

Andy joined the others holding onto the struggling Bernie. Slowly they forced him back to the wall, tying his hands and feet to the rings in the wall. Stepping back, they watched the struggling man. There was concern in their eyes as they saw Bernie exerting much more strength than they suspected he could. However, the rings held.

Motioning Andy to follow, Sarah went out the door behind her. The incoherent growls and shouts followed them out the door.

"That was incredible!" Andy gasped after closing the door behind him. "Sarah, I'm so sorry. I thought he was okay—I mean, I had no idea. Should we kill him? I've heard of people being possessed, but I never actually saw it—never actually believed it, really. When he started speaking in that deep voice, I was scared—I don't mind admitting I was scared to death. I never heard such a thing. What are we going to do? If we have to kill him, I think I should be the one to do it. It's my fault he's here, only makes sense I should have to remedy that."

"Andy!" Sarah's voice had an edge to it. "You're babbling!"

"Huh? I am? Sorry."

"Yes," said Sarah quietly, "he's possessed. Within him right now is the evil one, Satan, the devil, the dark angel, or any other name you care to use. I wanted you to see that, and I want you to watch what we do next. It's important that you pay very close attention."

"What exactly is next?"

"Have you heard of exorcism?"

"Oh yes, exorcism. Yes, I've heard of it. It's when someone casts an evil spirit outta someone else. Can that really be done?"

"Yes, certainly. Christ did it, the apostles did it, and many of their followers did it. It's a well-recognized procedure in churches. In the very early Catholic Church they even had a small select group of priests whose sole responsibility was to cast out demons."

"You can do that?"

"Yes. You can do it too, all men and women of faith can do it."

"I don't think I can do it."

"You will. That's why I want you to watch and pay close attention. I think the time will come when you will need to do this. True, now you don't think you can, don't understand it, even fear it; however, in the fullness of time, you will do it."

Sarah went to a table where her Bible lay. Picking it up, she turned the pages until she was satisfied. "I am going to pray. Please be quiet as I do. I simply am going to call upon God to strengthen me to this purpose. Remember Andy, though many think there are a lot of preparations to be made, physical things like certain branches, or drinks, and so forth, they are not necessary. The key ingredients are only two things: faith and God's word." With that she knelt down and read softly to herself as Andy stood by watching.

Rising, she opened the door to the adjoining room. Against the far wall, Bernie seemed quiet, but upon seeing Sarah began to struggle again with the lines that bound him. His red robe was disheveled, and near the hem, a tear had been ripped, probably by his foot stepping on it while he struggled.

Silently Sarah approached until she was within 6 feet of him. "I've come to set you free, Bernie," she said, her voice almost a whisper.

Immediately, Bernie began screaming and struggling against the chains that bound him. His curses reverberated off the barren walls. Then, leaning forward and staring directly at Sarah, he vomited, spewing dark bile like a projectile at Sarah, but the putrid liquid splashed down at her feet. She looked him in the eye silently for a minute or two, then spoke. "I come to you by the authority of Jesus Christ, Satan, and with the power of His word, I speak to you. Loose this man from your grip, I command you to leave this body that belongs to Christ!"

Suddenly Bernie's struggling stopped, and he leaned forward in his lines and the deep raspy voice of Satan came from his lips. "Who do you think you are?" he snapped. His voice was deep, rumbling through the room with a volume that made Andy want to cover his ears. "I am no servant to you, you piece of dirt made to walk! I do not serve you!" Bernie's head pushed forward until it could reach no further, then a shape detached from his face. It was that of an animal, the likes of which Andy had only seen in horror films. It came toward Sarah until it was within inches of her.

Sarah did not flinch, but maintained her steadfast gaze upon him.

"So you are Sarah. Why have I feared you—you are nothing!" A sound resembling a low chortle rumbled from his turned-up lips escaping through his jagged teeth. "The end is near Sarah, it is near. Soon you all will die, and then your God will have no one to speak his name, except to curse him."

Finally, Sarah spoke. Her voice was steady betraying neither fear nor anger, but had an air of authority and power about it. "I speak to you with the authority of Jesus Christ granted to me by his sacrifice and empowered by the holy word of the Almighty Creator, the living God Yewah, and to His words, and to His authority through Christ, you must yield! Release this body and depart!"

Bernie roared as though in pain. Focusing in on Sarah again, his bright red eyes mere slits, his face contorted by hate, spittle dripping from his lips. "I'm coming for you, Sarah. Do you hear me, Sarah? I'm coming for you, and I'm going to kill you. I am going to kill you!" Suddenly a dark shape, not solid, but darkly translucent, flowed out of Bernie. It was only for a second, but the face was awesome, appearing like some prehistoric gruesome terror, then it was gone as quickly as it appeared.

Bernie sagged in the shackles, hanging unconscious.

Sarah seemed to weave for a moment, and Andy rushed forward to steady her.

"I'm fine," she said. "Release him and get him to the couch in the other room. Get that robe off him, clean him up, and get him some suitable clothes. And clean up this filthy mess."

The men rushed to meet her demands. Sarah turned and smiled weakly at Andy. "Did you see it all?"

"Yes, it scared me half to death."

"The first time I saw it, I felt the same way. I want you to commit everything you saw here to memory and when the time comes don't let your fear prevent you from doing what has to be done. Lost souls depend upon it."

"I understand."

"I hope you do, but if you don't, you will. Now this Bernie fellow here—I don't want you or anyone else to hold anything against him. He was taken over and did the bidding of Satan, but now he is free. Now he will serve God, and Andy, he may help you. It was important that you went for him, important that you brought him here."

"Why?"

Sarah smiled small, but did not answer. Instead, she quietly left the room, obviously exhausted.

Andy rubbed his head. Why couldn't life be simple? Why couldn't he grow old and die peacefully? Why was Sarah talking to him like he was going to take over some job? He didn't want a job. All of this seemed to coalesce inside his stomach where he felt a tiny, but growing, ball of fear.

CHAPTER 13

Last Day

ANDY PAUSED BEFORE softly knocking. He waited, then knocked again. Still no response. Slowly he opened the door. Bernie Krantz, dressed in new jeans and a red-and-white checkered long-sleeve shirt, was standing, staring out the window. If Bernie knew Andy was there, he gave no indication. Andy waited a few moments before he spoke.

"Bernie, it's Andy."

Bernie did not reply, only a slight movement of his shoulders indicating he'd heard.

"I hear you're not eating much, and you rarely go outta this room," continued Andy. "Word is, if they didn't bring meals to you, you'd probably starve. So tell me, what's up? It's been nearly three weeks you've been here."

Turning his head, Bernie looked at Andy, then turned away. "Please leave," he muttered.

"If that's what you want, I will—but let's talk just for a second."

Bernie turned slowly to faces Andy. "And what is it you want to talk about?"

"Well, you. What are you feeling, why aren't you eating, when are you gonna leave this room? People want to meet you and they want to welcome you."

"Welcome me? No, I don't think so."

"Of course they do. You're thinking they don't want anything to do with you, right?"

"Of course—and I don't blame them. I would feel the same way. I'm responsible for betraying their hideout—do they know that?"

"Yes, we know."

"You know? You know! Don't you understand what that means? Any day now, they'll be here and who knows what's gonna happen when they arrive. At the very least, you'll be put into prison, or worse, killed on the spot!"

"We know, Bernie, we've known that for a long time now."

"I don't get it."

"Brother, do I know what you mean. Here I am explaining something to you that I am only just beginning to understand myself. All of these people here have been waiting for someone to come and get them, and they know they will die when it happens."

Bernie ran his right hand through his thinning hair. "They know that, and still they want to welcome me?"

"Yes, I know, it's hard to understand, but that's how it is. They're all followers of God's word, and believe God's word speaks of forgiveness. Let me ask you this: Are you sorry you brought this upon them?"

"Oh god, yes. I am so sorry, Andy. You don't understand how I feel. These past weeks, it's as though I'm alive again. Actually me again."

"The way you put it, sounds like you were drugged or something."

"No, no, not actually drugged. I wish I knew how to put it into words. When they came to me and said I had been selected for regional director, I was thrilled. I didn't have any idea what they were talking about, except it was an honor and it would bring me great authority and power." Bernie stopped for a moment, shaking his head. "Those are powerful drugs in themselves, Andy. Very powerful. Up until then I had a little radio show that had a small but loyal audience and my weeks were a string of TGIFs come and gone. That's all. Going nowhere, doing nothing. Now, here comes this power and prestige beyond anything I'd ever dreamed. Yes, I suppose I was drugged with pride. Finally, after all these years, I was going to really be somebody." Bernie paused for a moment, then nodded toward the window looking out on the neatly kept grass and Sarah's garden. "Whose garden?"

"Sarah's. I'll tell you about it sometime."

"Yes, Sarah." Bernie mused, allowing her name to die on his lips. "I was told about Sarah, you know—she's the one they sent me to get. Do you understand that?"

"They think she's that important?"

Bernie nodded. He took a deep sigh, and turned. "There's more: I knew her husband—and I knew your name as well."

"Really? Where did you know her husband from and how did you know my name?"

"I met him aboard ship before we went inside the pyramid. He told me his name was Cho or something like that. I didn't know it was TJ until later. They came and took him away and I never saw him again. He had a message I was supposed to give to you—he told me your name."

"Really, a message for me?"

"The message was: 'Sarah was right.'"

"That's what he told me to tell Sarah if he didn't return too," mused Andy. "So he gave you the same message to give her."

Bernie nodded

"Have you told Sarah this?"

"No. I will though."

"Tell me about these demons, these so-called aliens."

"What do you want to know?"

"I've only seen them on TV and a few pictures here and there, including a couple of posters. It's hard to really know what they are like in person. Are they as big as they appear?"

Bernie nodded. "Yes, very tall; and oddly, all the same height—except for Abdon. He's quite a bit taller than the others are. I'm told there are six more of the same rank as Abdon, with a seventh, the leader and commander of all, Eli. I hear that he's even bigger than Abdon—a lot bigger. I've never seen Eli, but they talk about him all the time. The rest of the aliens, or demons, are about six feet five. They are handsome people, all built like Greek statues. But, you know, I never see any women, just males. I always thought that was odd."

"Where did they tell you they were from?"

"They didn't. Always said it was too complicated for us to understand but promised to tell us soon, when we could understand."

"And now, you understand where they are from?"

Bernie sat down on the bed, nodding his head. "Yes, of course. They come from the bowels of hell itself."

Andy nodded in agreement. "Yeah, the first time I heard that it blew my mind." He sat down on the bed. "I just couldn't accept it, I guess. So I wonder if they are apparitions? You know, change shape and everything when humans aren't around? What do they really look like, have you seen?"

"I wish I could tell you, but I've never seen them, except as they appear to you. There was one time, but that was probably just an illusion, I mean I can't say I really saw them as different."

"You did, you didn't—what?"

"It was shortly after I was made director. I was in my office and had a visit from one of their messengers—sort of checking in to see how I was. It was all very friendly. As he left, I thought I saw an image out of the corner of my eye that wasn't human, something animal—like one of those dinosaur types with the big uglies. But it was only for a split-second 'cause when I turned to face him, he was just at he had been."

"What you're saying suddenly makes more sense to me than you might know. It's something that Sarah says now and then. I thought it was a little joke, but maybe it's not. I think we should go see Sarah. You can tell her about TJ and I can ask her something too."

"I don't know. The others, what do they think of me? Because of me, this place has been revealed, and they will be coming. Believe me, Andy, they will be coming."

Andy walked over and placed his hand on Bernie's shoulder. "First, once you get to know the others, you'll see that many have backgrounds every bit as bad as you think yours is. Understand one thing: Satan identified most of the people who became or will become enemies of evil long before they were aware that they were involved in a contest between good and evil. They are seduced, just as you were, into a life that should have kept them from ever discovering God's plan for them, but God found them, and rescued them—as he has you. Therefore, their past is often as bad, if not worse, than yours is. You are among friends here, people who understand what you are going through, because they've been there themselves."

Bernie smiled, then nodded. "Okay, let's go see Sarah."

Andy led Bernie out to the main room where several of the camp members sat around the main table chatting. Seeing Bernie and Andy enter, they rose and smiled. The first to greet Bernie was Jeff Clawson who approached and extended his hand. "Welcome. I hope you'll be happy here. Now, if there's anything any of us can do, please don't hesitate to ask."

Bernie shook his hand.

"Our friend Bernie is a little shy right now. He's afraid we will hold his past against him," volunteered Andy.

"Look, Bernie," said Clawson, "before coming here I was a detective with the New York Police Department. I was part of a special unit that sought out Anti-Unity people. That's what they were called then, you know, Anti-Unity. Our job was to identify them and bring them in. The ones who wouldn't change were put in prison—or worse." Clawson seemed to be stabbed by a moment of inner emotion and waited until it passed. "I felt just like you do now. I didn't think I would be accepted—how could they? I was one who persecuted them. But they did, and they have others too. Let's not talk about past sins anymore, okay?"

"Yes, agreed," said Bernie smiling. "Let's not."

"After all," Andy heard himself chime in, "I read where Paul, one of the great heroes of the Bible, was first a persecutor of Christians before becoming a hero of the word."

"Exactly," said Clawson's wife from the table. "So many of the heroes began on the opposite side of the tracks. Where are you two off to?"

"We are on our way to see Sarah."

"Ah, very good. I think she's upstairs in her room."

Bernie followed Andy up the stairs to one of the two doors. Knocking softly, Andy waited until he heard Sarah call them in. Opening the door, he found Sarah seated in her favorite high-back chair sipping a cup of tea. She smiled when they entered. "Well, I see our guest is up and about now. Tell me, how do you feel?"

"Very good, thanks to Andy here and the people downstairs. I can't remember when I've felt better. I need to tell you something before I am sidetracked. I saw TJ at the pyramid."

Sarah stopped midway in lifting her cup, remaining motionless for a moment. "You saw TJ?"

"Yes, we talked and teamed up."

Sarah put her cup down, then sat back in her chair. "Tell me about it."

Slowly at first, then with growing confidence, Bernie told about the helicopter, their assigned room, the speeches made, and finally how TJ was escorted out. "I never saw him again after that. But he did tell me about you. He asked me to give a message to Andy here and hopefully it would get to you. He said, 'Tell Sarah she was right.'"

Sarah remained quiet for a few moments. Finally, she reached over and retrieved her cup. "Thank you, Mr. Krantz, for telling me that. What are your plans now that you're whole again?"

The question seemed to take Bernie by surprise. "Plans? I don't have any. I thought I'd stay here with you, if that's all right?" The last said with a tone bordering on a plea.

Sarah put her tea down again. "Of course, that would be fine. However, understand, now that our hiding place has been discovered, they'll be coming for us. When they find us, I must tell you, they will kill us—and you."

Bernie instinctively put his hand to his mouth as though holding in the involuntary gasp he took. He stood silent for a moment staring at Sarah, then nodded. "Yes," he said softly, "that's what they will do." Bernie looked at Andy then back at Sarah. "Why don't we just leave? There must be other places we could go. It would at least buy some time until we could think of a plan. Surely you aren't going to stay here and simply wait?"

Andy cleared his throat. "That's exactly what they're doing. They're all waiting, and have been waiting for quite a while. They wait for a caravan of vehicles to come in the night."

"But we must all leave!" The urgency in Bernie's voice was obvious.

"Mr. Krantz," began Sarah patiently, "we're not running anymore. Dying is not the terrible thing you seem to imagine. We are going to be with God, and with our loved ones who have preceded us. Death is not a terrible monster. It's merely a portal through which we travel toward a wonderful reunion. Allow death a home in your mind and you'll find

there are many good things about death that make it almost a friend."
Sarah paused and smiled. "Now, the actual dying part, that's the
toughie." Sarah rose from her chair approaching Bernie. "Mr. Krantz,
you don't have to stay here and die with us. Andy isn't."

"You aren't?"

"No," said Andy. "I'll be leaving, and so will Stephanie."

"And you may leave with him," added Sarah

Bernie turned to Andy. "You and I? When?"

Andy shook his head, shrugging. "I don't know."

Bernie looked back at Sarah, confusion on his face.

"I see this is a bit overwhelming for you. I suggest you not worry
about it. All will be as it should at the right time. Your job is not to
figure out what, when, or how, but to be patient. Now, Mr. Krantz, if
you will excuse Andy and me, we have some things to discuss."

Bernie nodded, still puzzled. Turning, he walked silently out the
door, closing it softly behind him.

Sarah placed the teacup on the end table, and walked over to the
window that looked down upon her garden. "Time is short, Andy, very
short."

Andy nodded. "I understand."

"So you still feel you want to leave?"

"Yes." Andy shifted to the other foot and took a deep breath. He
hated disappointing Sarah. "I guess you must think I'm a coward or
something. I'll fight if you give me the opportunity, but I won't allow
them to kill me without that fight."

Sarah nodded thoughtfully. "I was certain you would feel that way,
and it has nothing to do with being a coward. Tell me one other thing,
what is it you are going to do? Do you know what lies ahead, do you
have a plan?"

Andy shook his head slowly. "I don't have a clue."

"Good. I find that hopeful." Sarah motioned toward a chair, telling Andy to have a seat, while she did the same, facing him. "I think
you are not going to stay because God has plans for you—and has had
them all your life, it's just now that your time is coming. Remember
our little talk about the flower blooming at the appointed time?"

"Yes."

"Now is your time to bloom. It won't be easy. It'll take a lot of courage and perseverance. You'll find you have a depth of faith you never suspected and you will need every bit of it. Andy, staying with us would be easier for you than what you will have to face in the future, but take heart: In the darkest days, remember death is your reward and it will be given to you when your task is done."

"Sarah, ever since I came here, you've sorta given me this mysterious air. Believe me, I'm not the man you think I am. I'm not out to change the world; I'm just interested in surviving. I don't want to die now, or even in the distant future. I want to live until I'm old and gray and die in my sleep holding a beautiful woman."

"Enough!" Sarah voice was stern and sharp. "We haven't time for your foolish denials. I'm not saying today what I expect you to understand, or believe. I only want you to remember what I'm saying so that as your life changes, you will recall my words, and take some comfort from them. Tell me, Andy, have you noticed a change in yourself since you've been with us?"

Andy instinctively smiled, he did notice a change. "Yes."

"So have I, in many ways. I think you are growing in the Word."

Andy laughed, realizing Sarah was right.

"Now," Sarah continued, her voice soft. "You will not be alone. Stephanie will be your companion; perhaps Bernie will be too, I'm not sure. Stephanie can guide you spiritually and her military experience will be helpful also, until you grow into your position. Bernie knows the workings of Satan from firsthand experience and will be able to guide you in avoiding them." Sarah paused, looking toward the floor while rubbing her hands slowly beneath her chin, lost in thought. "I don't know what your task is. It's not for me to know; though I wish it were, so I could share it with you. Perhaps what God wants you to do will be revealed to you through faith, and therefore, it would not be good for me to tell you, even if I knew. Whatever the reason, keep your soul's ear open for God's voice. Depend upon His ability to save you from yourself as well as others. You must have faith."

Andy nodded. "I'll try. I'll try my best."

"That's all we can do, isn't it?"

Andy smiled.

"Now, as to time," continued Sarah, "I feel it's very soon. We must act quickly. I've already talked to Stephanie; she will be a great help to you. I will send for Bernie soon and talk to him also. Go to the garage now and see Dave Clawson. He's getting a vehicle ready for you. Look over everything and let him know if there's anything you think you will need. Which reminds me, I want you to take some firearms with you."

"You do? Guns?"

"Yes, you will need them. Oh, don't look so surprised. David was a great warrior, so was Saul, and others. God will show you when to use them. Now, when we see them coming, I will meet you here and we'll get the guns from the basement."

"Right, when we see them coming I'll meet you here."

Sarah nodded.

"Let me ask one thing, Sarah, must you die? Why don't you come with us, you could do so much. You could lead us—we would do whatever it is you asked. I don't understand. Here you are, so much more in tune with the Lord than I. Why do you stay here, and me go? I just don't get it."

Sarah laughed. "Yes, sometimes it's confusing. Let me tell you something that should guide you the rest of the time you have here. Human logic is not God's logic. What seems logical to us, is not necessarily the correct conclusion. We let our human logic determine too much of our daily lives, when it's faith that should be our guide.

"I suppose, from the human point of view, we should all pack up our trucks and head for the hills—live another day, fight another battle. However, Andy, that is not going to happen. Our journey has come to its end. We know this not by logic, but through prayer. Now, if some should, at the last moment, decide they want to join you, then let them join you. However, I don't think there will be any."

Andy nodded. "I understand—actually I don't really understand, but I accept. But it's easier said than done."

"Yes, that's true. But it's not as hard as one might think. It takes practice. Living a life of faith will never be easy, but it will be exciting, and it will be fulfilling. Go now, see about the transportation. Also, see who's in the kitchen—maybe you should have something packed to eat later on."

"Really? You think it might be tonight?"

"Nothing's for sure, Andy. I just feel that it could be tonight."

Andy left Sarah, making his way toward the garage. He felt a growing excitement within him.

At the garage Clawson was expecting him. He showed Andy the vehicle he'd been preparing. "She'll do the job for you, believe me. She's a Jeep with four-wheel-drive and all the horses you'll need."

Andy nodded in agreement. "Sure is pretty. How many miles on 'er?"

"Less than ten thousand. Now I've changed the oil, checked over everything I could, including tire pressure. She's as ready as she'll ever be," he smiled. "Oh, and we've filled the gas tank, plus I have two eight-gallon cans tied to the back."

Andy shook his hand. "Thanks, Dave. Let me ask you, given any thought to coming with us? We got room, or if you prefer, there are plenty of other vehicles here you could take."

Clawson smiled. "No, don't think so. This is it for us. The Mrs. and me, well, we just think the time has come. Can't say I'm looking forward to it really, the dying part, I mean. That could be a little nasty, but as for death itself, we're ready. We've talked it over a thousand times, and that's our decision."

Andy nodded. "Well, if you change your mind, you know you're welcome."

Leaving the garage, he found Stephanie waiting for him. She smiled as he approached. "I understand Sarah spoke with you?"

Andy nodded. "It seems a little unreal to me, frankly. I know they've all been talking about their coming death, but I guess I never really believed it. Life here has been good, peaceful, with lots of laughs. I guess I just pushed the future out of my mind and lived day by day."

"Yes," agreed Stephanie. "Me too. I think most of us did."

"Sarah thinks it will be real soon, maybe tonight."

"Yes."

"What do you think of Bernie Krantz joining us?" asked Andy.

"Mixed feelings, I think. I can't quite get it out of my head that he was a regional director for those jerks. How do we know, for sure, that he's one of us now? He could change again at any moment."

Andy grunted in agreement. Those were his thoughts exactly. The two walked in silence for a while, then Andy stopped. "Steph, I just had the oddest feeling, scary too. It was as if I suddenly knew something I didn't want to know. It's a little frightening."

"What? What is it? That you should not call me Steph, I hope?" She smiled.

"I'm serious. It's going to happen tonight. I could see, inside my head, the headlights coming in the dark, a long line of them, and I knew."

Stephanie looked at him silently. "You think it's tonight?"

"Yes. Somehow, I just know. Maybe I'm having a mental breakdown, you think?"

"Maybe you had a vision."

"No, no. Believe me, I don't get visions."

"I think we should tell Sarah."

"No, definitely not. I don't want her to see she's dealing with a nut here. Let's just forget it. I'll tell you what it is: anxiety. I have more fear than I know, I'm internalizing my feelings, and they're escaping this way, sorta leaking out."

Stephanie crinkled her brow for a moment, then announced, "I'm telling Sarah," and she began running toward the big cabin.

Taking a big breath, Andy slowly exhaled trying to rid himself of his frustration then began chasing Stephanie. He caught up as she entered the main cabin and headed for Sarah's rooms.

"This is silly, Steph," gasped Andy.

"Maybe," she said. "We've got too much going on here not to take everything seriously. Then too, maybe you are just nuts." She smiled and knocked on Sarah's door.

A muffled greeting was her signal to open the door. Sarah was sitting in her rocker, an opened photo album on her lap. "Well, hello again. Seems we are seeing a lot of each other lately." Her smile came easily and naturally. "By the way, I spoke to Bernie. I'm not sure he's at all convinced about being part of your team, but time will help—how much of that we have, I'm not sure. Now, what brings you here again?"

"Andy here had a vision."

"No, I didn't," protested Andy. "I'm sorry, Sarah, I just think they might be coming tonight. It's just an opinion. I thought the Detroit Lions would win the Super Bowl once—that was a nutty opinion too."

Stephanie explained how Andy had stopped, and how he looked, and how his voice sounded when telling her. Sarah nodded, but did not smile. "So you thought this out of the blue, and you saw it clearly, and it frightened you?"

Andy took a deep breath. "Yes," he said, with a note of resignation.

"Well, if you expect me to tell you one way or the other whether you had a vision from God, I won't—can't. It indeed could be, or it could be gas. That's for you to decide. You will have to come to your own conclusion. I will tell you one thing though, if you finally decide these things you see are visions, you will never get a sign you can hang your hat on. That is, God won't give you a special, conclusive sign He is speaking, but you can bet the house on what He is telling you. All visions, all words of wisdom, all contacts with God's kingdom are accepted and acted upon through the exercise of faith. Faith is our path of communication. Get a grip, if God is speaking to you, it will not be easy to hear, even more difficult to relate and frightening in anticipation."

"You think it could have been a vision?"

Sarah shrugged her shoulders. "Could be."

"But how am I supposed to know whether it is or not?" Andy asked.

"God's word tells us the proof is in the pudding. If it's a vision, then it will come to pass—if not, it won't."

"Doesn't seem like a very good system to me. How are we to warn others of what's coming when we won't know if it's true until after it happens?"

Sarah smiled. "Now you understand the problem. However, don't worry, God will teach you well, and when you are ready, you will use it. If there's one mistake we humans have consistently made over the centuries, it's thinking our understanding is crucial to the process. It isn't. Only our obedience. Stop thinking you have to understand, to figure out, to plan, or act from your own strengths, intelligence, or understanding in order for God's will to be done. You don't. Stop wasting your time trying to be an equal partner with God in accomplishing anything. You are merely a vessel, a conduit, get your logic outta the way and allow God to use you as He wills, and not only as you understand."

Sarah stood up and approached Andy, then hugged him. "You have difficult times ahead of you, Andy Moore, but you also have great joy— let it all happen."

Andy smiled. "I'll try."

"That's all God requires, nothing more."

"So," interjected Stephanie, with an edge of excitement, "you think maybe it was a vision from God?"

Sarah smiled "Possibly. Time will tell." She looked around at the clock next to the couch. It read 6:30. "It'll be dark soon."

Andy and Stephanie left Sarah to her photo album and went searching for Bernie. They found him sitting, legs crossed, on the hill in front of the cabin. As they approached, he looked over his shoulder and without a sound went back to gazing out over the valley below toward the mountains in the distance.

"Bernie," began Andy, "Sarah talked to you, I hear."

Bernie nodded silently.

"So, tell us, what do you think?"

For a moment, Bernie was silent. "I don't get it. I really don't. What am I supposed to do with you guys?"

"What're we all supposed to do?" asked Stephanie. "None of us knows what anybody's suppose to do, including ourselves. This is the step of faith that Sarah is always talking about."

"You don't understand how I feel. I don't think I can leave all of these wonderful people. It's my fault, and now I'm leaving. It doesn't make sense to me, doesn't seem right.

"Look, Bernie," said Andy, "If we only allowed ourselves to do what makes sense, God's kingdom would never have blossomed. You know your Bible; did it make sense to have a 'virgin birth'? Did it make sense to choose fishermen to lead the world to Christ? He had a whole bunch of educated, dedicated priests He could have chosen, but He chose some fishermen who weren't even having a good day."

"Yes," chimed in Stephanie, "how about arranging for the son of Almighty God to be born in a stable? Or the feast of the fishes, or the making of wine, or almost anything else—it all doesn't make sense, it's just not reasonable."

"That's the point, Bernie," said Andy. "I think God made sure that we wouldn't come to him out of human logic, but out of faith. The three of us going off to do something we don't know, doesn't make sense, yet we are going to do it because we have faith that it's what He wants."

Bernie was silent for a moment, then nodded slowly. "Yes, I know. That's what Sarah said too. But it's hard, friends, just very hard."

Andy put his hand on Bernie's shoulder. "Come with us, Bernie; let's give Sarah a chance to be right. Give God a chance."

Bernie smiled. "I suppose I should do that for once in my life."

Stephanie put her arm around Bernie. "I know, let's go up to the cabin and have a big meal. If tonight's the night, we'll need a full stomach, don't know when we'll get a chance to have another!"

The three returned to the cabin in time to smell aromas of the impending dinner. Although tonight wasn't their turn to help in the kitchen, they pitched in anyway. Fewer people than usual were showing up, and by the time dinner was ready only families with children had come to the dinning room. Their mood affected Andy, Stephanie, and Bernie too, and the three silently ate their meal, lost in private thoughts.

When finished, the clock's hands indicated eight o'clock. It was dark outside and the three followed the others to the bluff. There, the rest of the camp was already seated watching, waiting, and silent. The clouds overhead hid the bright light of the orbiting alien ship. They too waited in total darkness quietly. An hour went by, and it seemed darker than it had been for a long time. Two, then finally three hours passed. At 11:30, there was a stirring and voices began chattering as finally the night was considered safe. Suddenly a woman's voice screamed, "Oh, my God!"

Andy looked toward the distant mountain and saw the source of her fear. Rounding the far turn, still many miles from actually entering the compound, was a caravan of headlights.

"Oh, Andy. Oh my God, Andy," said Stephanie softly.

The headlights counted out to be more than twenty vehicles, all traveling in a tight procession up the road. They appeared as a serpent of lights, one behind the other, bending with the road.

Andy turned quickly for the cabin and saw Sarah was standing in front with her arms folded. Turning she began walking back to the cabin, then broke into a run. Andy and his two companions ran after her, looking back as they did at the coming procession. Reaching the cabin, and bolting inside, they saw the door to the basement already open. Dashing down the narrow wooden steps, they found Sarah waiting for them.

"Pick out what you want, and hurry!"

"Sarah, please come with us," pleaded Stephanie.

Sarah shook her head. "Don't waste time, get the things you need! I'll make sure the vehicle is ready." Quickly, she made her way up the stairs; the screen door slammed closed a second later.

Bernie picked out a rifle. "This looks like the M-1 I had in the service. It's old, but I know this rifle. He also grabbed two revolvers, sticking them in his pants.

"Grab some of those boxes of ammunition too," yelled Andy.

It only took a few minutes for them to load several boxes and haul them outside for the short trip to the garage area.

"Where did they go?" asked Stephanie as she saw the headlights had disappeared.

"They must be around the mountain, ready to come out at Pinchins Bluff over there," he said, referring to the section of road that snaked behind the mountain. "Once they emerge from that bluff, it will only take a few minutes to reach the camp," added Andy as they half ran, half stumbled their way to the garage where eager hands met them and threw the boxes in the rear of the Jeep.

Stephanie met Sarah and hugged her. Andy heard a sob escape from Stephanie's lips. Sarah let her go and in turn gave Bernie and then Andy a hug. "God be with you, Andy, and He will be. Don't give up on your faith."

"Come with us," urged Andy.

"Hush, now get going!"

Andy did not hesitate, climbing behind the driver's wheel and bringing the Jeep to life. He took a moment to look at each of the people gathered there, knowing this was the last time he'd see them. Finally, without headlights, he put the Jeep into gear and stomped the accelerator. He felt the vehicle leap forward, spewing dirt and gravel behind them. He headed, not for the road where the approaching caravan would be coming, but for the field behind the cabin leading to a small logging road and from that to the gravel road some distance above them. All three had their seatbelts on, still each put a hand on the Jeep's ceiling to prevent from hitting their heads as the vehicle bounced and rocked its way through the field toward the logging trail.

Several times Stephanie and Bernie looked behind them for the headlights, seeing each time they did that they were drawing closer.

Suddenly, Bernie's voice barked out. "Stop the Jeep, Andy! Now!" His voice showed he meant business, as did the gun he held pointed at Stephanie.

Andy applied the brakes and the vehicle slid to a stop. "What are you doing?" demanded Andy.

"Stephanie! Don't make any moves; this is not the time for heroes. I can't go on. I gotta get out. I'm going to kill as many of those bastards as I can. I may go to hell, but I wanna make sure I send a few of them there too!"

Andy and Stephanie looked at each other as Bernie opened his door and got out. "Bernie…" began Andy.

"Shut up and get outta here!"

Andy hesitated then put the gear into drive and the Jeep leaped forward again.

Bernie watched the Jeep leave. Then, after checking his two side arms for ammunition, began running toward the road that the caravan would travel before reaching camp. It was nearly a quarter of a mile, and though out of shape, he reached the road before the caravan. He stood gasping for breath, feeling he might pass out before they came. Gradually he began to recover. Suddenly a flash of headlight swept over the road and Bernie knelt by the side of the road to wait, still panting.

Within a few moments, the trucks appeared from around the bend, their headlights feeling out the road. Bernie could see they were army trucks, what the military referred to as quarter tons, having a cab able to fit three people in front and a flatbed in back with a canvas covering fitted over metal ribs. The trucks were traveling an easy 30 miles an hour. Quickly he checked the forty-five caliber pistols he held in each hand. Bernie waited. He was sure the bastard would be in the lead truck—he wouldn't permit himself the indignity of being anywhere other than in the lead. He would be on the passenger side.

The lead truck was fifty yards, then thirty—finally, when only ten yards in front, Bernie leaped out with both guns firing at the passenger side. Initially the truck veered to the left, but then back toward Bernie, accelerating. Bernie stood his ground firing both guns toward the right windshield; he saw it shatter and kept firing. He was so intent upon aiming, he didn't realize his danger until the front bumper smashed into his right thigh. The force of the impact threw him back, and up. He fell to the ground, still in front of the truck, only a few feet ahead. The pain assaulted his senses, just as the truck hit him again. Within a heartbeat, the wheels crushed Bernie beneath their weight, first with the right front tire, and then the right rear tire. Bernie never felt the rear wheel.

The trucks continued toward the camp, less than 1,000 feet ahead. Making the final turn, their headlights illuminated the camp, washing it in harsh white streams. They lit up the group of people waiting in a line stretching across the grassy parking area. The lead truck slowed as it approached the group, then halted some 50 feet from them. The two following trucks went to either side of the lead truck, but did not come even with it. The three trucks came to rest forming an arrow pointed at the silent group, while bathing them with their harsh beams. The rest of the trucks formed a double line behind the lead trucks, then turned off their engines though keeping their headlights on. For a few moments neither the people in the trucks, nor those facing the trucks, did anything. Finally, the door on one of the side trucks opened and the security chief of the region stepped out; it was John Trombley.

From the back of the trucks, more armed men emptied out of the covered beds. They formed a silent line behind Trombley, waiting their cue. Each was armed with an automatic rifle, which they allowed to droop before them.

"Which one of you is the leader?" shouted Trombley. "Which one of you is Sarah Jenkins?"

Sarah stepped forward, tightly holding the small hand of the child at her side. "I'm Sarah Jenkins," she said calmly.

THE JEEP BOUNCED onto the logging trail that proved not much better than the open field, it but did allow them to go a little faster.

"Anything?" Andy asked without taking his eyes off the trail.

Stephanie craned her neck to glimpse the area beneath them. "Yeah, I can see a line of headlights. Looks to be about twenty or thirty vehicles, but I can't see what kind they are."

"Can you see the camp, any people?"

Stephanie shook her head slowly. "Yeah. Seemed gathered in front of the trucks."

Andy followed the trail around a bend, causing them to temporarily lose sight of the camp. The trail abruptly ended at a gravel road, the same gravel road the vehicles approaching the camp had used; however, they had turned off the gravel road onto the camp entrance some three miles down the road. At this location, the two were above, and nearly a mile from the camp. The night was black and the camp could not be seen.

Andy stopped the Jeep and leaped out with Stephanie following after grabbing a pair of binoculars. Andy led them down the embankment veering off to his left in order to get a clear view of the camp below. He stopped where there was an opening in the trees allowing them a full view of the camp below.

"Where's Bernie? Where did he go?"

"Don't know, I don't see any sign of him at all," said Stephanie, the binoculars glued to her face.

"Let me look," said Andy reaching for the glasses. Quickly fixing them to his face, he searched the darkness, but there was no sign of Bernie. Shifting his gaze to the camp, he saw the trucks had come to a halt. Their headlights illuminated the group of people gathered in front. "Looks like our people are still lined up."

Stephanie, taking the binoculars, looked for a moment then nodded. "Yeah, too far away to recognize faces. Looks to me like some other people, soldiers I think, facing them from the trucks—hard to tell, the headlights don't show a lot."

SARAH STOOD QUIETLY facing the headlights. The visitors appearing no more than dark images lit from the back by the headlight's glare. Others in the camp, taking her cue, waited silently with only an occasional sniffle from a child breaking the quiet.

The armed soldiers encircled the group.

John Trombley walked slowly in front of the group, surveying them as if looking for something or someone. When he reached Sarah, he stopped. "So you are Sarah?"

Sarah nodded.

Trombley looked at her for a second or two before continuing. "So this is the famous Sarah. You know, we've wanted to meet you for a long time. Yes, a very long time, and now here we are."

Trombley wore his cape of office, which billowed out now and then in the evening's fitful breeze. The cape's hood was scrunched down on his shoulders, revealing his unkempt hair and two-day growth of beard. As he talked, Sarah could see that he was missing his right incisor tooth.

"So, Sarah, are you happy to see us? Are you as happy as we are to see you?"

Sarah remained silent, fixing her stare not on Trombley, but on the passenger side of the lead truck. even in the dark his white robe could be seen.

"Ah, I see you might not be. Well, I suppose that's to be expected."

The figure in the truck moved and the door swung open. Getting out of the cab, his robe nearly touching the ground and its hood holding his face in black shadow, he stood for a second. Then he moved slowly toward Sarah until he faced her, a few feet away. Giving a quick flick of his hand, he dismissed Trombley, who dutifully withdrew into the shadows.

"Hello, Sarah," Abdon spoke slowly, his voice was deep carrying a tone of familiarity.

"So you came at last," replied Sarah.

A sound that might be called a chortle came from the darkly shadowed face. "Yes, you knew I would—you know we would, for Eli is with us too."

"Yes, I know," said Sarah softly.

"So now what are we to do?" He clasped his hands behind his back then took two slow strides to his right, turned, and took two strides back. "Under the law—your law, I should add—you are now fugitives, subject to the death penalty for the crime of not permitting this new era of human glory to come about. You know that too, don't you?"

"I've heard such laws were passed. They are not my laws, as you put it, but they are the law."

"Yes they are. I am not the wicked entity you imagine. If I were, I would order your execution without discussion. However, I am not going to do that. I believe in mercy, does that surprise you, that I would show mercy?"

Sarah remained silent.

"So I will give you a chance to save yourself and your followers." Abdon paused.

Sarah continued to remain silent, knowing this was some sort of play to be performed and any response on her part would only delay the inevitable.

"Renounce now your silly religion, and have your people do the same, and we will leave you undisturbed, in fact we will wish you a pleasant evening. Moreover, Sarah, I will make you the overseer of all the land for five hundred miles in any direction."

Sarah's face showed no emotion. Finally, taking a deep breath, she shook her head, "No, never."

"Yes, so I expected." He looked up and beyond to the people gathered behind Sarah. Taking one step, then another, he addressed them. "And so, is there none among you who will come with us, join us, renounce this foolishness?" He waited a few moments, but no one responded. Turning, he placed himself in front of Sarah again. "Yes, as I thought. It's sad, really very sad. He motioned to a group of men, who quickly ran behind the group toward the buildings.

Turning, Sarah saw they were lighting torches as they ran.

"I like fire, don't you? Hotdogs and all that, isn't that what people do—cook hotdogs?"

A moment later Sarah could see flames licking at the main cabin, followed quickly by other structures. Slowly at first, then rapidly, the buildings began to be consumed by hot hungry orange tongues eager to feast.

Sarah turned back to face Abdon.

"Yes, too bad, but if I do not eliminate those infected with this religious zeal, others might fall victim and we'd just have to do this over again. However, Sarah, all is not lost. I have a special treat for you," he said. The sound of his voice betrayed a hidden smile, "I wouldn't want this experience to be something entirely negative for you. I suspected before I even came here that you would not change your foolish allegiance, so I prepared something special for you. I thought about this meeting a lot, you know. Trying to think of what we could do to make it appropriate. And I came up with something I think you will find very appropriate: Probably a privilege you didn't expect. But, I did it just for you, Sarah, so that you could meet your God in a manner I'm sure you would consider a treat." Turning, he nodded at the gathered men by their trucks, saying "Have that Jerry and his friend come forward."

Immediately two men dragging a heavy object approached, but not until the headlights lit them up did it reveal they were dragging a large cross, expertly crafted with brass fittings on the blunt ends.

The two men stopped, and behind them others went to the back of the trucks and began dragging their own crosses, one end on their back while the other end dragged on the ground behind. These crosses were smaller than Jerry's and showed a rougher hand had made them. There were some gasps behind Sarah and not a few whimpers. A woman screamed, "Oh, my God, no!"

✧ ✧ ✧ ✧ ✧

"WELL?" SAID ANDY, his impatience showing in his voice. "What's happening?"

"Not much. Looks like the big tall one is talking to someone, probably Sarah. The rest are sorta just standing there."

"Here, let me see."

Stephanie handed over the binoculars to which Andy glued his eyes. It was as Stephanie said, nothing appeared to be happening. Then suddenly, the headlights went out.

"Uh oh," said Andy

"The lights went out!" gasped Stephanie. "Can you see anything?"

"Not a thing, nothing," said Andy, taking down his glasses and handing them to Stephanie. "I'm sure they haven't killed them yet, we would have heard shots."

"Yes, I'm sure you're right. Wait, I see something—look," Stephanie said as she hastily focused the binoculars. "They are torching the camp. Oh God, they are burning everything there!"

As she spoke, Andy could see with the naked eye the growing flames. Higher they reached, casting the whole hill in a red-yellow glow as if the sun were about to rise.

SUDDENLY ABDON LEANED forward toward Sarah and a loud voice shouted, "Renounce, Sarah, renounce!"

Abdon's command was met with silence, unbroken except for a stifled whimper here and there.

"Now, remember it is not my law, but the law of your people that condemns you to death—and I am bound by your edicts. I have no choice but to allow such a lawful sentence to be carried out." He paused a moment, as though in thought. Then, he lifted his hand, saying "Ah, but wait. You might think I was playing favorites if I were to enforce your laws on you, and not on others, including my own. Am I right?"

Again Sarah remained silent.

"Yes, yes I'm sure you would." Pausing he looked over to Jerry and John balancing their large, brass-tipped cross. "And do you think I should enforce all laws too?" he asked.

For a moment both Jerry and John were struck silent. Then Jerry ventured an answer. "Yes, sir, of course. You should enforce the law." The last was said with a growing grin.

Abdon nodded, his face still hidden within the shadows of the hood. "Yes, of course. And all in heaven know I am a creature of the law. Yes, I'm glad you agree. Now, you will recall that several weeks ago, you murdered your father. Am I correct?"

Jerry hesitated. It was obvious he understood the direction of the question. "But he was a Christian—he was considered a criminal, he was under a death sentence." Jerry's voice began to show signs of fear growing inside him.

"Well now, Jerry, that's not exactly true is it? It was not until last week that your High Council and World Court declared the death sentence to all who were not Brothers. Last week, right? And you murdered your father before that."

Jerry looked at John who wore his own face of fear. "But we did it for you, sir. We did it for you!"

"I understand that. Your motives were fine, but the law is the law." Abdon nodded to guards who'd quickly grabbed both men before they had a chance to resist. The cross fell to the ground with a thud as the two were wrestled to the ground.

Abdon looked down at the two men, who began to sob. "No, no please, I beg you."

"Crucify them," said Abdon in a flat voice

STEPHANIE WATCHED FOR several minutes while the cabins burned. Then suddenly she gasped, then screamed, falling to her knees and covering her face.

Grabbing the binoculars, Andy searched the scene for the reason for her screams. He found it, and uttered his own gasp. A cross was being raised. On either side of the cross were two figures, each writhing in pain. Suddenly the cross dropped into a hole that had been dug.

For a few moments no one moved watching in astonishment the crucified men wither in agony. Suddenly pandemonium broke out as soldiers rushed the group grabbing individuals. Andy saw crosses rising with outlines of bodies nailed to them writhing in pain, silhouetted by the flames. Some individuals made a break for it, but it was all in vain. More and more crosses rose, one by one. Several shots ran out. Still more crosses rose—some with children on them. Each cross had two bodies, back to back. Andy's eyes filled with tears. He was too far away to hear the screams, yet they reverberated in his head. Each cross rose slowly and paused as the workers repositioned themselves for the final push. Finally, the cross resumed its vertical climb until reaching the edge of the hole, then dropped, slamming the bottom of the pit, adding pain to the struggles on the cross.

Dropping the glasses, Andy hung his head, while his tears flowed. He could hear Stephanie sobbing next to him. He sank to his knees where he and Stephanie remained for a long time, even past the dying flames, until the embers could not be seen. Still they did not move, could not move. Finally, Andy raised his head, took a deep breath, and stared into the dark night, which now cloaked the butchery below. "We have to go," he said softly.

Silently Stephanie got to her feet, turned, and walked past Andy toward the Jeep above them. Andy raised the glasses one more time, but the dark of the night had swallowed its shame.

From above, he heard Stephanie shout his name, fear clearly in her voice.

Running, he found her standing in front of the Jeep, facing a tall man some 15 feet away from her dressed in dark pants and a white, opened-neck shirt.

"Good evening," he said softly as Andy rushed to Stephanie's side.

"Who are you?" demanded Andy, feeling a rising fear. He calculated whether he could reach one of the guns before this man could, and decided he couldn't. The tall stranger appeared athletic.

As the man stepped closer, he appeared to be in his middle thirties, with a soft smile on his face and large blue eyes. He stood silently as both Andy and Stephanie surveyed him. Finally, satisfied the two had had enough time, he spoke. "I am here to tell you that God is with you."

"Who are you!" demanded Andy. "Wait! Wait a minute, I've seen you before, right?"

The man nodded.

"Yes, I remember now, the train station—right? The train station?"

Again he nodded. "Who I am is of no concern, but listen to my words. I was with Sarah and I shall be with you. I, and ten thousand like me. However, beware of the days that lie ahead. Trust not to your own understanding, but to your faith. Your way will be made plain when it is time, not before. Trust, and all will be done, until your appointed day."

"Are you an angel?" asked Stephanie.

"One of millions. Fear not, though the enemy has legions, we have God's word. All is not lost, all is being won. Don't let your senses of today judge the outcomes of tomorrow. Now, go quickly, you are still in danger here. Go!"

The last was said with such force that both hurried to get in the Jeep. Andy stopped and turned back, but the man was gone. "Where is he?" he demanded. "I got some questions!

"Who does he think he is! If there are ten thousand of them, why didn't they rescue those people down there! Why did they have to suffer? Come back here!" he screamed, but the night remained quiet.

"Andy, get in!"

Andy opened the door and got in, and for a few moments, neither said anything. Finally, Stephanie broke the silence. "Start the car, Andy, and just go."

Taking a deep breath, Andy turned the key until he heard the engine came to life. "So now just exactly where is it we are to go? I wish he'd have at least told us that."

"Let's just drive west and trust."

"West and trust?"

"Or east, or north, or whatever. Yes. Trust is what he told us to do, and maybe this is the first lesson."

"I don't get—or maybe it's that I just don't wanna get it."

"Meaning?"

"This whole thing—I mean I'm no heavy-duty Christian—I'm just me. I swear, I like a drink now and then, I screw up. I don't think I'm the right guy for this."

"I'm getting a little tired of this whining."

"Okay, you wanna know the truth?"

Stephanie nodded.

"I'm scared. I don't want this responsibility. I don't think I'm up to the job. I'll tell you what I want. I wanna find a real bar, have a cold brew, and watch football. I wanna go to McDonald's and get a burger. I wanna listen to C-Span and curse the jerks on it. That's what I want, that's what I can do. I can't do this charging around fighting Satan and his angels, and talkin' to God and His angels—I'm just no good at it."

Stephanie smiled, nodding slowly. "I know what you mean." She leaned back against the car seat and closed her eyes. "I'd like to be on a sailboat somewhere in the South Pacific; I want to go to a sale at Hudson's and be the first person in the door. I would love to have a cool glass of red wine and listen to music all night by a fire; I'd like to eat a huge big meal at least once in my life and not think about the consequences." She sighed and let the silence that followed hang over them.

Finally Andy smiled. "Well, I guess what we want is not gonna happen."

"Nope, don't think so."

Andy thought a moment while the engine smoothly idled, then nodded slowly. "Yeah, maybe you're right. How we got selected, I don't know. But here we are and I should at least give it my best, whatever that is. But I'll tell you this: If anything worthwhile is gonna happen, God sure is gonna have to do it 'cause I think He chose the wrong guy."

"And He will, Andy," smiled Stephanie as she squeezed his hand.

Returning her smile, Andy took his foot off the brake, made a U-turn on the gravel road, and headed west.

Give the Gift of

Comes the End

to Your Friends and Colleagues

CHECK YOUR LEADING BOOKSTORE OR ORDER HERE

❏ **YES**, I want _____ copies of *Comes the End* at $14.95 each, plus $4.95 shipping per book (Michigan residents please add 75¢ sales tax per book). Canadian orders must be accompanied by a postal money order in U.S. funds. Allow 15 days for delivery.

My check or money order for $_____ is enclosed.

Please charge my: ❏ Visa   ❏ MasterCard
                   ❏ Discover ❏ American Express

Name _____

Organization _____

Address _____

City/State/Zip _____

Phone_____ E-mail _____

Card # _____

Exp. Date_____ Signature _____

Please make your check payable and return to:

House of Stuart
64155 Van Dyke • Washington, MI 48095

Call your credit card order to: 800-247-6553
Fax: 775-256-8997
Online: www.comestheend.com